The Keyman

by

Kamal M Malak

Fern Publishing Limited,
Edgware, Middlesex, UK

All characters and places are fictitious; any resemblance to any person or place is coincidence. Any references to any regulatory or other law enforcing body, any well- known case, person, incident, and historical facts which may not be accurate, are used fictitiously to support the story, and no offence to any person, organisation or sect is intended.

ISBN 978-0-9954528-2-4

First Printing- Printed in the United Kingdom

Fern Publishing Limited,
Edgware, Middlesex, UK

www.fernpublishing.co.uk

Chapter 1

In the St James's Park area, a number of hedge funds and asset management companies are based. This is one of the best areas of London's West End. A number of cordon bleu restaurants, five star hotels, casinos, night clubs and offices are based therein. In one of the regency style building, on the fourth floor, there were offices of Chezan Investments Ltd. The whole floor was occupied by the company. In the board room there was a meeting taking place. Around the large hard wood table, Jimmy Noble and Pearce Noble were sitting, the joint CEO of the company. Next to them, was Sam Holworth from new Country Bank Plc who was the banker responsible for the account of Chezan Investments Ltd.

Sam Holworth took a sip from the glass water and said in a sombre voice, 'I believe we have been very patient with the company, the bank has to clean up its portfolio; there is really not very much of a choice.'

Jimmy looked up at his younger brother who was supposed to be the financial brain but before Pearce could speak, he pleaded, 'look Sam, we are doing our best, we know the pressure you are in but I can assure you we are even under greater pressure to bring the company back to profitability and tidy our balance sheet.'

Pearce was pleased with his brother's comment. He added, 'you see Sam, we are reviewing a new project in Caribbean and this should bring real gold into the business.'

'What is this project?' Sam looked at them with surprise, 'you never mentioned it before.'

Pearce rang the telephone in front of him and spoke to his secretary. 'Jackie, could you please bring in the 'New Heaven' folder.'

They continued to talk, and in a minute, Jackie entered the boardroom with a folder in her hand. 'Sorry, I have not made any copies yet, do you want me to make copies?' She asked politely.

Seeing Jackie, Sam's eyes brightened up. He had met her many times in the office and knew her reasonably well. 'No, it is not necessary at the moment, thanks Jackie.' Pearce looked at her. Jackie knew that they did not want her there anymore so she walked out of the boardroom.

'I am going to review the project, and then we will present it to you in detail.' Yasin Kanji who was the unofficial financial director of the company, explained.

Pearce did not like his remark, 'We had a meeting with the promoters recently, once we establish the basic facts then the details would be prepared with all the financials including short term and long term forecasts.'

Sam Holworth opened the folder, looked at the pictures of the area and an architect view of the hotel and furnished apartments. 'You guys don't really have much experience of the property and hotel business.'

'We believe that the diversification is necessary to make some real bucks; this is the only way we can repay the bank its debts' Pearce showed his enthusiasm.

'Look there is local management meeting of the bank in two days' time, and the next month, there will be board meeting at the head office. I really need some real numbers to please them; otherwise you will need to find me a job in your company!' Sam showed his desperation.

'Don't worry Sam, we will not let you down, let me get this project's copy with additional details to you in couple of days…'

Before Jimmy could finish his sentence, Sam interrupted, 'Please let me have something tomorrow, so that I can get it into my presentation for the next day.'

'Look how about by close of the business tomorrow? I will send it to you by hand.' Jimmy offered.

'I am staying at the company's flat at Marble Arch, and will be working in the evening, do you think you could send it to me there by hand?'

In the meantime, Jackie entered the room with fresh coffees. She gave one cup to Sam. Sam felt her perfume and while she bent over to put the cup in front of him, he felt the softness of her breast on his shoulder. He was wondering what it would be like to put his hands on those two rocks.

Jackie walked along and put the cups in front of the other three men, and walked out of the boardroom.

They continued to discuss for a while.

A little later, Jimmy Pearce and Yasin were sitting in the board room, Sam Holworth having left.

Pearce looked at Yasin. 'Get these tidy up and get some proper cashflow projections in it, I need it by close of business today.'

'How can we do it so quickly, I need to understand the project?'

'We can review in detail later on, for the time being, get some projections. Just put some assumptions and show the detailed projection for one year and then five years long term projection on a yearly basis.' Pearce did not see any problem.

Yasin looked at Jimmy seeking his help… 'But the figures need to make sense.'

'Yes, yes, they will, you better get on with it' Pearce showed his impatience.

Yasin got up, picked up the folder of New Heaven and walked out of the board room.

'What do you think?' Pearce looked at Jimmy.

'I think we need to give Sam something to chew over, otherwise, he is going to be in problems at the bank.'

'Yeah, I agree. We should give him the glossy picture of this project. I will say that bulk of the profits will be used to repay the bank loan.'

'But how are we going to convince the bank to give us more loans in the first place or are you thinking of bringing the money from Switzerland?'

Jimmy looked at his brother like telling him off. 'We must not mention about our funds in Switzerland, that is not the idea. They do not know about it.'

Pearce shook his head, 'yeah silly of me; if they find this project very profitable then they will fund it; from the profits we not only repay the new loan but also existing loan or at least part of it.'

'That is it, now you understand.'

They were quiet for a while. 'What do you think of this 'Moonie' (referring to Yasin); do you think he has got what it takes to manage our business financially?' Jimmy showed his dislike of him.

'I am also thinking, maybe we need another sharp accountant.'

'I agree this guy is an old dog.'

'But he knows too much about our business and a lot of our secrets.'

'We do not need to get rid of him as yet, let's get another controller type person and this guy stays as our financial right hand man, when the time is right we get rid of the dead wood.' Jimmy confided in his brother.

Pearce smiled, he understood his brother well.

Later in the late afternoon, Pearce was in his office sitting in his chair behind the large desk, looking at some papers. Jimmy entered the room and sat down opposite him.

‘Did you get the New Heaven’s projections?’ Jimmy asked.

‘No, Yasin has been working with the accounts office and has been asking many questions. Frankly, this guy has no imagination!’

‘Well, we need to really find another person. Jimmy waited ‘we must get the figures by tomorrow. I think I will send Jackie to the bank’s flat to deliver it…. on her way home?’

‘Yeah, it will be late to send by courier; Jackie will be the right person.’

‘She is really sharp, beauty and brain.’ Jimmy showed his admiration for Pearce’s secretary.

‘Well, delivering a project report does not require a lot of brain!’

‘No, fool, you don’t understand…. Did you never notice how Sam looks at her? I bet he really fancies her!’

‘You are a vicious man……. He has normal behaviour giving pleasant look to a pretty woman. It is called politeness.’

‘What I am saying is that Jackie’s delivery could be more fruitful to us.’

Pearce went into some thoughts. He liked Jackie and had slept with her many times discreetly. Even Jimmy did not know about it. He did not like the idea Sam jumping over her. ‘You know Jackie is a respectable woman, we are not going to use her to bribe the banker.’

‘No Pearce, I do not mean it. But I think it is not much point sending any of the office clerks or even Yasin there. Jackie is far smarter if Sam asks her any questions she will pretend that she does not know about the project. Yasin or any other person might spoil it.’ Jimmy lied to his brother.

‘Yes… I think you are right, tomorrow I will send the report with her. I will also inform Sam about it. He said that he is going to be working in the night for his presentation.’

‘I know he spends quite a few nights every now and then, there in the flat. I don’t know what his wife thinks of it.’

‘That is why I am not going to get married as yet.’ Pearce laughed.

‘Fine.’ Jimmy got up and left his brother happy.

Next day, a taxi stopped in front of a luxurious block in the West End. Jackie Breton got out of the taxi carrying her handbag and a small file. Jackie paid the fare and walked quickly into the block where a concierge was sitting behind a table with CCTV screen and telephone. He looked at her with an enquiring face.

‘Good evening, I am Jackie Breton from Chezan Investments to see Mr Sam Holworth of New Country Bank’.

‘Good evening madam; please wait I will call him’, the concierge said politely. He examined her carefully realising that she was not the hooker type who occasionally visited in the evening, and he had to follow special security procedures for them or even refuse them the entry.

He rang on his phone, and in a moment, ‘please take the lift to the fifth floor, flat number fifteen on the right, he is expecting you.’

‘Thank you.’ She walked towards the lift.

In a few moments, she was met near the lift by Sam who was only wearing a trouser and shirt. ‘Hello Jackie, what a pleasant surprise, Pearce did not tell me he was going to send you.’

Jackie smiled, and they walked towards the flat.

About ten minutes later, Sam and Jackie were sitting in the lounge of the flat where there were couple of desks with chairs and on one side, the sofa. This was the three bedrooms flat of the New County Bank for their executives to stay in the town near the office, so that they did not have to spend a lot of time commuting to their homes which often involved an hour's journey and some times more if the rush hours were missed. Senior executives used it to work in the evenings when there was some urgency or if they were working late at the office, they could stay there overnight. Sometimes, some executives spent the weekend with their wives, girlfriends or some office colleagues.

'Do you know much about this project?' asked Sam.

'No, I was only involved in typing it. Pearce and Yasin are the ones who prepared it. Do you want me to wait till you have looked at it?'

'That is going to take some time but I thought I might go through some of the basic points with you… look while I look at it briefly…. Oh sorry, let me get a drink for you what would you like?'

'I am on my way to home… how long is it going to take?'

'About fifteen minutes… I won't keep you long…. Let me get you a drink.' Sam got up from the sofa and went to the kitchen next door, and came back with a glass of cold white wine.

'Oh just a cold drink would have been okay' she said while taking glass from his hand, 'thank you… you are not drinking?'

'I just had a glass, it is on the desk.'

He sat down next to her on the sofa and started looking at the folder. 'Do you know who owns the freehold?'

'I have no idea, I just typed what was given to me… however, I believe that the promoter's uncle owns it.'

'Thanks...I think what I will do… make a list of the questions and then ring Jimmy or Pearce. Do you know where they are?'

'Pearce was in the office when I left, Jimmy had gone to some meeting. I believe they are having dinner with their parents tonight.' Jackie took the sip from the glass.

'Maybe, I should leave them in peace. I am going to make a list of questions and will ring them first thing, Sam said. 'But I won't have much time in the morning, the meeting is fairly early, and I will not have much time to update.'

'Perhaps, I can help you. I know a little bit about the project.'

'That's great, have you got some time?'

'Yeah... Sure but not too long. My husband was going with his friends to a football match. He should be back about nine thirty.'

'That's excellent', Sam continued reading the folder.

In a few minutes, Jackie had nearly finished her drink. Sam asked, 'do you know if they will sell the apartments or rent these out?'

'I think they plan to sell some and rent out the others for the continuing income stream.' Jackie was happy what she had learnt during the discussion in the office.

'You seem to know quite a bit, I wonder why they have not mentioned it in the project?'

Before Jackie could reply, Sam noticed her glass 'Oh... let me get you another drink… we also have some smoked salmon, would you like some?'

'No thank you… I am not very hungry.'

'Oh come on, I am also a bit hungry… let's go to the kitchen.' Sam got up.

Jackie reluctantly got up and they both went to the kitchen where there was a small table and few chairs. She sat down on a chair while Sam took out the smoked salmon and bread from the fridge, and took out two new glasses and filled them up with the white wine from the fridge.

'That was a quick break!' Jackie smiled.

'Not really, I have been working for some time', Sam smiled back.

While they were having salmon and drinking wine, they started talking non-business. 'What does your husband do, if you don't mind me asking?'

'He is a salesman in the local dealer of Ford.'

'That's an interesting job!'

'But not very well paid….. We have been saving for the house deposit but can't really manage.' Jackie confided in him.

'These days banks are difficult, they have to comply with all kinds of regulations and lending criteria. Our bank is the same.'

'I did not know your bank gave mortgages', suddenly Jackie saw an opportunity.

Sam looked at her while taking a sip from the glass. 'Yes we do, but unlike high street bankers we tend to give mortgages to our customers with whom we have business relationship or their staff in some special cases.'

'Do you think you could help us? Basically we do not have enough for the deposit even though, we should be alright for monthly instalments.' Jackie was happy she came.

Sam was quiet for a while, his mind working quickly. He also saw an opportunity. 'Yes sure, perhaps after a few days, once this saga is over (implying the forthcoming meetings), you can get in touch with me.'

They both took another sip of the cold wine. Jackie was feeling a lot more comfortable. After finishing the salmon, they moved to the lounge to continue, taking their glasses with them.

'Sorry Jackie, I won't be long.' Sam started looking at the papers again.

'Please take your time, as I said my husband will not be home till late.' Jackie wanted to oblige him.

'Thanks.' Sam continued with his review. Jackie was wondering why Pearce did not arrange a late meeting in the office, so that the whole thing could be done a lot easier. Anyway, I am free and now perhaps we can get a mortgage and have our own home at last. She started dreaming.

Sam was finding difficult to concentrate. He could not forget that a beautiful young woman was there in the flat alone with him. She seemed to be quite relaxed. How important is this bloody meeting, I can always bullshit my way out of it. He pretended to look at the papers but his mind was working fast.

'Would you like another drink?' He decided to make a move.

'No thanks, I already had two glasses.' Jackie knew the cold wine made her very hot!

'Look I am also having another, it is really nice.' Sam got up from the sofa.

'Alright then, just a few drops.'

Sam went into the kitchen and opened the fridge. He noticed that the wine bottle was almost empty. But there was a champagne bottle in the fridge. The maid always kept couple of wine bottles and champagne in the fridge. He opened the bottle of champagne and poured it into two glasses. He brought the glasses to the lounge.

'You broke something in the kitchen I heard some noise?' Jackie asked.

'No, it was the cork of the champagne.'

'Do you always keep the champagne ready in the fridge?.... What are we celebrating?'

'Well I thought I will thank you for the visit and helping me out with my review….' Sam smiled.

Jackie took the glass from his hand. 'That's very kind of you…. I am just doing my job.'

'So am I…. Cheers.'

After a few sips of champagne, they looked at each other. Sam looked into her eyes to read if she was ready for the next stage. He realised that she had taken her jacket off while he was in the kitchen, showing her satin blouse with a firm pair of breasts in full view. He came close to her. 'That is very nice blouse' touching the blouse close to her breast. While he moved a few drops of champagne fell over her blouse. 'Oh I am sorry ….so clumsy of me.' He took his handkerchief out and rubbed it on her blouse without realising what he was really touching. Jackie was trying to work out if he had done it intentionally but this middle aged man was not bad looking and he is definitely going to come handy for the mortgage, her mind worked quickly.

'Please don't worry', she took his handkerchief and opened one of the buttons of her blouse and wiped it on her breast. Sam saw inside half of her breast. He brought his glass forward and poured a few drops of champagne on her breast. Before Jackie could say anything, Sam put his lips on the champagne licking it on her half opened breast.

'What are you doing Sam', Jackie raised her voice.

'Oh it's just that champagne really tastes better on a woman's body.'

'Don't be cheeky', she moved his head gently. Do you do this to all your customers?'

'Sorry Jackie, I don't. You are such a pretty young woman, I couldn't control myself.' Sam apologised without meaning it.

'Alright… let's see how does the champagne taste on a man's body?' She threw almost quarter of the glass on his shirt.

Before Sam could reply or react she opened the buttons of his shirt and put her lips on his chest. Sam did not expect and he felt a beautiful woman's lips on his chest. She showed quite a bit of expertise the way she licked the champagne. 'It certainly tastes better on you', she exclaimed. Sam was pleased that he did not have to work hard to get her into the right mood: No music, no dim light no soft talks. Jackie continued opening his shirt even more. It wasn't long before Sam picked her up in his arms and brought her into the bedroom.

While they were kissing passionately and taking each other's clothes off, Sam searched something in his side board drawer. 'I am on the pill' Jackie whispered softly into his ears. Sam closed the side board drawer. He decided that he could take the risk with her.

Two bodies, one mature and the other not so mature worked hard in the bed. Sam thought she was really sexy. She had no inhibitions like she had known him for a long time while Jackie thought that she needed to give him some good time, after all, a mortgage was worth it? Besides, Tom (her husband) had not been very active in bed recently; he seemed to be always tired.

About half an hour later, Sam and Jackie were in the bed completely naked. The hard exercise session was over and they had explored each other's bodies, tasted it and were satisfied with each other's performance.

'I hope I have not been too presumptuous?' Sam asked her gently while one of his hands was on her tummy, not letting go a beautiful young woman's body and continued to explore the surroundings.

'Don't spoil it…let's make the most of the occasion.' Jackie was unrepentant.

Sam kissed her passionately and they went into their second round happily.

About an hour later, Sam was at the door of the building where a private cab was waiting to drive Jackie home. The driver opened the door and Sam kissed her gently on the cheek. 'Thank you Jackie, you are a wonderful woman!'

'Bye Sam, you are not bad either.' Jackie replied with a slight smile.

In the cab, Jackie was thinking what a clever person Sam was. Her evening was going through like the film screen in front of her. How he threw the carrot of mortgage, how he accidentally dropped some champagne on her blouse, and how he tried to wipe it by stimulating her breast and how….. and how….. She kept on thinking. She was sure that it was not the first time he slept with a woman in the office flat. How come he was searching for the condom in the drawer? She was sure he was quite used to that activity. Then suddenly she thought of Tom, what explanation she was going to give him for being late. With a bit of luck, he would not have arrived home. Maybe, she will have time to take a quick shower. The cab continued as fast as her thoughts, on the road.

In the flat, Sam Hollworth was sitting after having taken a quick shower. He could not concentrate on the work in hand. He was thinking what a lively body Jackie has got. God, the way she did the trick with champagne, his wife never had done that. He was going to suggest to her next time. The wife's thought disappeared as quickly and the firm breast of the young Jackie took over his mind. He was thinking what an actress, she pretended to be unhappy when he dropped the champagne intentionally on her and then tried to remove it by his mouth. But how quickly she changed the tempo. He was also sure that it was not the first time she slept out of her marriage, in the office or away from home environment. And she was honest with him not to use the condom, it certainly increased the pleasure.

He did not do much of his presentation any more. He was going to enclose the summary from the client's folder as his exhibit. He will promise to explain any questions later. He put his presentation and other papers on the desk and moved to the bedroom where the sheets were in a mess and some tissues lying on the floor. He put the tissues in the waste basket, made slightly the bed, changed his clothes and went into bed. He could not sleep for a long time. Jackie's beautiful naked body kept on coming into his mind. He was wondering how he was going to get her into the flat, next time.

After a short time, the banker finally fell asleep happy. He had worked out the next meeting!

Chapter 2

A few days passed- Jimmy and Pearce Noble were in their office. They were having a meeting with Sam Holllworth, the banker from New Country Bank about their New Heaven project. Sam had explained that the bank was under a lot of pressure to tidy its books. Chezan Investments Ltd had already defaulted on its obligations to repay the loans. So the bank was looking some extreme measures to sort it out.

Sam Hollworth took a sip of the coffee in front of him and said, 'you see the bank cannot wait much longer, something needs to be done either we have to restructure by taking equity in the company or find some fresh source of capital injection by you guys or your family.'

'Look we have been working very hard to find some new opportunities, our investments and the trading activities in the commodity market are generating funds but not enough to repay any major part of the loan…..' Jimmy also took a sip of the coffee and continued. 'It is just keeping the boat sailing.'

'I think the solution lies in this new project, if the bank approves it and invests a few millions, we are not talking hundreds of millions just twenty-five million. This will produce a remarkable return. We should be able to repay a chunk of your loan from its profits.' Pearce did his sales talk.

'But how…..? I am finding it very difficult to ask the bank for more money for your company. The credit committee is almost ready to cut the losses and call for administration.' Sam showed the hopelessness of the situation.

'Surely they would be able to see the profitable returns, the investment is in property, even if we don't make fabulous returns, the downside is really low', Pearce continued with his argument

'Besides, putting the company into administration route can only increase the losses. Redundancies, office rent, break of lease etc etc…' Jimmy said.

'Yes, I know I did point it out to the committee….', Sam was quiet for a few moments…'Look can we say that you are adding some new blood in the business which will improve the financial control and also bring in some more business.'

'We have been thinking on those lines already. I have already spoken to a lawyer who works for financial services. He is very well thought of, and maybe, we will soon make him an offer.' Jimmy said exactly what the banker wanted to hear.

'What about the finance? I regret your current guy does not seem to be quite up to it.'

'Agreed, we are planning to bring in a new financial guy, first hire him as financial controller then if he is good, promote him quickly to the CFO position. I have already spoken to one of the head hunters.' Pearce added.

'Why you guys have not mentioned all these in your project?' Sam asked quickly.

'You see this has really nothing to do with the New Heaven project, it is to do with the future operations of the company. But with hindsight, you are right, we should have mentioned it, Pearce said, 'we can revise the project; the one we gave you was done in a rush.'

Sam Hollworth was making some notes while they all kept quiet. ‘Yeah okay, so you revise the project and financial projection including other points I sent you by email, and then I will present it to the credit committee. I have to put my head on the line for you guys.’

‘Will do straight away,’ Pearce promised.

‘We know if we convince you, the bank will agree to it. You control the bank.’ Jimmy buttered him.

‘Shall I send the new folder with Jackie again? She said she helped you the other days.’ Pearce asked.

Sam Hollworth was suddenly quiet; he was wondering if they knew what had happened in the flat the other day. He looked into their eyes to read if they knew but both brothers kept straight faces. ‘Well, she is a nice girl…yes she seemed to know quite a bit about the project.’ Sam said it in matter of fact voice, ‘you guys decide if we are pressed for time, do send it by hand, otherwise, you can use the courier service or even post.’

Jimmy and Pearce also could not read from his face if anything had happened in the flat, the other day. Jackie had not told them anything except that she delivered the papers and stayed for a while to assist Sam.

Both brothers knew that it was time to change the subject. ‘Are we getting late for the lunch?’ asked Jimmy.

‘No, the table is booked at ‘Red Sea’ for about one thirty; we still have fifteen minutes or so.’ Pearce replied.

They started collecting their papers, and shortly afterwards they left for the restaurant.

The next day, there was an interview in the board room. Jimmy was with a new candidate called Dean Rowe for investment business manager position. He was to be responsible for the brokers and help the management in drafting and reviewing the contracts.

‘So you have been investment manager at this… Safe Investments... did you look after any staff?’ Jimmy asked.

‘Yes, I supervised, under the Equities department manager, a few of the traders and analysts’, replied Dean.

‘It is a bit strange for a lawyer to be in the investment business? No!’

‘Not really, I am more of an investment person than a lawyer. Even though, I did review a number of contracts in the previous position. But I really want to be in the investment business.’

‘We have a diversified portfolio. We are looking at some profitable new projects; the idea is to diversify even more and not rely on commodity trading.’

‘I believe I would fit in well, I have all round experience, mainly legal but in the past couple of years, more in trading and broking …. Besides, I really want to play a managerial role in a smaller organisation compared to be a specialist in a small area.’

They continued to talk for a while. After about fifteen minutes, Jimmy who was very satisfied with him but did not show it, said, ‘I think I will ask Pearce to join me, he is my younger brother and also joint CEO.’ Jimmy picked up the phone and spoke to Pearce. What Dean did not know that Pearce has been listening to their conversation from his office. Jimmy and Pearce, both were able to listen to the conversation clearly from their office via their telephones or in the loudspeaker so that others could also hear it. A few telephones were kept in the boardroom; one of them contained a powerful microphone. This fact was not known to anybody else in the office. In the meantime, Dean took a sip from the glass of water in front of the table. In a few moments, Pearce walked in. Dean got up and they shook hand.

‘We find that our traders and brokers are not being supervised properly since we do not have much time. The business is expanding and as Jimmy must have told you that we are diversifying, so it will require long hours and strict commitment,’ Pearce wanted to see how committed he was going to be.

'In finance, people work long hours, I am willing to put in 120% of the efforts and am used to long hours in the office…. That is why I am not yet married!' Dean showed his sense of humour.

Jimmy and Pearce both laughed. 'We have some beautiful women working in here but I suspect not many unattached but you still will have a fair chance.' Jimmy threw a carrot.

Pearce liked his sense of humour and thought he was not going to be a boring type person and will fit in well in the organisation. 'A good sense of humour will come very handy.' Pearce added.

They continued to talk. About an hour later, all three went to the restaurant nearby which Jimmy and Pearce had arranged if they were interested in the guy they will take him out for lunch.

A few hours later, Jimmy and Pearce were in the office. It was Jimmy's office which was slightly more elegant and bigger than his younger brother's office. They were discussing Dean's position. Jimmy had already spoken to him.

'He seems quite a nice chap, good personality and a combination of legal brain plus finance I think he would fit in well,' Jimmy said.

'I think so too, I was impressed. Do you think he will accept it?'

'Well it is about 20% more than what he is earning at present, you recall I said to him that small equity will be considered after one year.'

'He also asked for certain benefits; we don't really have a proper pension or life assurance.' Pearce recalled the discussion in the restaurant. 'We need to look into that area.'

'Well that is your area; you need to look into it, maybe before we look for a controller.'

'I am going to look into it straight away; maybe, I will get Yasin involved.'

'I don't think we should get that Charlie involved. Otherwise, he will feel that we are doing this for new hires. And maybe, he will feel that he is being sidelined for the top financial position.' Jimmy was not impressed with Yasin Kanji at all.

'He is still a good man, and he knows too much about our business and dealings. He knows all the overseas contacts and the special payments we make to various officials!'

'You can buy good people penny a dozen. We need people who can make a positive contribution. He always goes on the wrong side of the brokers. He lacks personality.'

'I am thinking we would 'promote' him and ask him to be overseas project manager for Middle East. This way he will be travelling mostly overseas, particularly the investment in Cairo'.

'I won't trust him with cash, one day he will disappear with a large amount of cash.'

'I will think of something.' Pearce did not want to continue with the discussion any more. 'Let's talk about it another day. Are you coming to the bar tonight? I am going out with some office people.'

'No, tonight I am meeting this guy from Boston. He is going to tell me about a new project.'

Pearce got up but before he could leave, Jimmy asked. 'I hear you are getting too close to Jackie? She is married woman and she is one of the employees.'

Pearce walked towards the door to ensure that no one was around. 'She is a neglected woman; she claims that her husband does not care much about her. She said that he has not slept with her for months.'

'But you do not need to take her husband's duties….. These days there are all kind of problems; women claiming that they are sexually harassed by their colleagues and employers.'

'She is not that type. Besides, I need to keep her interested in the company. Do you know Sam is also interested in her? She is a useful person for the bankers!'

'Just be careful.'

'Will do.' Pearce left Jimmy's office with a smile.

There was a party in a Mayfair house. This is the exclusive sought after area of central London close to all amenities. It has a good mix of offices, banks, art galleries and residential apartment blocks and some town houses. In one of the houses, belonging to Mr & Mrs Noble senior, Firoza Noble was surrounded by young men. It was her birthday party and they decided to do it in their own house rather than in a hotel. The young ladies and young gentlemen, showing the cultural diversity of London, were there in smart clothes. The air had got luxury and affluence. The white uniform dressed waiters were there to serve the drinks and the canapes to the guests. In the lounge where the party was held, the partition with the dining room was removed to expand the area. The pink champagne was the theme specially bought from the famous Knightsbridge department store. People mostly were standing and talking in the small group. Jimmy and Pearce Noble were there. The staffs from the office were not invited except Shan Reza, an executive in the business and Shrute Sting, a hatchet man who also acted as the muscleman for the brothers.

'Ladies and gentlemen, cake time' Mrs Noble announced. Everyone moved towards the table where there was a beautiful birthday cake with a few candles. Firoza, surrounded by her friends, stood there with a smile. Soon there was a chorus of 'happy birthday to you', and Firoza cut the cake after blowing on the candle. The cake pieces were served to the guests and they all dispersed in small groups.

After a short while, the music was put on and some couples started dancing. Jimmy danced with his sister then at the change of the song, Shan Reza came to her. 'May I' Shan asked Firoza politely.

'With pleasure', she took Shan's hand and moved to the dancing area. After the dance, they moved to a corner and started talking.

'How have you been keeping?' Shan asked.

'Okay, nothing much really. How about you?'

'I am okay, still busy with the divorce case. You know she is behaving like a bitch (referring to his ex-wife with whom there was a court case).'

'You should have married me!' Firoza smiled.

'I wish I could… you were always too busy with so many boyfriends!'

'Yeah, I know I am not the marrying kind… I just want to be surrounded by good looking rich men.' Firoza sounded serious.

'You don't mean that? Do you.' Shan was surprised with her honesty.

'No seriously, you should have not married, maybe; just maybe, I will let you ask me…' Firoza laughed.

'Anyway what are you doing after the party?' Shan brought the main point of conversation.

'Nothing much…. The party is going to last late.' Firoza looked into his eyes.

'I don't mind waiting, my apartment isn't very far.'

'I don't know, maybe one of the young men will ask me the same question…. If he is not better looking than you, then yes.' Firoza teased Shan.

'I will take the chance.' Shan went along with it.

'Fine….' Before Firoza could say anything further, her father's friend came and asked her for the dance. She could not refuse him and with an 'excuse me' she went with him.

Shan was thinking what to do, suddenly he saw Mrs Noble coming close to him. 'Hi Shan… paying attention to the wrong person, you should be dancing with me', Mrs Noble smiled.

'Of course, you are my favourite person… I always love to dance with you' Shan took her arm and went to the dancing area. Mrs Noble squeezed him discreetly. She always liked him but was always disappointed that he will always be polite but very reserved.

The beautiful evening, in a very beautiful part of London, with equally beautiful people, continued.

After a few weeks- There were three new recruits in Chezan Investments Ltd.

Masood Panji: a qualified accountant, the new accounting manager. Yasin Kanji finding out that the accounting and finance was going to be out of his control insisted Pearce to hire one of his recommended candidates with similar background as him. 'This guy is going to do whatever you want… you see what I mean.' Yasin had explained to Pearce. Yasin knew that with Masood, he will know what is going on in the company.

Vincent Muller: the new financial controller affectively in charge of all the finance and accounting department. Jimmy and Pearce were both impressed with his qualifications and experience. He was strongly recommended by the headhunters. Sam Hollworth also had a look at his CV and had approved him.

Dean Rowe: the new investment manager who was a lawyer by training but had moved to investment, responsible for the brokers and the traders, affectively in charge of that department.

A staff meeting was being held in the board room. A number of staffs of Chezan Investments were sitting and some standing. The objective was to introduce the three new members of the company who had joined in the last couple of weeks.

Jimmy was standing at the end of the board room near the TV screen which was used as projector and computer terminal for various presentations. 'Ladies and gentlemen, it gives me great pleasure to introduce the new members of Chezan Investments Ltd. Dean, could you please stand up.'

Dean stood up, Jimmy continued. 'This is the executive responsible for new investments and supervising the brokers and analysts. He has a distinguished background and is a lawyer by training. Dean has been working with one of our competitors and is well known in the industry. Please join me in welcoming to our company. He will be a very important member of our investing team.'

Dean smiled while the staffs clapped to show their appreciation. Dean sat down.

Soon Pearce walked over to the place where Jimmy was standing and took over from Jimmy. 'It is my great pleasure to introduce to you another important person in our company. Vincent, could you please stand up.'

Vincent stood up. 'Vincent Muller is a chartered accountant and a member of chartered management Institute. He has had experience working with professional firm, and international conglomerate. He will be responsible for the finance and accounting of our company. All the accounting and finance staff will report to him. If ever you need to know about tax, accounting or finance he is the man.' Pearce praised the new man.

Everybody clapped. Vincent smiled mutely and then sat down.

Finally, we have replaced our accounting manager who recently left, by Masood Panji, a qualified accountant with a number of years' experience. He will be supervising the accounting department and report to Vincent Muller.'

Masood Panji stood up, and after a smile, sat down. He did not like that no one clapped.

Pearce moved back to his seat while Jimmy continued. 'Ladies and gentlemen let's just congratulate our finance guy Yasin Kanji who is being promoted to be responsible for the project in Cairo. He will be reporting to me and Pearce and will spend bulk of his time in Cairo. He will continue to do ad hoc work for us. Please join me in congratulating him.' Jimmy looked at Yasin who stood up, everyone knew him and they clapped on his promotion.

After a few minutes, coffee and fine cakes were served and Chezan staff left the board room. Most of them thinking that maybe, they should stop applying for other jobs.

A month passed. Yasin Kanji made visit to Egypt and stayed there for most of the month. The new executives at Chezan seemed to be settling down well in the company. Masood Panji was a very ambitious person, he began to feel that he did not really need a financial controller above him; he could do most of the work himself. He started thinking of ways to get rid of Vincent Muller. One day, he had an argument with one of the accounting clerks. He came to Pearce's office and complained about him. He was standing in Pearce's office. Pearce did not ask him to sit down.

Pearce listened briefly to his complaint. 'Look Masood, you need to sort these things out yourself. Secondly your supervisor is Vincent, and if you must, then you should speak to him.' Pearce knew if he does not stop him there, he will be in his office every day.

Masood did not like his reply but he knew that he did not have much of a choice, so instead of arguing he decided to play another trick. 'Vincent is always busy, he is looking at the cashflow projections and revising them, so I thought I will just bring it to your attention.'

'Sorry, Masood I am even busier!' Pearce started looking at some of the papers in front of him. Masood knew that it was the signal for him to go. He left the office immediately.

About an hour later, Vincent was in the accounts office where there were four clerks and Masood the accounting managers sitting. He did not know that earlier Masood had been to Pearce.

'The companies list you gave me, I noticed that for one of the group companies, last year's accounts are not signed by the auditors, and also these are not in the Companies House.' Vincent asked Masood.

'The auditors do not submit the accounts to the Companies House, I think the company does. I will look into it.' Masood replied.

'Don't worry I will check with the auditors and deal with it myself. Here are some expense claims authorised, one of these requires Pearce's signature, please give it to Jackie.' Vincent gave him the expense claim forms. He walked out of the office noticing the desks of the clerk were full of papers.

Vincent came back to his office and rang the auditors. The auditors said they would look into why one of the company's accounts was not signed. He started working on the cashflow projection. His telephone rang and Jackie informed him that Pearce would like to see him in his office. Vincent got up immediately and went to his office.

'You see, the bank is quite happy with the original cashflow projections. What we need is to give them 'New Heaven project', revised business plan including some very specific cashflow projections.' Pearce explained.

'I think, in order to do a good business plan we should visit the site, and then we can work out how we are going to present it. I understood the bank is not very keen to give substantial funds upfront.'

'Not only that you will see that our past losses have put us in critical position. We are funding the Egypt project, Yasin is there and soon we should have substantial receipts there, but the new project requires a lot more.' Pearce never told him that they had substantial cash reserves sitting in the Swiss accounts.

'Well Yasin is coming back soon to update us over Egypt. We need to seriously consider visiting Caribbean.' Vincent advised.

'Yes I agree with you, I will speak to Jimmy and let you know. I strongly think that you should go there. You are okay with a few days trip?'

'No problem, I am used to travel quite a bit in the past positions.'

'Good, I will let you know.' Pearce finished the discussion.

Vincent got up and left the room.

Next day, Pearce was in Jimmy's office. They had been discussing the New Heaven project. Jimmy already had discussed the position with the promoters and they both were willing to visit and show them. It was also agreed that Jimmy and Vincent should visit with two promoters for two to three days and get a good feeling and plan for the project. Pearce was to hold the shop while Jimmy and Vincent were away.

'Alright then it is decided, should you take also Dean with you?'

'Not really, I think we need to economise, besides, he is too busy sorting brokers and analysts out', Jimmy grinned.

They were interrupted by the phone. Dean was on the line 'Jimmy, I just read the report on Bloomberg that the crop in Brazil is bad, it has been damaged by the bad weather.'

'God, no! …. But hang on we have more long positions than short, right….?' Jimmy immediately got tense.

'I am going to look at the positions; we have forward buy contracts, some of these are not yet sold.' Dean explained.

'Thank you Dean…somehow it is not bad news for us after all.' Jimmy put the phone down.

'I think the luck is favouring us, we should be able to sell our forward contracts at substantially higher prices.' They both immediately started looking at the computer terminal.

'We should make a bundle,' Pearce could not hide his happiness.

'Let's see, could you ask the Swiss people to transfer about three million USD to our Swiss account. We should not bring that profit to the UK.' Jimmy whispered looking into Pearce's eyes.

'I think Vincent will pick it up and then we will have to explain it to him about our Swiss account?' Pearce warned Jimmy.

'No, let me handle it, Vincent would not know, and even if he does, we will tell him that we needed some funds for some project and let him account for it in the books.' Jimmy was not used to anyone looking deeply into his affairs.

'What about the auditors?' Pearce was still nervous about it.

'Don't worry they never picked it up before, let's us worry about it later.'

'Fine.' Pearce got up.

Soon Pearce was in his office he started reading all about the crops and the coffee prices, the coffee futures had gone up substantially. A discreet smile came into his face.

It was evening; most of the staff had left the office. Vincent was still working in his office. Jackie entered Pearce's office. 'I am off; would you like me to do anything before I go?'

'You know Jackie today I am very happy.' Pearce wanted to share his happiness with someone.

'Did you win the lottery?' Jackie, who was quite frank with him, asked.

'We don't play lotteries' we play market… my dear.'

'Then you do not need anything to take your frustrations out?' Jackie looked into his eyes.

'Nervousness is a double edged sword when you are worried you are nervous when you are too happy you are nervous… just in case that happiness does not materialise.'

'Really… 'Jackie did not understand his philosophy.

'Who is in the office?'

'I think only Dean, rest of them have already left.'

Pearce got up from his chair and locked his office from inside. He came close to Jackie who did not seem to be surprised. 'You could do something to relax me tonight,' Pearce hands touched her breast.

'I could make you a nice cup of tea. That should do it.' Jackie played with him

'No my darling, today I need something special, his hands moved south from her breast.'

'Sorry, I have my….. ' Jackie whispered.

'Gosh… why do you women have to have this at the wrong day?' Pearce showed his frustrations.

Jackie did not move his hand but her quick mind immediately worked out. 'I can do something to relax you. Just sit down on you chair.' she moved towards the door and ensured that it was locked.

In the meantime, Pearce went back to his chair and sat down wondering what she was going to do? Jackie came back quickly and moved his chair towards her and sat down on the carpeted floor in front of him. She opened his trousers' zip. 'Don't make too much noise', she whispered. Soon she brought his pants down and worked efficiently with her lips and then with her mouth. Pearce's nervousness was quickly gone; he kept on putting his fingers in her beautiful hair while the efficient secretary continued to work hard to please her boss. It wasn't long before he held her head tight with his hands and closed his eyes. Soon the boss climaxed in her mouth.

About half an hour later, Jackie left the office noticing that Vincent was still in his office and also working hard to please his boss but in a different way!

Chapter 3

There was a meeting in the office of Pearce Noble. The insurance broker, Marc Kohnvich was sitting in front of the desk. Pearce and Marc had been discussing the private pension and the insurance of the employee. Jackie had already served them coffee.

Pearce looked at one of the papers, 'so we do not need to go under auto enrolment, these pensions will suffice.'

'Yes of course, the auto enrolment is pretty basic.'

'Let me call Vincent.'

Before Marc could reply, Pearce already pressed the buzzer on his phone, 'Jackie, could you please ask Vincent to join us briefly.'

In a short while, Vincent Muller entered the office, 'Vincent, this is Marc Kohnvich, the financial adviser for pensions and insurances.'

Marc immediately extended his hand, and they shook hands.

'Glad to meet you.'

Marc nodded.

'Look, Vincent, you are the one who is going to be reviewing all these documents and tell me whether the company should go for it?' Pearce explained the reason for meeting.

'Sure.' Vincent said.

'Tell me if we have this private pension do we need to take auto enrolment as well?'

'No, it would suffice, as long as the pension is adequate.'

'Okay, how about the life insurance of the employees, as we discussed in the last meeting. The company does want to make up for years of neglect in this area.'

'I will need to review the provisions but it might be an idea to have a life insurance for accidental death or disability based on the times of the annual salary of the individual.' Vincent replied.

Marc Kohnvich looked at Vincent seemingly impressed with his quick grasp of the matter.

'I will include those provisions in my detailed quote, how many times do you think will be appropriate?' Marc asked hiding his delight that Vincent was going to help him in making a very profitable deal.

'I will have to review all the papers but in a number of companies have five times of the yearly salary as accidental death and a little less for permanent disablement.'

'Fine, let me get some more details from Marc, and then I can hand over the whole package for your detailed review.' Pearce looked at Vincent who understood that he was no longer needed for the discussion.

Vincent immediately got up and with a slight nod at Marc, left the room.

'He seems very intelligent', Marc observed.

'Yes, he is very sharp; we are hoping that he is going to help us to get out of this mess.' Pearce praised his financial controller.

'How will you tie him up when he realises that the company is nearly bankrupt!' Marc knew the financial position of the company.

'You know we have a lot of support from overseas, we got some important contracts and recent bad weather in Brazil has been a blessing in disguise!'

'Why don't you take Keyman insurance on him if you believe that he is going to turn the fortunes of your company?' Marc looked into his eyes.

'That's a good idea, say if we take a large policy on him or one of us (meaning his brother) then what is the position?' Pearce suddenly became excited with the idea.

'It is not very expensive, say a two-million policy will cost you about a thousand pounds, he seems to be young and reasonably fit.' Marc tempted him thinking about his commission. 'I can give you precise quote if you let me know the figure.'

'Good.... but that small amount is not going to help us.'

'Well, there is no limit for a ten-year term policy, say five million or even ten million should not be very expensive.'

'Okay I will let you know but why don't you give us a quote on ten million, fifteen million and twenty-five million then we can decide depending upon the cost etc.'

Marc was extremely pleased but hid his happiness. 'How are you going to show that he is worth that much money?'

'We are going to promote him to the chief financial officer soon, may be in a few days. We definitely want him to turn our company around. We have been discussing a few strategies. Not long ago we hired a new investment manager.'

They continued to discuss for a while. About half an hour later, Marc got up.

'I will get you all the papers within two days, maybe tomorrow.'

'You will remember our arrangement', Pearce looked into Marc's eyes.

'Of course, you will get 5% commission on all the business I do with you.'

'I do not want anyone else to know about our arrangement.' Pearce whispered. 'Not even Jimmy.'

'Of course not, this is between two of us!' Marc's eyes explained more than what he said.

'Excellent.' Pearce said while Marc left the office saying 'see you.'

About fifteen minutes later, having worked out the plan in his mind, Pearce rang for his brother. Jimmy's secretary said that he will be back after lunch around two thirty. He asked her to let him know as soon as he was in. Pearce was getting more and more excited about the fruitful meeting he has had with the insurance broker.

About two hours later, Pearce was in Jimmy's office. The door was locked and they made sure that the internal telecom was not on which sometimes they had used for their secretaries to hear what was going on in the office, specially, when there were some visitors. Pearce had explained his brother about the life insurance, pension and the Keyman insurance.

'I think it is an excellent idea', Jimmy also got excited. 'What happens when the Keyman dies accidentally?'

'Well, according to Marc, we get the insured sum! No questions asked.'

Jimmy was quiet for a while. 'Do you want me to give you time to think it over?' Pearce asked.

'No, I have worked out a plan.' Jimmy whispered and got up and went to the door to check it was locked, and that no one was close to his office. 'I think it is wonderful …man, this is probably the most profitable project we are going to have!'

'What do you mean; it is going to cost a bit.'

'Okay listen, the bank is going to pay all the costs we will ask them for more money claiming that the new project and the new team require further investment. In worst case scenario, we will bring in some of our reserve money from Switzerland. The Keyman is going to die in due course, and then we can either repay the bank or close down the company before repaying the bank.'

'God, how quickly you worked out all these things. Why should a young and healthy man die?'

'Don't worry, it is going to happen; we will send him to the Caribbean and perhaps, a rock might fall down, or a jealous husband might do the job or he might have a heart attack, there are all kinds of possibilities.' Jimmy sounded confident.

'But for a large sum, the insurance company will need to be sure that he is the Keyman?'

'Of course, we will offer him the seat on the board and he will be the CFO of the company….. If they ask more questions we will tell them that we do not even sleep with our wives without consulting him…. That should prove he is really the Keyman!' Jimmy smiled.

Pearce burst into laughter; he still did not believe what his brother was saying. 'We are not even married … how anybody would believe it?'

'Listen man I am serious.'

'Let's talk about it another day, Marc is going to send the quotes then we can review the position.' Pearce knew the whole thing required a lot more serious thought.

'You know in couple of days' time, there is a presentation. Sam Hollworth and two other bankers are visiting. We need to present to them.' Jimmy reminded Pearce.

'Yeah I know, I need to sit down with Vincent and Dean. I am going to make Vincent as our main focus.'

'You see how quickly you learn!' Jimmy teased his brother.

Pearce got up. 'What is the update on Egyptian project?'

'Oh, didn't I tell you; tomorrow Yasin is coming and will update.' Jimmy pressed the button, 'Sandra did you hear from Yasin?'

'Yes Jimmy, he is arriving later today in the afternoon in London, and should be in the office tomorrow morning.'

'Thanks, Sandra.' Jimmy looked at Pearce 'Alright then, I will talk to you tomorrow; let me get ready for the meeting as well'.

Pearce left the office wondering how his brother's brain works. How he considered so lightly the life of an innocent man.

Next day, Yasin Kanji was in Jimmy Noble's office and had been updating Jimmy about the overseas project.

'You see, these guys want more kickback, they said that they have to bribe some very senior politicians.'

'Nonsense, this guy (Egyptian project manager) has been pocketing all the money. Did you not notice the car he drives and his clothes?'

'But he is from a wealthy family.'

'No my dear Yasin, he is not. All this cash you take with you to give to these..... mother f... (He changed his mind and used) bloody crooks. How do we know he gives it to them or keeps it himself?'

'Well the contract continues, we kept on supplying the grain to the army, and no stock was lost at the port.'

'Maybe so....Anyway, what about the cashflow?'

'The payments were received for the long outstanding invoices, I transferred some of the funds to Switzerland, the balance should be in London soon.'

'How are you going to explain the transfer to Switzerland? Vincent is really sharp; he seems to be doing an internal audit!'

'I raised a fictitious invoice from Swiss agent for his commission … anyway the amount is not so substantial, no one is going to notice.' Yasin said proudly.

'The bankers were questioning last time that we continue to have profitable projects but we still can't manage to reduce their loans.'

They continued to discuss the project in more details. Jimmy made some notes. Sandra entered with two cups of coffees.

'Thank you Sandra.' Yasin smiled at her.

Sandra looked at him but did not say anything; she just put the cups in front of them and walked out.

They started drinking coffee.

'Look Yasin, you are doing a great job. You are our confidant and know a lot more about our family's dealings. But for tactical reasons, we need to appoint Vincent on the Board and make him the CFO.'

'What…? Last time you said that I was going to be the financial director of the company.' Yasin could not hide his displeasure on this news.

'Well, for all practical purposes…you are… of course you are, but the bank needs some new blood, they want to see that we are doing something about it. Sam is under lot of pressure, he thinks his job is on the line.' Jimmy tried to cool him down.

Yasin was disappointed. He was told that after some more field experience he will be made the CFO of the company. He hid his disappointment. 'When is the meeting with the bankers?'

'Day after tomorrow… let me assure you again that you are part of the inner management team...you know what I mean!'

'I guess the official title does not mean much.' Yasin put up a brave face.

'Now you understand.'

Shortly afterward ,Yasin left the office of Jimmy thinking he needed to get more cash for Egypt and also take his 'commission' from it. Somehow, he felt that he was never going to make a director of the company.

Two days later, there was a meeting in the boardroom of Chezan Investments Ltd with banker Sam Hollworth and his team of two assistants. From the company, it was Jimmy, Pearce, Vincent, Dean and Yasin.

'We cannot go on financing and increase our loans to you, the Board will not have it, I really need to get some ammunition to satisfy them.' Sam expressed the hopeless situation the bank was in, for the past loans made to the company.

'As I said, Vincent is going to explain to you the current position, and our future plans. The bank already knows that we have some new blood in our management team, and the company is going to be transformed soon. We are not saying that we will repay all the loans soon but within twelve months, we should be in a very strong position.' Pearce said it confidently.

'Let's hear the presentation of Vincent and then discuss, May I add he has been promoted to CFO position with immediate effect with a seat on the board.' Jimmy added.

'Congratulations', Sam and his colleagues said.

Vincent got up and went to the TV screen used for the presentation. He highlighted the 'New Heaven' project, its cashflow presentation, the positive impact it will have on company finances.'

'But these projections and the business plan is not really very specific there are so many ifs and buts in it, shouldn't we have a more specific plan laying out the details?' commented one of the bank's assistants.

Before Vincent could reply, Jimmy interrupted. 'Look we are planning to visit Caribbean, and look at first hand the land and local environment and the business plan will be updated immediately on our return. I am sure we will provide you all the details you need.'

'Who is going?' Sam asked.

'It will be Vincent, the promoter and his assistant and myself.' Jimmy explained.

'Let me continue now with our existing projects, Egyptian project, the project is running smoothly and we have received funds in London and you would have noticed that the company's overdraft is considerably reduced.' Vincent continued with his presentation.

'Yasin, would you like to add something?' Jimmy looked at Yasin.

'Basically the project is running smoothly, old outstanding invoices have been settled, the funds being transferred to London, the country is a lot more stable now, and we hope to increase our business over there.' Yasin said confidently.

'Good.' Sam praised Yasin.

Vincent continued with his presentation, and after they discussed the bread and butter of the business, the commodity trading and equities. 'We are going to have some very favourable cashflow from the coffee contracts. Perhaps Dean can explain it better.'

Dean immediately looked at his papers and explained how the bad crop in Brazil has increased the coffee prices and that they had not sold all their future contracts, and therefore, their new sale contract were a lot more profitable.

'How much profit we are talking about?'

'I would estimate it to be about US eight million.' Dean smiled. 'I must say that it is not me who has done it we should thank the Mother Nature!'

'But we will have to settle for one short contract,' Jimmy added, 'so the profit will be reduced.'

Dean was surprised about this short contract, he did not know. Before he could say anything Pearce said, 'I will fill you in, there is a short contract… maybe, the copy was not given to you.' Dean kept quiet and decided to discuss the contract later with both of them.

'So how much profit is going to be there?' Sam asked.

'I think we are probably looking around US five million.' Pearce did the quick calculation in his mind regretting that he should have told Dean about the three million transfer to 'pay' for the short contract.

'That is excellent.' Sam praised. 'God, we have some good news today.'

The serious meeting continued while Sam and his assistants made some detailed notes. Jackie and Sandra served them coffee and light refreshments. When Jackie came close to Sam he looked closely at her but did not say anything. Jackie acknowledged him with her eyes.

The bankers left happy knowing that Chezan Investments Ltd was going to be back on a lot better footing soon, so further investment in their new project should be easier to sell to the credit committee.

Late in the afternoon, Yasin Kanji and Masood Panji were sitting in one of the offices. Masood used to sit in a large office which he shared with a few accounts clerks and the petty cashier. Yasin wanted to know what has been going on during his absence.

'This bastard is really doing well.' Masood confided in Yasin referring to Vincent.

'Is he good?'

'He seems to be…. He was questioning the large sum of cash you took to Egypt. '

'Don't worry about that, let I or Jimmy explain it to him.'

'He is promoted, no?'

'Yeah… anyway, I am managing the Egyptian project…Are you not going to Caribbean?'

'I did the basic business plan but Vincent has hijacked it, they did not even tell me that they were planning to visit the site.' Masood complained.

'The higher they fly, the quicker they fall!' Yasin consoled him, 'don't worry he is not going to last long.'

'This petty cashier keeps on buying things for his personal use and charges to the company. I am going to report to Pearce.'

'These are small amounts, he is one of us, don't waste your time on it.' Yasin advised him. 'Think big man,' he added.

They both were quiet for a few moments. 'Look if I make the FD, you will be my financial controller,' Yasin threw the carrot at Masood.

'I get it; I am going to make sure Vincent does not settle in the job. Sooner you are FD, better it is.' Masood promised his 'boss'.

Two days later, there was a private party in one of the exclusive halls of the famous hotel in Park Lane. The hotel is probably the most exclusive in London. In the basement they had a large ball room, and two smaller halls designed for smaller parties. The hall was well decorated.

The Noble family was there: Albert Noble and Alisha Noble (the parents), Jimmy Noble, Pearce Noble and Firoza Noble. All were well dressed. There were Mr & Mrs Dean Rowe, Mr & Mrs Vincent Muller, Yasin Kanji and Shan Reza. From New Country Bank, Sam Hollworth and his wife, his two assistants and their wives and the member of credit committee at the bank, Jeffrey Anderson. For security reasons, the muscle man Shrute Sting was also there. All of them were in smart evening suits and long dresses.

They were sitting in luxurious chairs behind a large well laid out banquet table. The finely dressed waiters and waitresses were serving them some of the finest foods available. Fine Bordeaux wine was served with the food. Everybody had a smile on their faces and doing small talks while eating.

About two hours later, the waiters cleared the big table and now a number of them stood, and some sat on the sofas nearby. There was a sound of a spoon against the glass. It was Albert Noble who wanted to address.

'Ladies and gentlemen, thank you very much indeed for coming tonight. It has been great pleasure to see you all. I understand that my sons are doing well and that all the debts I left behind are going to be cleared by them… (Some guests laugh). In our kind of businesses, there are always circumstances beyond our control which affect our business, even though, we try to diversify the business, the commodity trading is very much of luck: if the weather is good or bad depending upon how you position yourself, the overseas governments and who is ruling the country, all kind of factors play part. (He pauses). Anyway, the company has been recovering and I wish you all a very pleasant evening, and to the managers of the company sincere thanks and a bright future…. Good evening ladies and gentlemen.'

Everybody clapped.

The soft music was played while all of them split into smaller groups.

Pearce came to Greta Muller. 'How nice to see you Mrs Muller, you look beautiful.' He praised the wife of Vincent Muller, a beautiful woman in her late twenties.

'Thank you… Vincent talked a lot about you.'

'I hope all good… where is he?'

'Yes it was all good, he is with your parents over there,' she pointed to Vincent.

'I did not know the accountants were choosing such beautiful wives!'

'I am sure you say that to all the women, men always do.'

'No seriously, you are very beautiful.'

'Thanks Pearce,' Greta began to feel more comfortable with the boss of her husband.

They continued to talk.

On the sofa, where Albert and Alisha were sitting, talking to Vincent, Sam came towards them with his wife.

'If you will excuse me,' Vincent noticed the banker coming with his wife, he got up.

'Okay son, take care.' Albert Noble said.

Vincent noticed his wife with Pearce so he joined them.

'Come my dear,' Alisha welcomed Davina Hollworth.

'Good evening Alisha... how are you?'

'Very well, thank you; and you my dear?'

'Good', Sam and Davina sat on the sofa.

'I understand, the company is doing well at the moment?' Albert asked Sam.

'Yes, I think we are getting somewhere, the new team is also making the difference.'

'Yes, I just met Vincent what a fine man?'

'Very impressive, I think they (his sons) have found a really competent person.' Sam also praised Vincent.

'How have you been keeping, there are lots of new regulations?'

'First we had to put up with all kind of rules and regulations from EU, and now we have to prepare for the Brexit. The shareholders seem to take a lot more interest in the company these days.' Sam had a lot to talk about.

They continued to talk for a while. In a few minutes time, it was time for Hollworths to move on, so they got up. 'If you will excuse us.'

'Nice to meet you my dear' Alisha added. And discreetly she brought out a small packet from her hand bag and gave it to Davina. 'I did not see you at Christmas, this one has been overdue.'

'Oh, no please, you have already been very kind.' Davina hesitated.

'You are like my daughter, please don't say no.'

'What is it anyway?'

'Oh nothing, just a small bracelet.' Alisha said in a low voice.

'Thank you very much,' Davina bent to kiss her cheek while handing the small packet to Sam who quickly put it in his Jacket.

'Good evening', they both said and moved on.

While walking back, Davina asked her husband, 'I wonder what type of bracelet it is.'

'Knowing them it has to be some nice one, most probably a diamond one.' Sam replied in a low voice. 'Wait till we get home you can have a look at it.'

'Can I borrow your husband for a minute?' They heard from Jimmy who walked to them.

'Sure, I will find a nice young man.' Davina grinned.

Jimmy and Sam moved to a lonely corner. They spoke to each other in a slow voice making sure no one was listening to them. Professional people with good food, excellent wine and excellent atmosphere had different things on their minds rather than listen to Jimmy.

‘Good evening Mr Anderson, how are you?’ Firoza came close to Jeffrey who had been to the toilet and had just walked in back.

‘Hello, hello, my dear, you should not call me Mr Anderson, Jeff will do’, Jeffrey put his hand on her shoulder. Jeffrey was in his mid-fifties, experienced banker and member of the credit committee which approved loans. Before Sam, he was the account manager for Chezan Investment. Once there was rumour that he was going to be made CEO of the bank but it never materialised. He had been a womaniser and probably that is why he was divorced. His only daughter having grown up, he was living alone. He had come to terms with his situation and was quite happy to toddle along as a senior member but with no prospects of further advancement. He was waiting to take an early retirement or made redundant. But for Chezan Investments, he was still very important since he knew the company and its owners well and was crucial member for the credit committee for the loans.

‘Hello Jeff if that pleases you.’ Firoza said in a seductive voice coming close to him.

‘Fantastic dinner; what a lovely people. Tell me, when are you going to get married?’

‘Oh you never proposed to me, I am still waiting.’ Firoza joked with him.

‘I wish I wasn’t twenty years too late, I would have not waited.’

‘You are not bad even now!’ Firoza played with him.

Jeffrey picked up a glass of champagne for Firoza from a passing waiter and one scotch glass for himself. He gave her the glass.

‘I really had enough… but thank you.’

‘Cheers.’ Jeffrey touched her glass.

They continued to talk for a while. Then after a few minutes, Jeffrey whispered something into her ear.

Firoza looked at him not quite sure but then she whispered back something in his ears and left him.

About two hours later, while the party had finished and most people had gone home, Firoza and Jeffrey were in the bedroom of the hotel where the party was being held. Jimmy Noble had hired the room for him to stay overnight. Some of the bank staff went to the bank's apartment which was almost a walking distance. Firoza was still in her evening gown while Jeffrey had taken his jacket off, both sitting on the small sofa.

'You know Firoza, I don't understand while there were so many good looking people around, you chose to come with me.' Jeffrey although half-drunk still managed to ask the relevant question.

'Oh…you don't know …I get turned on by mature people, it is your intellect which stimulates my…..,' she did not finish her sentence.

Jeffrey was experienced enough not to let such an opportunity go by. He immediately put his hands on her shoulder and kissed her. It was a kiss which showed experience. She put her hands on his hair. They continued to kiss for a while. After a few moments, Jeffrey knew she was there for what was coming, no pretentions. Jimmy had arranged the room for him and she was there. There was no time to waste. He got up, excused himself and went to the attached bathroom. He took out a pill from his pocket and put it in his mouth. He came outside and picked up a bottle of water from table and poured some water and swallowed.

'Sorry would you like some water?' Jeffrey asked Firoza.

'No thank you. I had too much to drink...I think I should leave, you probably are tired.'

Jeffrey did not reply, he grabbed her and brought her to the bed. He kissed her hard and put his hands on her bottom.

Firoza knew when she came to his room what she was expecting; her instructions were to make the old man happy. This is the work she has had done for the company and for herself many times. She did not stop him and put her hands on his shoulder. Shortly after, Jeffrey put his hands on her breast and started playing with them while kissing her. Firoza did not want to make it too long she started opening his shirt. Soon they helped each other undress and went into the bed.

About an hour later, Firoza was tired. She could not believe that an old man will make her work so much. Two rounds of full blown passion. Shan definitely needed to learn something from Jeffrey, she thought in her mind.

In the lounge near the entrance, Shrute Sting was waiting to drive Firoza home; an impressive Rolls was parked near the entrance. He was wondering why Firoza was in the hotel so late at night while all the other guests had left. He knew Jeffrey was also there. What does she see in him, he complained to himself. 'Shit, I could keep her awake the whole night if I had a chance, that woman can give a hard on to any man by just looking at him.' He could not continue with his dream much longer when he saw a tired Firoza getting out of the lift. He immediately got up, leaving his drink unfinished.

Chapter 4

In a beautiful island called New Island in Caribbean, three men were waiting anxiously at the arrival lounge of the airport. Bradley Connors, a man in his early sixties, was a rich man who inherited a large number of properties in Caribbean going back to the British time. He had sold some of it and developed some. Although he lived mostly in London, he had a large villa in the island. His nephew Baxter Connors was in his early forties, a fitness fanatic who looked after his body well. He was now doing most of the management of the properties which Bradley had. It included some land near the beach. Also waiting was Josh Kunta, the local manager of Bradley in the island who was from Caribbean and well connected.

There was an announcement about the British Airways flight arrival from London. After a few minutes, the passengers started walking out in the arrival gate. The immigration and customs was very quick especially for the flights coming from Europe. Soon, Jimmy Noble and Vincent Muller walked out from the arrival gate, greeted by Bradly and Baxter with a warm handshake.

'This is Josh Kunta, our manager in the island', Bradly introduced Josh to Jimmy and Vincent.

They both warmly shook hands with him saying, 'how are you?'

'Would you like something to drink before we go?' asked Baxter.

'No, thanks, we had plenty to drink in the plane', replied Jimmy.

In a few minutes, a polished Range Rover driven by Josh carried all the five men to the Villa of Bradley Connor which was close to the beach on a small hill.

'It is lovely, what a beautiful island?' said Vincent.

'Is it your first time here?' asked Baxter.

'Yes, I have never been here before.' Vincent looked at Jimmy.

'It is my first time too.' Jimmy added.

'Look at the weather, so pleasant!' Baxter said.

'Beautiful, not too hot, just right, I am glad we brought our light clothes with us.'

They continued to talk while the Range Rover, very smoothly driven by Josh, brought them to the villa.

They all entered the villa, greeted by the housekeeper, Ashani, a middle aged Caribbean woman. While Josh was bringing the light suitcases of Jimmy and Vincent, they sat in the lounge. Ashani served them immediately, the local passion fruit juice. Josh also came in, leaving the suitcases just outside the lounge.

After a few minutes, Bradly asked Ashani, 'could you please show Jimmy and Vincent their rooms?'

'We will meet around six thirty and then go for dinner in the restaurant. I have already booked a table. This restaurant is close to the 'New Heaven' project.' Baxter looked at them. 'Is it okay or you want me to delay it?'

'No, that should be okay, we have more than an hour to refresh and relax.' Jimmy looked at Vincent who kept quiet.

Several thousand miles away in London office of Chezan Investments Ltd, Marc Kohnvich was sitting in front of Pearce in the office. They had finalised the pension and insurances of the staff.

'I am surprised that you have taken such an expensive Keyman policy, twenty-five million.' Marc could not hide his surprise.

'You see he is the new CFO as well as a Board member. He is going to be the key person in our company's turnaround. He has got cost cutting and very good financial control experience.'

'I thought you were carried away by your commission!' Marc joked.

'No, I am being serious; in fact, we were thinking to increase the sum. Do you know right now he is in Caribbean doing probably a great job with my brother Jimmy. We got a very important project starting soon and he is going to be the key person to sell it to the bank!' Pearce highlighted the importance of Vincent in the company. 'And yes, you must be making a bundle out of all this, no?'

Marc felt a little embarrassed about his joke. 'It's true I shall earn a good commission but I must tell you the number of hours I have put in it, and the competitive rates I have got for you.'

'Sure, we shall be doing more business in future. You know we are always interested in all kinds of financial proposals.'

But I thought your company's finances were a little tight (he did not tell Pearce that he had done a company search at the Companies House for the company).'

'Between you and me … we have plenty of funds available from a number of investors who do not wish openly to invest, we do it for them.' Pearce confided in him in a low voice.

Marc was quiet for a while. Then he realised how they maintain a beautiful office in one of the most expensive areas of London, Rolls Royce, Bentleys and Ferraris. 'Sure, I come across a lot of projects while visiting companies.'

'We also give a good commission to the introducers.' Pearce tempted him.

'By the way, does Vincent know how much policy you have taken for him?'

'He does not need to know the sum; he knows we have taken a pension, life assurance and Keyman policy for him. We do not want him to get too big headed!'

'I see… anyway he signed all the papers and we have used the same data for the Keyman insurance policy as well.'

'Please if you ever speak to him do not mention the amount; I am not giving him the papers of the Keyman policy.'

'No I will not have much to do with him, the payment has been received in the bank, and the formal policies should be with you soon. These papers are basically complete.'

'Good.'

'Finally, your share has been transferred to the bank account you stated. He took out a piece of paper from his wallet, do you want me to send you the details.'

'No that's fine; I do not need any paperwork. I have checked with the bank and the amount is in line with our agreement.' Pearce was happy with his efficiency.

'Okay, then I shall be off.' Marc got up.

The insurance broker left happy, having earned a fortune in the commission.

After briefly looking at the papers, Pearce took out the detailed papers of the Keyman insurance policy papers and filed them in his desk drawer and locked it. Then he pressed the buzzer and asked Jackie to call Masood to his office.

'Masood, these are the papers of staff pension, life assurance and Keyman policy. Please go through with the bank payments to ensure these are all in line and then leave these for Vincent to review on his desk.'

Masood took the papers from his hand. 'When will Vincent be back?'

'I don't know it may take a few days, depends what they find in Caribbean.'

'We need some new computers in the accounts?' Masood pointed out.

'Prepare the capital expenditure forms and let Vincent sign them on his return, and then I or Jimmy will approve it. At present, we need funds for the new project so it may be after it has been finalised.'

'Thank you.'

Pearce started looking at his desk; Masood knew that he was not needed so he left the office. His efforts to come close to Pearce, so far had not materialised.

An impressive white Jaguar was carrying five people along the hilly area close to the beach in the New Island. The car was driven by Josh Kunta, and next to him sitting was Baxter Connors; Bradley Connors, Jimmy Noble and Vincent Muller were sitting at the back.

'Look this is the site of 'New Heaven' do you want me to stop here?' Baxter pointed out to the area close by.

'We are going to spend quite a bit of time here tomorrow, so let's leave it for today, Josh can you drive a bit slow.' Bradley said.

'It's getting a little dark, so tomorrow should be fine. But it is a fantastic location. You can have a reasonably good view from here and the mountains at the back. Just like Cote d'Azur really!' Jimmy showed his enthusiasm.

'And at a faction of the cost! In fact, from a little height you will have a completely unobscured view of the sea.' Baxter added.

They continued to talk while the car continued to be driven slowly by Josh.

After about half an hour, they were in the luxurious restaurant with a view of the beach and the sea. The waiter had served them the aperitif, and they were talking.

'It is a nice place.' Jimmy said admiring the view from the restaurant.

'You see Jimmy, Caribbean is a second home to me. I live here quite often and from the young age I have been coming here. I think the area has got more potential than the people realise.' Bradley wanted to convince Jimmy about the viability of the project.

'I am sure ..... What do you think?' Jimmy looked at Vincent.

'I am sure the place can be further developed, it has got the natural beauty and a beautiful weather.' Vincent was also impressed.

Soon the waiter arrived for the order and they started ordering the food. They continued to talk about the project and later about their personal lives. Bradley explained that he did not have any children of his own so basically he saw Baxter as his main heir. Vincent couldn't help noticing that in one of the tables two men were discreetly observing them. He did not think much of it and ignored it. He also noticed some well-known Hollywood stars enjoying the meal close to their table.

'Oh... the area is very popular with Hollywood. There are always some film stars and crew dining here.' Baxter noticed Vincent looking at one of the tables frequently.

'I think that should be a plus for our project, no?' Vincent immediately started thinking of the business they were there for.

Bradley admired the way Vincent was conducting himself and how he connected everything to the business at hand. No wonder they think so highly of him, he thought.

‘Yes of course’, Baxter said.

They continued with their meals and the conversation shifted from business to the local drinks.

It was quite late when they returned to the villa.

It was sunny morning; Jimmy, Vincent, Bradly, Baxter and Josh were visiting the site of the proposed ‘New Heaven’ project. The site was slightly on the hill and had a reasonable view of the sea. However, once the building was done from a certain height there would be a clear view of the sea. Towards the back about half a mile or so there were some high hills sparsely habituated. There was a small cabin constructed from the prefabricated units to be used as the office, and the rest of the area for the security man who looked after the site.

The security man had placed a few folding chairs and a table for them to sit in the open. He also served some cold drinks from the small fridge he had. They walked along the site stopping at different places and discussing various aspects. Jimmy and Vincent were really impressed with the site and they could see huge potential. About half a mile or so, there was a hotel but lacking grandeur. There seemed to be a good opportunity to either build a hotel or serviced apartments.

After a tour of the site looking at all angles, they retired to the chairs and were discussing the project. ‘So what do you think?’ asked Bradley.

‘I must admit it is a fantastic site, but I can see a few issues. How easy is it to get the planning permission from the council; secondly, what is more viable a hotel or services apartments or indeed villas.’ Jimmy gave his first impression.

Bradley looked at Vincent for his opinion. 'I also think so, the other point is that the terrain is a bit rough, how is going to affect the construction cost?' Vincent spelled out his opinion.

'You see the government here is encouraging investment, they badly need some employment here, the island is suffering from huge unemployment... there might be some tax incentives as well.'

'I see…. but I think not very suitable for luxury villas.'

'Yes, you are right; the land is not big enough; the luxury villas here are rather spacious. The site is really more suitable for a hotel or apartments.'

'Who owns the adjoining land?' Jimmy looked at the side site.

'I own it…. It is considerably smaller.' Bradley replied.

'Why did you not include it in the project?' Vincent asked.

'I think, in the initial phase, the current site is sufficient. It is very valuable piece of land… it is naturally divided from this land by the small hill in between….maybe, we can talk about it later.'

They continued to talk and drink the cold drinks provided. After a while, Vincent got up with his notepad and pen. 'I am going to walk along the site and make some notes.'

'Do you want me to come with you?' enquired Jimmy.

'No, I should be okay it is rather long walk, I should be back shortly.'

'All right, I will give you company in case you want to ask any questions', Baxter also got up.

They continued to talk while Josh also left to collect some raw coconuts for juice and some light refreshments. He knew they were going to stay there for a while.

Vincent started walking, and Baxter joined him.

While Jimmy and Bradley were alone, they started discussing some more serious business.

'Look Jimmy, you are just like my nephew, I think it is a wonderful opportunity for you!' Bradley tempted him.

'Sure…. You know all these adjoining lands and nearby area are going to appreciate in value if this project takes place?' Jimmy showed his sharp brain.

'Yes…of course.'

'Who owns these?'

'Well you know the immediate adjoining land belongs to me, the rest, slightly further away, are owned by various people, a piece is also owned by Josh Kunta…. Anyway, what it has got to do with it?' Bradley seemed confused.

'You see, if we are going to invest substantial amounts here, I was wondering if I could buy the adjoining land myself, provided of course, the current project is firmed up.' Jimmy said seriously.

'Well, I was hoping to sell it myself at an increased price once this project gets off the ground.'

Jimmy was quiet for a few moments, 'you see Bradley, we are going to risk quite a lot of funds here, in order for me to really convince myself that it is going to be profitable, I need to make some money personally. If we invest here, it seems everybody else is going to reap the benefit….'

Bradley was still not sure what Jimmy was trying to say, he interrupted him. 'Please say it clearly what do you mean.'

'Basically, I want to buy the adjoining land at a reasonable price, let's say a small discount to the current price, without taking into account any future developments in the area, so that I might build a villa for myself here…I love the place.'

'I see… is it for your family?'

'No, I want to keep this for me…and of course, this will be between you and me. I would not like anybody else should know about it, neither Baxter, nor Vincent or anyone else including my family.' Jimmy whispered.

Bradley was surprised; he never expected that he will be putting this condition for the investment, and not for the family business but for himself. He stayed quiet.

'You can think about it… you can let me know before I leave for London.' Jimmy did not wish to force him to make a quick decision.

'So do I understand correctly that this project is only going to kick off once I agree to sell the adjoining land to you?'

'Look Bradley… you are an experienced businessman. One has to exploit the opportunity. You see I could have asked you to increase the price of this land and give me the adjoining land at a peppercorn… but I want to be fair.'

'I guess I am getting old… but come to think of it I am also used to all kinds of arrangements and facilitating payments.'

'There you are, the way we conduct business is changing… you see you are not going to lose out…you are selling the current land at a good price, you will share in the project, if I make some money as well, what's wrong with it?'

Bradley was quiet for few moments. He was thinking fast and wanted to close the deal. If this project does not take off, he will have to spend a lot of time to find another investor. These guys are young with plenty of energy and connections…. 'Look I am going to make a very quick decision I hope I do not regret it…' Bradley took a sip from his glass.

Jimmy saw his CFO making notes and discussing the site with Baxter from the distance. The guy seemed to be right into it.

'Okay, I am willing to sell the adjoining land to you provided this project materialises within a month or so... the price will be the current price without taking into account the potential increase due to current development…and yes… a small discount of 10%.'

'Thank you so much, really obliged.' Jimmy could not hide his pleasure. He knew the land was going to increase at least double in value once the current project starts.

'Do you want me to speak to my lawyers?' Bradley asked.

'No, perhaps you can confirm it to me in writing by email. Of course, I will not take it up unless the current project is completely agreed… then we can deal with the lawyers.'

They continued to talk about it for a while until they saw Josh coming towards them with lunch and drinks. Soon Vincent and Baxter also joined them. The security man, from distance, saw Josh so he walked towards him to help. Serious business was forgotten while they enjoyed the lunch.

After lunch, they talked a little bit about the New Island.

'I saw you making quite a lot of notes; so what do you think?' Jimmy asked Vincent.

'I think the land is big enough to make a two-phase project. In half of the land, we can build luxurious furnished apartments with gym, swimming pool, tennis court and a first class restaurant.'

'Why not a hotel then?'

'I think initially in order to attract families the furnished apartments will be more competitive; if the people are coming from thousands of miles they want to hang on for a few days. The services of the hotel make it more expensive.' Vincent explained.

'We can sell some of these too?'

'Yes of course, when the tourists come here and they like the place then some might be interested in buying the apartment.'

'I will get you the planning permission whether it is hotel or furnished apartments… I know the minister of tourism and development personally. You have seen in the package the understanding that they will approve any development: be villas, apartments or hotel.' Bradley added.

'Yes, I have seen it… look I have just roughly set out the area to build in the first phase including outside tennis court and lawns…..' Vincent showed his note pad to Jimmy.

'Where will be the land left for the second phase?' Baxter asked.

'All these lawns will not need to be there, part of the lawns will be converted in the second phase.'

They all seemed to appreciate what Vincent was saying. The discussion continued. About two hours later, they decided to call it a day and returned to the villa. When in his bedroom, Jimmy immediately rang Pearce to know what has been happening. He updated him about the visit to the site and briefly about Vincent's idea of phased development. Pearce informed him that all the pension, life insurances and Keyman policy were all finalised. Vincent and others also spent some time on their mobiles.

In the evening, there was a dinner at home. Minister of tourism and development, his wife, the local mayor and his wife and another couple were invited. Josh's wife, Thema and Ashani had done all the preparation. A maid was there to help in serving the food and the drinks.

During the dinner, Bradley asked the Mayor, 'could you please reassure our guests here that there would not be any problem for the planning permission.'

Mayor smiled, 'of course not, we are looking at some major inward investments and creation of the jobs. I can't see any problems, do you?' he looked at the minister.

'You are absolutely right; we are already aware of the planned construction, and a letter was issued by the ministry that they will encourage the new construction there… we know Mr Bradley Connors for such a long time…. How can we refuse him anything? He has been a wonderful person assisting the local economy,' the minister said it proudly.

Jimmy was pleased that Bradley did have some important contacts, and that they were all willing to endorse the investment there.

After dinner, Vincent retired to his room while the others continued drinking. He had to make some notes; Vincent was very work orientated.

The next day, a private jet was hired and all of them went to the island of Mustique. Bradley wanted to show how Caribbean had developed. He also knew the promoter of the island who developed that small island a few decades ago. The view from the jet flying low at the various Caribbean islands was fantastic. In a clear day, they could see the beautiful beaches, impressive boats and villas and natural beauty. Jimmy was wondering why he never came to that part of the world.

After flying on a large area of Caribbean, they descended into the Mustique Island. This island was amazing, small but full of natural beauty. They stayed in a small hotel there. After refreshing themselves, they went to the tour of the island. They saw some very impressive villas owned by the royal families, billionaires and important politicians. A number of these had their own private beaches. They swam in the sandy beach, and had dinner in Bradley's friend's house in the evening. Vincent took a lot of photos with his mobile.

After dinner, they were all sitting in the lounge and discussing.' So how do you feel now?' Bradley looked at Jimmy.

'I think the place is wonderful…do they have any land to develop in this island?'

'Sorry, no, it is fully developed. The only option will be to demolish one of the villas and build something but that would be a real pity. The island will lose its character… frankly they do not want any intrusion here, it is rather a members only club… you know what I mean!'

'I see…anyway, I think the New Island is good for us. It is more open and I think it will attract more tourists.'

Next morning, they flew back to the New Island. They were sitting in Bradley's villa.

'Vincent I am going to meet someone with Bradley. I suggest you go to the site and do some more detailed study, make your plans take photos etc. After that, I am planning to fly back to London in the afternoon.'

Vincent did not know that he was going to leave early. 'Yes, it would be better to do a little more study here.'

'You want to meet the architect, get some rough drawings, cost estimates, look around the Island a little more, so that when we submit the plan this time to the bank we have all specific details.'

'Fine, I think we need to explore the Island a little more to put the info in the project.' Vincent agreed with Jimmy.

'Well, spend as much time as you like. There is no urgency in London at the moment.'

'I am also off to New York, I need to meet someone over there…but Baxter would look after you. But be careful the island ladies are as hot as the weather over here!' Bradley looked at Vincent.

'Especially with those good looks, you should be very popular.' Baxter laughed.

Shortly afterward, Bradley and Jimmy left in the car driven by Josh.

'So what is the plan?' Baxter asked.

'Let's fix up a meeting for tomorrow with the architect, and then we can go to the site.'

'It wouldn't take that much time at the site.' Baxter pointed out.

'We can visit a few places in island once I finish at the site.'

They also left in the Range Rover.

At the site, Vincent got busy just like he was working in the office. He sat down with his laptop in the shade of the small structure. Baxter sat down on a chair and started talking to someone. After looking at his emails, he started on the project. He entered the rough size of the plot, nearby land and other buildings and other details. Then he took his mobile and went out walking alongside the border of the land and took several photos of the site nearby area. He brought a chair and stood on it and took the photos of the sea. Baxter was impressed with his dedication. He answered many questions Vincent asked about the site and their own plans. 'Do you have subsidence here due to very uneven land?' he asked Baxter.

'We can check with the architect tomorrow, he would have better idea.' Baxter admitted his lack of knowledge.

'Do you get sometimes storms over here? I understand that these are rather frequent in Caribbean?'

'Not really, just like anywhere else; you see these are islands and the sea plays quite a bit of a role on the weather over here.'

Vincent continued to work. It was nearly lunch time. Josh joined, and they had light lunch.

'Are you going to spend more time here?' Baxter asked him.

'I guess I could do some of the work back at home in the evening.'

And after a short while, Josh, Baxter and Vincent left in the Range Rover. Baxter wanted to show him some important places in the island. They started at the beach which wasn't far from the site. A number of holiday makers were there. All kinds of shapes: women in their bikinis at the beach, people swimming and sunbathing. Vincent took photos of the beach. There was an impressive restaurant on one of the heights. 'What is it?' Vincent asked.

'Oh this is a popular restaurant, and it gets real busy in the evening. We will be dining here tonight', Josh replied.

They moved on to the next place, a few miles further in. There were mountains and just at the bottom, there was some smoke.

'This isn't really very interesting but I wanted to show the view from here of the sea if we climb a little on the hill,' Josh said.

'No it is very interesting these are some minerals underneath with which the fumes come out. This is really very interesting, why this has not been developed?' Vincent showed his interest in the site.

'We do not really think much of it; most people think this is not something to show. In fact, there is a plan to dig it out about half a square mile and take out whatever is causing all these steams.' Josh said it seriously.

'I think it can be a tourist attraction, you don't find these kinds of sites everywhere!' Vincent gave Josh some idea.

'Do you really think so; I am sure I can buy or get a lease of the place if you think people will visit here. Maybe I can make a little money here....'

'Well, let's say if I was visiting the island I will visit this site too.'

Josh made a mental note to pursue it as there seemed to be some business opportunity. They climbed the hill and Vincent continued with his photos.

A little later, they moved to a natural spa which was nearby, where the warm water with all kind of minerals was used to improve your health, skin and the body.

'Have you been here?' Vincent asked Baxter.

'Once or twice, I prefer to swim in the sea.'

They continued with the major sites of the island. Soon they arrived at the ruins of an old castle which was also on a small hill. The ruin was not in good repairs, and no one was allowed to get into the ruin, just look from outside. 'This is going back to hundreds of years, the local ruler once had this castle but it seems that it is going to be completely damaged, there is not much maintenance of it.' Josh explained.

'I think the Island is waiting to generate some more funds by increasing the tourist trade, then they can afford to spend more on these sites.' Baxter added.

'Yes it is chicken and egg situation, more tourists will come if the sites were developed; more sites will be developed if there were more tourists.'

They continued to discuss and visit the various places of interest, and after collecting substantial information, notes and the photos Vincent came back with them, happy with the knowledge that he has made a good progress and will be able to put up a decent business plan for the bank.

Chapter 5

Vincent Muller, Baxter Connors, Josh Kunta and Thema Kunta were in a beautiful restaurant with a fantastic view of the sea. They were having aperitif, the rum punch with fruit juices a speciality of the restaurant.

'Gosh, it is really nice here.' Vincent exclaimed.

'Yeah, it is very nice, wait till it gets a little late; all the beauties of the island will descend over here.'

'We already have got one over here.' Vincent looked at Thema who was a young attractive woman. She had been married to Josh for a year or so.

'Thank you; I like people who appreciate women.' Thema looked teasingly at her husband.

'This is their mannerism; they don't mean it. European people tend to pass these kinds of compliments regardless.' Josh teased her as well.

Baxter chuckled, 'I never pass a compliment unless I mean it.'

'Sure we know you are a playboy. Didn't you say last time, you knew too many beautiful women you do not know which one to choose.' Thema grinned.

In the meantime, a waitress came there to take their orders.

About an hour later, the restaurant was very busy hardly any table free, and the bar area was crowded. Next to the bar, there was an area which was used for dancing. A live band had come there and started playing the music. A few people started dancing. They had nearly finished the meal.

'Thank you, I would love to…I thought you will never ask?' Thema got up and extended her hand.

Vincent was surprised; he went along with the ploy. 'Of course, how could I let such an opportunity pass by.' He got up immediately and walked with her to the dancing area.

Vincent had never been close to a black woman before. As soon as they started dancing he felt that she was really sexy. Dancing closely he could feel her firm breasts. The next dance was slow rhythm and they continued the dance. 'Gosh, this woman is hot, Baxter was right the black women are too hot!' He thought. While dancing closely Thema looked at her husband who was busy talking with Baxter. Suddenly she felt Vincent's body against her, she realised that he was a handsome man, and although she had been intimate with many white men before, she felt his masculine body very tempting. Well, Josh is going to have a good time later, I am going to take my time tonight with him', Thema decided. She felt his hands brushing on and off on her nipples. She had to hold them, in case, she also got carried away.

After the song finished, Thema and Vincent came back to their table. Before Thema could sit, Baxter got up extending his hand and she went back to the dancing floor with him.

'You got a very pretty wife!' Vincent remarked.

'Yeah, I know I have been very lucky that she chose me….She is also a good wife.' Josh knew, although well-built, he was very ordinary looking. And he always thanked God that he had a wonderful wife. Of course, his sexual prowess played a big role in it too.

'How do you get along with Bradley and Baxter?'

'They have been very good to me. You see since the time they started investing in the island themselves, and now bringing some more investors, the Island has improved. The unemployment has fallen and the property prices have also gone up. My own piece of land has gone up too… I am hoping that it will increase substantially once you guys do some new projects over here.'

'I see…' Vincent took a sip of his drink.

'Mr Connors (Bradley) is a very influential person here. Everybody in the government knows him. He has very high level contacts.'

'He has got other properties in the close-by islands too?'

'Yes, he is very wealthy… he could invest in the project himself but he likes to bring in the new blood.'

They continued to talk. In a few minutes, they saw Thema and Baxter coming back.

'Well it is my turn now… 'Josh said when Thema was about to sit down.

'Sure, in a few minutes…' she sat down in her chair and took a sip from the glass.

About an hour later, the dancing floor was packed; some women had let their hair down. Baxter, Josh and Vincent were all dancing with different women. Vincent's partner was a woman called Talisha.

'Do you come here often?' Vincent asked.

'Yes, it is very nice here… I used to come here with my husband....' Talisha replied.

'What happened to him, Is he travelling?'

'No I am separated from him; he is too jealous. He wants me to stay at home all the time. Sometimes, he went out with his friends and I waited at home alone.' Talisha complained. 'Anyway what are you doing in this island?'

'Oh I am just visiting… my company is planning to do some project here.'

'That's very interesting, so you would come here often', she asked innocently.

'I don't know....perhaps…'

She came close to him. Vincent was thinking how come he is feeling so aroused here? What is it with these black women! You touch them and you feel the heat inside you. It does not give you much time. Thema gave him the same feeling and now Talisha. He felt heavier in his pants. He was thinking how his boss used to joke in the office a few years ago. 'I like my women young and black!!' Now I know where that came from.

Talisha felt him, and joked, 'so you are happy to see me!'

'Sorry, you girls here are too sexy' He tried to distance from her but she did not give him the chance she brought her body forward. They continued to dance.

It was quite late when they all returned.

In London, Pearce was with Greta, after a dinner in a restaurant he had persuaded her to come back with him to his apartment which was located near Kensington Park. It was a small apartment but very nicely located in a luxurious block with a view of the park. Greta did not really want to come to his apartment, but being alone at home was not a better option. She missed Vincent, prior to Vincent going to Caribbean, she was not very well, and they had not had sex for a few days, and now he was away.

'You are going to be bored at home, he had said to her, just a nightcap…then you can take a taxi or I will drive you home.' Pearce had said.

They were sitting in the lounge decorated very tastefully. Pearce had served her some Scotch. Jackie had been in the flat many times and used to make sure that the place stayed in good décor and well stocked with the drinks.

'What are you thinking?' Pearce came a little closer on the sofa.

'I was wondering what Vincent must be doing.'

'He is probably having his dinner... '

'Why is he still there when you said Jimmy is already back?'

'Don't worry about him Greta, he is okay... he is in good company, Baxter is there, and it is a very romantic place.' Pearce wanted to bring Greta in the mood.

'Oh yeah, romantic without his wife... not much use really.'

'You don't know these Caribbean women they are too sexy and really hot.'

Greta knew her husband was very faithful, she had not known him to be indiscreet since they were married. 'He is probably still working...that man is a workaholic!' Then suddenly she realised that Pearce had come very close to her, and their bodies were touching. She moved slightly away.

'Let me get you another drink...'Pearce realised that her glass was almost empty, the whisky and wine at the restaurant and now the Scotch did not affect her very much. She was still very sober and was not responding to his efforts. He poured some more scotch in her glass from the bottle at the coffee table. He got up. 'Let me put some more ice in it.' He took the glasses and went into the kitchen. He put some ice cubes and then discreetly took out a pill from a drawer and put it in Greta's glass. Quickly he came back.

'Cheers', they both took a sip.

After a few minutes, Greta felt a little dizzy. 'I think I should go back, could you please call a taxi?'

'No, I will drive you myself it is not very far…anyway I tend to sleep late.'

'I know you want to take advantage of me…' Greta felt her drink and her voice shaking. The drinks finally had affected her and she was feeling a little tipsy.

'No I never take advantage of anybody…' Pearce came close to her he knew it was the right time to move. He pushed her gently on the sofa and put his body over her. Greta did not want but she hardly could say no… she felt the masculine body and suddenly felt the heat. Her body was reacting strangely. When Pearce kissed her she responded with great energy and passion. They continued to kiss for a while, then Pearce just spread her legs and went on top of her. They continued to kiss and feel each other's bodies and Greta did not object when Pearce put his hands inside her bra.

For an hour, two young persons touched each other, felt each other and tasted each other. Greta could not remember the last time she has had sex with anyone with such enthusiasm. She did not feel any inhibitions and did everything which she had done many times with her husband who was not coming at all to her mind at the moment. At present, it was only Pearce, nice, handsome very willing very passionate. They did not bother to go to the bedroom, the sofa in the lounge made some heavy noises to accompany Greta's moaning.

While Pearce was in the shower, Greta dressed herself. She put back her clothes; she could not remember when she or Pearce took them off. The physical activity had taken some effect of the alcohol off. She sat down on the sofa. Soon Pearce was back.

'Would you like something to drink before?'

'No...I had enough drink for one night...Perhaps a glass of orange juice or water.' Greta got up and they both went into the kitchen. Pearce served her in the glass the orange juice from the fridge. She sat down on the chair in the kitchen while Pearce was standing close to her. After a sip, she put the glass on the table and noticed Pearce standing close to him. Pearce intentionally brought himself forward in such a way that her mouth was touching his thigh. It was not long before Pearce's trouser zip was opened and Greta felt him in her mouth. The alcohol could not be blamed this time.

About twenty minutes later, Pearce was driving Greta back to her home in his Ferrari car. 'You said you will not take advantage of me..?' Greta complained.

'I don't know who took advantage of whom.' Pearce laughed.

'How did you know, I was on the pill?'

'I did not...These days there are so many things…but it is good you were on the pill. I do not like those bloody rubber things.'

'I was not the first woman there, was I..?'

'You know I am a bachelor…'

'No I mean …wives or staff from the office.'

'No Greta…you are the first person from the office.' Pearce lied.

Greta suddenly felt the guilt when she remembered her husband. Why has he not called her, normally he rang her every night at her mobile. Soon they arrived at Mullers' home which was a small detached house in Primrose Hill.

'Would you like to come in for a coffee?' Greta showed her politeness.

'No, I think that bit we did in my flat.' Pearce smiled, and got out of the car to open the door for her.

'All right then,' Greta got out of the car too.

'Why do you have such a big house for both of you?'

‘We are planning a family, you see.’ Greta confided.

‘So why are you on……’

‘No I am not……’ Greta replied quickly, and moved towards the front door. ‘Good night.’

‘Good night.’ A confused and worried Pearce got back to his car.

Following day, Pearce and Baxter had meeting with the architect firm. They also visited a local construction company and got certain information about the cost but they both thought that it was not a suitable company. They would enquire in the main island of Barbados or some other larger companies. They visited briefly to the site, Vincent made his final note. About lunch time they got back to the Villa.

After lunch, Vincent went to his room to do some work. He also rang the office and spoke to Pearce and Masood to get an update about the office. Baxter had a meeting with someone in the town. Vincent continued to work on the business plan and downloaded photos into his laptop. Every now and then he was thinking of Talisha whom he had met in the restaurant the other day.

About an hour later, he received the call from Baxter that he was held up and would not be back at home until late at night. He said that Josh will come to the Villa and will take him out for dinner. Vincent told him that his work was completed and that he will leave for London next day. Vincent rang the airline and confirmed his flight details. Everything was making sense and he was happy that his visit had been successful. It was nearly time for Greta to get back home so he rang her.

‘Hello darling, sorry did not ring you yesterday.’ Vincent apologised.

‘Well I also went out for a meal yesterday so I also did not ring you.’ Before Vincent could ask the details of her previous evening she quickly asked. ‘Oh I am missing you, are you coming back tomorrow?’

'Yes, I have finished my work over here; I should be home tomorrow night.'

'I will pick you up from the airport?'

'No, don't bother; you will be tired from the office and then driving… I think I will take a taxi.'

'Alright then, I will prepare your favourite dish tomorrow.'

'Okay darling, I can't wait to be with you. I have been missing you.'

'So am I…. the nights are too long without you.' Greta said it in a charming way.

'What are you doing tonight?'

'Nothing; would have an early night I suppose...maybe watch a TV or read a novel.'

'Alright darling, see you tomorrow.'

'See you ...bye.'

'Bye, love you.'

'Me too.'

Vincent disconnected the phone.

In the early evening, Josh came to the villa. They talked a little bit. Ashani, the house keeper served them drinks. When asked about the choice of the restaurant, Josh wanted to take him to an exclusive French restaurant, well known for its cuisine and run by a Michelin chef. 'Why don't we go to the same place as yesterday?' Vincent suggested Josh.

'I see you are hooked on those beautiful women!'

'Not really, I go to French restaurants often in London. That place seems very pleasant and it will be a good place to remember when I get back.'

'Fine, let's go then.'

'Are you not going to pick up Thema?'

'No she is rather tied up today, family commitments.'

'So it is going to be two single men alone.'

'I bet we won't be alone for long time.'

The restaurant was full as usual. Vincent & Josh had a light meal in the restaurant and moved to the bar area after. The live music was on and there were a number of people dancing. Vincent noticed Talisha was dancing with a young man. He wanted to go and speak to her but he waited. When the music stopped for change of song he saw her coming towards the bar, the young man following her. She noticed Vincent and said something to her companion, and came straight to him. The young man seemed disappointed.

'Hello, Vincent you were trying to ignore me.' Talisha complained.

'No …it's not like that at all. I saw you dancing with that good looking young man so I did not wish to disturb you.'

'I see these young men all the time. It's you I have been thinking.' She extended her hand.

Vincent got up and looked at Josh, who with his eyes encouraged him to go with her. Soon they were dancing. Vincent felt really happy with her. She had such an outgoing personality. The next song was slow rhythm and they held each other. Talisha looked into his eyes but did not say anything. Vincent held her closer; he also looked at her but kept quiet. He was thinking if he was not married she would have made a very good Mrs Muller. After a while, Talisha held him closer and they could feel each other. The weather was excellent, neither hot nor cold, the atmosphere was romantic; and the restaurant with a view of the sea and the beach with pine trees created a Hollywood scene, the moon lighted up the area. It wasn't long before they started kissing each other and held each other even closer.

Time flew, they continued to dance for half an hour or so. They returned to the bar where Josh was talking to another couple sitting close by.

'I thought you guys are going to stay there the whole night?' Josh looked at them.

'Talisha is just magic, she dances so well I never noticed the time.'

'No, he is such a wonderful man.' Talisha complimented.

'I guess I lost my chance.' Josh laughed.

'No, after a drink I will be happy to.' Talisha smiled.

They had some more drinks. To Vincent the rum never tasted so good.

After about couple of hours, the night was getting darker and darker. Josh had couple of dances with Talisha and then with another woman while Vincent danced all the time with Talisha. They did not notice the time. While they were having a break from dance they sat on the table. Josh looked at his watch, 'let's get go man, tomorrow you are travelling', he asked Vincent.

'No, please let us stay for a while God knows when I will see Vincent again,' Talisha pleaded.

'You see, I have to go and pick up Thema,' Josh replied.

'You go ahead; I will drop Vincent to his place.'

Josh looked at Vincent who has been quiet. 'Maybe it is too late besides, I do not have a car and I don't really know my way around.' Vincent was also disappointed.

'Don't worry I got my 'old lady', I will drive you to your place.'

Josh and Vincent were quiet for a few moments. 'What do you say?' Josh asked.

'I guess I can trust my new friend here, I should be okay', Vincent looked at Talisha.

'Okay man, if you need me, give me a call.'

'Sure, will do.'

Even though, he was not very happy with the arrangement Josh left shortly afterward.

'Now I have got you all to myself.' Talisha looked at Vincent mischievously.

'I am sure I am in good hands.'

'You are… my darling', she came close to him and kissed him lightly. 'Let's dance', she got up.

Soon they were dancing; the band was playing a romantic slow-rhythm song ….Hold me tight…

"Excited, aroused, feeling tipsy, can't cope with the sparkling wine,
Touch me, feel me, taste me, yes baby yes...I am no longer mine,
Dreaming, imagining, on my clouds, floating in the sky,
I am getting high, nothing to hold me, I can't feel my spine,
I am falling darling, please hold me tight,"©

'Are you holding me tight?' Talisha whispered while increasing the pressure of her grip on him.

Vincent held her even tighter and put his lips on hers. 'Is that tight enough for you?'

'I think my drink is going to come out. You are such a strong man!'

Vincent loosened his grip and they continued to dance. Their thin material clothes on the bodies let them feel each other without obstruction. The kisses became longer and the bodies getting closer. Talisha had not been so happy for a long time. Vincent was enjoying himself oblivious that he was married. He thought for a moment of Greta but the drink and the sexy woman with him, his mind did not stay longer on her. 'Anyway I am just dancing we have done this with other partners many times', he said to himself. Greta came and went back as quickly.

About an hour later, near the beach which was deserted, Talisha's 'old lady' was parked. The pine trees and a small rock almost hid the car. Inside, Vincent and Talisha were making love. Vincent wanted to do it on the beach but Talisha warned him that on these beaches, even late at nights, people walked around, and it wasn't very prudent to do it on the beach. So old lady's back seat had to do. The car was moving with the jerk and one could not see except two shadows inside. Talisha had opened her dress and taken her pants off so she was literally naked while Vincent had taken his trousers down but let the tight light shirt still on with its buttons opened. Vincent thought she was really beautiful and he tasted her beauty to his heart content. Talisha, since her divorce was although quite desperate, but still was very choosy with whom she slept. When they had finished making love suddenly, they were interrupted. There was a bang at the window. To Talisha's horror it was her ex-husband. Vincent came out of the car putting his trouser quickly.

'What's the matter?' Vincent asked angrily.

Instead of replying, the man gave him a punch on his face. Vincent avoided bulk of its force by moving his head but the drink and the activity in the past hours, had made his reflection a little slow. In the meantime, Talisha came out putting her dress properly. Vincent did not retaliate, his mind planning an action. 'Don't be fucking mad, Rocky', Talisha roared.

'Do you know this man?' Vincent asked.

'Yes, he is my ex-husband.'

Rocky did not reply, he lunged on Vincent again. This time his punch was accurate and it landed on Vincent's face; this followed by another punch into his groin. Vincent felt the pain, and the effect of rum and Taisha's perfume seemed to disappear. He retaliated and tried to punch

Rocky who seemed to be quite used to street fights, he avoided the punch by bringing his head down. Talisha moved and covered Vincent with her body. 'Stop it you fool', she screamed. Rocky did not pay much attention to her plea, he came forward and pushed her on the side, Talisha fell down. Vincent realised that Rocky was not going to stop; finally, he pulled up his courage and punched hard on the face of Rocky who could not avoid it since he was not ready for it having pushed Talisha. His lip was torn and he started bleeding. He wiped his lips and seeing the blood on his hand immediately took out a knife from his pocket.

'You mother fucker, I will teach you how to fuck our women.' Rocky barked.

Talisha, seeing the knife in his hand, immediately got up and stood again in front of Vincent. 'Please Rocky don't do it…I am not your wife any longer', she pleaded.

'Listen man, it has nothing to do with you.' Vincent tried to argue with him planning in his mind how he was going to deal with a strong man with a knife. He had seen a small stone nearby; he could also use the sand to throw at him.

'She is my wife, you think you white fuckers can come here and fuck our women…man I am going to cut you into pieces.' Rocky threatened and raised the knife in his hand in a menacing position.

'No please don't, Rocky please.' Talisha begged him.

Vincent pushed Talisha gently and picked up some sand in his hand and threw at him. The quantity of sand was not enough, and rocky received some of it on his face, and the rest on his neck and body. Rocky had not expected it and it made him really angry, seeing Talisha out of the way, he lunged at him with knife. Vincent tried to hold his hand holding the knife but Rocky was strong; the knife touched his hand and cut it slightly. With the other hand Vincent pushed him back, and was looking for the stone nearby when Rocky raised his hand to stab him again. Suddenly, there was a gun fire and a bullet passed very close to Rocky's hand holding the knife.

'Drop your knife, otherwise I will shoot you.' Rocky heard a cool menacing voice.

Rocky stopped and turned back and saw a man holding a revolver in his hand. He could not recognise him but he was well built, and seemed very confident the way he looked. Rocky thought quickly whether to throw the knife at the intruder but his mind as quickly told him that the man was serious. Talisha came close to Vincent again. When the intruder saw Rocky not dropping his knife, he warned him. 'Look you mother fucker, I am not going to ask you again, drop the fucking knife and move back.' Rocky listened to the voice, he could not recognise the man but he felt a chill in his veins the way the man spoke. He dropped his knife. The man came closer, picked up the knife and put it in his pocket.

'This is my wife, and this man has been raping her.' Rocky lied.

The man came closer. 'He is my ex-husband, and this is my friend.' Talisha pointed out both men.

'Yes, I know all of you.' The man replied.

Suddenly, a car stopped by and Josh came running. He looked at all of them and having recognised all of them, he punched hard on Rocky's face. 'How dare you attack my guest, you son of a bitch.' Josh shouted. Rocky's cut lip started bleeding again. He realised his helpless position quickly, he was outnumbered and had very little choice, he also knew Josh, and knew that he was very well connected and equally strong as him. He wiped his lips with his hand. Josh having realised that Rocky was not going to retaliate, he came close to Vincent and examined his hand, 'are you alright?' Josh asked anxiously.

'Yeah, I am fine; this cut is not very serious.'

Talisha came close to Vincent and started talking to him with tears in her eyes. Josh came close to the intruder who was still holding the gun in his hand. They moved slightly back and spoke to each other in whispering voices.

In a few minutes, Josh started his car taking Vincent back with him. Talisha also started her car at the same time. Rocky looked at both cars moving with a great speed, feeling helpless to stop them, his injured lips not bleeding any more. The intruder, who had put his revolver in his pocket, brought out a badge from it and showed it to Rocky. Then he said something to Rocky and pointed towards a car parked nearby. Rocky did not argue, and started walking with him towards the car.

Chapter 6

A week passed. Vincent was in the office, he had been working hard on the 'New Heaven' project. He looked at his work admiringly. It was a neat booklet, in the beginning, summary then detailed cashflow projections, architect report and the plan for the new site, a projected photo of the building, gardens swimming pool, tennis courts and the résumés of the key managers. The plan was divided into two phases, on the success of the first phase; the second phase in the form of a hotel would be constructed. Vincent took it as personal pride to do his best for the plan so that the bank could approve it, and Chezan Investments makes huge profit.

He was going to have a meeting with Jimmy Noble and Pearce Noble shortly. He looked at the photo of the sight and suddenly he remembered Talisha; what a woman! He remembered touching her curly hair and short curly pubic hair, and he felt the heaviness in his trouser. He also remembered their lovemaking in the car and her pleas for his safety. That woman is worth something, he thought. She had called him once but of course, he could not encourage her very much since he did not want Greta to know anything about it. He promised to meet her when he visited next time Caribbean. While he was thinking about Caribbean, Talisha and her body, Jackie entered into his office. She gave him some papers. 'They are ready for you.'

'Thanks…I will be there in a sec. I was just reviewing the business plan again.'

'Are you sure…you seem to be lost in some thoughts, did you meet some Caribbean beauty?'

Vincent immediately put his hand on his trouser to ensure she does not notice what Talisha's thought had done! 'No Jackie I was just doing some calculations in my mind.'

Jackie smiled, 'sure', and left his office.

Vincent looked at the papers briefly what Jackie had given to him. He put them on one side of his desk. He picked up three copies of the 'New Heaven' project, his pad, pen and his mobile, and left his office.

About an hour later, Jimmy, Pearce and Vincent were sitting in Pearce's office. They have been looking at the business plan prepared by Vincent. They were impressed by the details and most of the aspects covered in the plan.

'I don't know what the bank is going to think of it, there is no return until late in the year two.' Pearce said.

'I think we can expedite the funds, even though, I have not put it in the projections, if we sell some of the apartments outright and take the deposits from the buyers.' Vincent explained. 'I have put this in the details.' He opened one of the pages of the booklet and pointed it out.

'Don't worry about the bank too much.' Jimmy assured his younger brother. 'We have got our man there.'

'You mean Sam?' Pearce asked.

'No, it is Jeffery Anderson.' Jimmy laughed.' We have been preparing for it for a while.'

Vincent did not quite follow. 'I think the bank should be very pleased with the high return and I think if we go on second phase, and it is successful, all their loans can be repaid.'

About half an hour later, they had nearly finished discussing the 'New Heaven' business plan. 'I think I will send this plan to Sam prior to submitting it to the bank officially. He can have a look and let us have his input.' Pearce looked at both of them.

'Yes, this plan is final, I will add straight away couple of points we just discussed, and then give you two copies.' Vincent showed his enthusiasm.

'I think it is probably too late to send the courier to the bank but let me ring Sam to see if he is staying in town.'

'Well done, Vincent, I think it is a great plan.' Jimmy praised Vincent.

'Yes, well done, I think you have done a great job.' Pearce added.

'Thanks', Vincent got up picking up the project booklets and left the office. Pearce immediately picked up the phone and spoke to Sam.

'You heard he is staying in the flat tonight.' Pearce said to his brother.

'Great… how are you going to send it to him?'

'I will ask Jackie if she could deliver it to him by hand.'

'Good.' Jimmy got up and left the office.

In the early evening, Jackie was in the flat of the bank where Sam Hollworth had received her. This time he was ready for her, a champagne bottle was there in the ice bucket. He served her the drink. He looked at the 'New Heaven Project' booklet. 'It seems very professional.'

'Yes, Vincent has been working hard on it; I helped him put altogether in this presentation folder.' Jackie said proudly.

'You are so good at putting the final touches!'

'My hubby does not think much of me.... Why are all the husbands like this?'

'I don't know about him but I can see a fine woman with lots of talents.'

'You have not seen much of it? Have you?'

'Well I have seen some and I am sure you will show me the rest in due course.' Sam looked at her meaningfully.

Jackie did not reply, she was thinking that he had not fulfilled his promise to get her a mortgage. Her application for the mortgage had been turned down. The bank only gave mortgages to their employees and in a very few cases, they did give it to the employees of the customers. While she was thinking Sam was looking at the project papers.

'Sorry Sam I have to get back, Tom should be at home.'

Sam was not expecting it. His minds ran fast, he was expecting her to sleep with him. 'Oh what's the hurry, I am sure he can wait for you, after all when he goes out for football or the pub with his mates you wait for him, no?'

'Yeah I know but then I am a woman.'

Sam did not know how to start, last time he played with her by dropping some wine. 'Look Jackie Pearce told me you do a great job at man!'

'What do you mean' Jackie raised her voice.

'Well, you know...'

Before Sam could complete his sentence, Jackie interrupted, 'bastard, does he talk personal things with you?'

'No, please don't misunderstand, he was praising you.'

'My foot, it's really amazing.' Jackie was annoyed.

Sam did not like the way she was talking. But he knew that he had to play cool in order to get her into the bed. 'Look …I know you are not very happy because the bank turned down your mortgage application…you see I explained to you before on telephone that they have changed their policy. I could not really do anything.'

'I don't know what you can and what you can't do…I did not get the mortgage, I am applying to other banks.'

'I have got an idea, I know a mortgage broker and I am sure he can get you the mortgage we have some relationship with them.'

'Why didn't you tell me this before?' Jackie changed her tone.

'Well I thought our bank will give it to you…and listen if I speak to him he will even lower the interest rate for you as a favour to me!'

'I see… that is interesting… alright then I will meet you once we got the mortgage.' Jackie got up.

Sam was disappointed he did not know how to get her in the right mood.

'Listen, at least have another drink with me then you can go if you so wish.' Sam got up and filled her glass from the champagne bottle in the ice bucket. He also refilled his glass and sat next to her.

'You are such a beautiful girl I don't know how men can resist you.'

Jackie did not reply and took a sip from the glass. Sam got up and put some music on. He came back. He knew he had to be very careful, otherwise, the good opportunity is going to pass. He sat next to her making sure he does not touch her.

In a few minutes, Jackie felt relaxed, her anger had gone, the prospect of the mortgage, the fine champagne and the music made her feel at home. A few moments later, 'Do you know it is not very nice for Pearce to disclose the personal information.' Jackie took a big sip of the fine champagne.

'No, it is not…I agree but to be fair with Pearce he was only praising you.'

'Alright let me show you a bit of my expertise.' Jackie showed her balls.

Sam was glad his strategy to throw the carrot of the mortgage and praises seems to have worked. 'Shall we go to the bedroom?'

'No, here is fine', she came close to him and opened the zip of his trouser. Sam was not expecting such a quick reaction but he kept quiet. She got up and sat opposite him on the carpeted floor in front of his chair. She pulled his trousers down. She picked up her champagne glass and dropped a little champagne on his penis. Then she held it gently in her hands and slowly rubbed against her cheeks, then to her eyes and then to her neck and gradually to her breast.

'Do you want me to take your blouse off?' Sam loved the gentle way she did it.

She did not reply but put the finger on her lips to stop him talking. Sam realised that she wanted to concentrate what she was dong, he kept quiet. She gently did the second round in the same way. Then with her lips she kissed his tummy and worked south. Sam started to have erection. She continued to kiss. Soon Sam was excited and he started to put his fingers in her hair, gently massaging her head. After a few moments, when he was fully erect, she opened her mouth and closed her lips tightly and with her tongue she massaged him. Sam was getting the real pleasure, he realised that Pearce was right Jackie had some expertise! While she put the pressure of his lips and increased the speed of her tongue Sam was thinking about his wife Davina. 'No she never did like that', he was sure. Suddenly Jackie stopped. Sam came back to the real world. 'What's the matter, do you wish to go to the bedroom?' he asked gently.

Jackie got up, and went back to her chair and picked up her purse nearby. 'No Sam I just wanted to show you a glimpse of what I can do!'

Sam could not believe that she would do such a thing, he felt really embarrassed.

'You see when the mortgage is done maybe we can revisit the position but please do not take me for granted. I do not have to have sex with you every time I deliver something here or we meet.' Jackie said it plainly.

'No you can't do that to me.' Sam raised his voice.

'Look Sam I am not a teaser, you almost seduced me the last time I was here. And you did not fulfil your promise of the mortgage. I am not the bribe from the company to you… that is not what they pay me for!'

Sam immediately pulled his pants and the trousers and got up. He came close to her and held her hand firmly. 'You are getting out of control, no? This is not the way to behave you should have not started anything?'

'You are hurting me,' she pulled her hand out of his hand. 'You bankers think that you can buy anything, don't you?'

Sam got really annoyed. He felt he needed to teach her a lesson in behaviour. How dare she puts him on and then leaves him cold. He grabbed her arm again, and with the manly strength he lifted her. He brought her to the bedroom while Jackie started to scream. Sam almost threw her on the bed. While he went back to close the door firmly, she got up and pushed him. Sam fell on the door but did not fall down completely. He was hurt in his head. 'You stupid bitch I am going to show you what the bankers can do!' He slapped her on her face. Then he pushed her back to the bed. Jackie was also very angry she started fighting with him by throwing punches at him while he sat on her. But she was not a match for a strong man. It did not affect Sam. He held her tightly.

'Sorry Sam, let's do it properly,' Jackie said it in a desperate voice.

Sam thought she had finally come to her senses. He got up from her and stood on the floor to take his clothes off.

As he was taking his shirt off, Jackie suddenly sprang from the bed and rushed towards the door. But before she could open it he grabbed her by putting his strong arm around her tummy. He lifted her again and threw her roughly on the bed. He put his hand on her mouth. 'Look if you do not behave I am going to hurt you.'

Jackie wanted to say something but the only voice came from her mouth. 'You fu….bas….gh……'

Sam increased the pressure of his hand on her mouth, Jackie was helpless. After a few moments, when her supressed sound died down he took his hand away from her mouth. Jackie was not sure what to do, the slap on the face and the strong body on top of her made her realise the hopeless situation she was in. Sam took her shirt off and the bra, then he pulled her skirt and the pants off and threw her clothes to the floor. While she was lying naked in the bed, Sam got out of the bed and took his clothes off. Jackie did not try anything this time she knew he was watching her very closely. He sat on her again and brought his penis close to her mouth. Jackie did not want to even see him, she will not open her mouth when he insisted and rubbed it against her lips. 'I will bite it off, you son of a bitch.' Jackie hissed like a snake.

'Alright…I do not like to be physical,' Sam said it in a cool voice. He moved and put his lips on her nipple while squeezing the other breast with his hand. Jackie stayed there helpless.

Jackie's nightmare was over in about half an hour time. Twice was all that Sam could manage. When he finished with her he left the room. Jackie got up and dressed herself. She looked in the mirror and saw some marks on her face. Sam had been quite rough with her, he not only wanted sex but also punish her for her bad behaviour. Before she could leave the room, Sam entered with two glasses of champagne.

'Look I am very sorry about it.' He handed the glass to her. Jackie threw the glass on the wall and the crystal glass with expensive champagne fell on the floor, broken, leaving some of the champagne on the wall.

'What are you mad about woman…you started something but will not finish it…is this the way to behave?'

Jackie did not reply, she had tears in her eyes. 'Can I go now please?'

'Do you want me to call a cab for you?'

'No, there are plenty of cabs in the street, I will take one.'

'Okay…as you wish.' Sam took a sip from his glass. 'But let me show you something.' Sam brought out the mobile phone from his pocket. He pressed the button and Jackie heard the voice, 'let me show you a bit of my expertise.' She heard her voice in horror. Sam pressed the button on his mobile and said, 'don't get any stupid ideas. Tomorrow you will thank me, you might not have noticed but your hungry body really needed me!'

Jackie did not reply she was thinking what a horrible man he was.

'And yes, my promise to help you with your mortgage is still good… I will text you the details tomorrow.'

Jackie kept quiet. Sam realised she was not going to talk, he opened the door for her and they both walked towards the front door of the flat. Sam accompanied her to the lift. 'Goodnight Jackie.' Sam said as though nothing had happened. Jackie entered into the lift and immediately pressed the button. She did not reply or look at him.

Going back in the cab Jackie was thinking, how horribly it had gone wrong. She just wanted to tease him for his presumption. Was she at fault? Should she go to the police? He had not used the condom so there was plenty of proof and the marks on her face. How conceited is he! How he had recorded her voice, it would be very difficult to prove that it was non-consensual sex. Maybe she will need to deal with him in another way. What did he mean when he said that my hungry body needed him, she did not recall participating actively in the process. 'Fucking liar' she thought. She knew what went on in the company; at a suitable opportunity she will teach him a lesson!

The next day while Jackie was in the office she received a telephone call on her mobile.

‘Hello, Jackie Breton speaking.’

‘Good morning Mrs Breton, my name is Charles Gongly, l am an independent financial broker.’

‘Hello.’

‘Mr Sam Hollworth has passed your details to me. He sent me the copy of the application to his bank with your mortgage requirement.’

‘Okay.’

‘I have prepared an application to my finance company, and if you agree I will send it to you to sign. Then perhaps you can bring it with your passport and utility bill and we can meet.’

‘I do not wish to waste my time. What are the chances I will get the required mortgage?’ Jackie was suspicious.

‘Mrs Breton , please don’t worry, we specialise in this kind of business, I am absolutely sure we can help you, the rate of interest may not be as low as the New Country Bank but it will be very competitive. Besides, Mr Hollworth has spoken very highly of you. We do a lot of business with their bank and we will make our best efforts to meet your requirement.’

‘I see….Does my husband needs to come as well?’

‘Not initially.’ Charles replied.

‘Okay, please send me the details and I will call you to make an appointment.’

‘Fine, will do.’

‘Have you got my address?’

‘Yes, it was included in the application.’

'Good, thank you.'

'I am looking forward to hearing from you.' Charles showed his professional courtesy. 'Bye.'

'Bye.' Jackie disconnected her mobile.

The thought of getting the mortgage pleased Jackie. And her plan to teach Sam a lesson has to be postponed till this matter was resolved. She picked up her phone and rang her husband.

About a week later, there was a credit committee meeting in the New Country Bank. The proposal of 'New Heaven' project was being discussed. Sam Hollworth presented the proposal with his observation and additional calculations. There was a heated discussion. A few committee members were unhappy that Chezan Investments had not, in the past, met their obligations. They had consistently failed to keep up their repayment of loans. They also questioned that in spite of the company giving them all rosy trading position, they were not able to reduce their loan and now they were asking for more funds.

'Look, the loan to them is already provided fully in our books.' Sam explained. 'This project is really good, and I and my team have looked very carefully, especially their cashflow projections. If it is successful this will bring a substantial chunk of our loan back.' He waited. 'In fact, in three to four years of the project completion, we should have all our loans repaid.'

'They seem to be playing lottery with our money, if they win they will repay our money keeping substantial amount of winning with them, and if they lose it is our money.' One of the members said.

'I don't think that is fair. You can't compare this with a lottery, the investment is in brick and mortar, I agree it is not in England, but Caribbean is a developed holiday destination.' Sam controlled his temper. 'Besides the promoters, who have a history of success, will continue to share in the project and will also invest some of their money.'

The heated discussion continued for another hour. The committee was split evenly. Jeffrey Anderson, the senior member, suddenly remembered Firoza and her beautiful body. I must do something to make sure I spend a few more nights with her, he thought. He raised his voice. 'Gentlemen, sorry and lady (looking at the only female committee member) I have been in the past their account manager. Chezan Investments Ltd is run by Mr Noble's sons, they are very competent, and although their loan history has not been very good, no one can fight with the nature. They have been unlucky due to crop failures, political trouble in Africa and so on. Now there is a good opportunity. I believe we need to give them the last chance. And as Sam mentioned the loan is fully provided. So really, in a way, we can look at it as a new client, rather than a delinquent existing client.'

The other committee members looked at him and were wondering why he has suddenly woken up.

Jeffrey Anderson continued. 'And if I may say so, this is a good opportunity for the bank to realise their more or less written off loan, and I am sure the Board of directors are going to be extremely pleased with it. Besides, the government will see that we are helping our customers rebuild and eventually, the profit from this venture will be like export.'

Sam looked admiringly at Jeffrey; he was pleased he had such a strong support from an experienced and well connected member of the committee. He had no idea what role Firoza was playing in it!

After further short discussion, the committee which could not agree unanimously went for a vote, and with a good majority the loan was sanctioned.

Jimmy Noble and Pearce Noble were overjoyed with the bank's decision. The decision was taken to hire another person familiar with the construction business who will report to Vincent Muller with a dotted line to the brothers. There was new enthusiasm in the business. The bankers and their client were all very happy and looking forward to various benefits which will accrue to them with this new venture. Jeffrey Anderson knew he will have to buy some more pills!

A few days later, Mark Kohnvich visited Pearce Noble's office. They were having coffee and discussing. It was really wonderful news about the new project.

'Yeah, please keep it to yourself, the lawyers are working hard and we think that the construction will start in a few days.'

'So I can bring my family to Caribbean for holidays.'

'Of course, but it will take at least nine months before the first phase is completed...' Pearce replied happily.

'I don't mind waiting… listen this project must have improved the position of Vincent, no?'

'Yes, he has become a Keyman now in practice as well. This project is a key operation for us.'

They both took a sip of coffee and were quiet for a moment.

'Look what happens if Heaven forbids, Vincent became incapable of working? Would the insurance company will pay up?'

Marc thought for a moment. 'Yes, I think the incapacity to work is included, and if I am not sure the benefit are exactly the same as death… but why do you say Heaven forbid!' Marc looked at him meaningfully.

'Well, the family believes that Vincent is a real contributor to the company and the future prosperity of the company is, to a large degree, dependent upon him.' Pearce tried to convince him.

'I will check with the insurance company to be absolutely sure. If in doubt, I will make sure that they add this clause.'

'Good… if we ever cash in that policy we will make sure that you benefit from it too!' Pearce smiled.

They continued to talk, and after half an hour, Marc left the Chezan Investments office as a happy man.

Chapter 7

In 1947, British India was partitioned and a new country Pakistan came into existence. Most of the British civil servants and personnel had left the country but a few stayed on, and some departed slightly later back to Britain. There was a large scale migration of people from Pakistan to India (mostly Hindus and Sikhs), and a large section of Indian Moslems moved to Pakistan. The migration was also accompanied with similarly large scale riots and lootings. The trains from India to Pakistan carrying Moslem passengers contained a lot of injured people as well as some dead bodies. Similar situation arose in the trains coming from Pakistan containing Hindus and Sikhs. No one knew who started this violence but the spiral of revenge and settling of the scores continued regardless. A large number of innocent people of all religions who had not participated in the decision to split the country, suffered. Lots of them lost their homes, loved ones, the established businesses and the farms.

During this time, a British Police officer, John William who was going to go to Bombay to take the ship from there to London was at Delhi railway station. His wife was with him. He was wearing his uniform with a revolver. While they were waiting for the train to arrive, they were sitting in the waiting room reserved for the first class passengers (in those days, these were mostly British civil servants, British soldiers and some rich Indians). The station was very busy, a number of people were waiting mostly to go to Pakistan and some others were waiting to receive their relatives and friends on the trains coming from Pakistan. John heard some noise and he saw a train arriving on the nearby platform. Suddenly, there was lot of noise and some people rushing towards the train and some getting out of it. He could see that some of the people getting out of the train were injured, some of them bleeding, and some women and children crying. There was a lot of shouting and screaming at the same time.

About fifteen minutes later, John saw, on the opposite platform, a large group of Indians arriving there, armed with knives and swords, and some had wooden batons with them. They were shouting and chanting the slogans which John understood from the little Hindustani language he had learnt. They were chanting 'deaths to the Moslems' and 'shove them all to Pakistan'. It seemed that it was the reaction of some of the people who were generally peaceful and non- violent but had turned into raging thugs in the light of the religious hatred prevailing at that time. Seeing the Hindus coming in train, some badly injured and some of the women scantily dressed and children crying, had turned them into mobsters. On the same platform, there were a number of people who were waiting to board the train to go to Pakistan. The mob started attacking these people. Some of these were beaten, some were thrown on the track of the trains, and some were stabbed. Soon four uniformed police officers arrived and tried to contain the situation.

The mob disregarded the police officers, and also attacked couple of them. The police officers retreated and went back to get additional help. Once the police officers had gone, the mob continued even more ferociously attacking the Moslems. Some of the young Moslems formed a small group and retaliated at the mob. But they were no match for the mob armed with knives, swords and large wooden batons, and physically fit. John wanted to help the people but felt helpless. The British were no longer in command and although, he was in the police uniform he had no jurisdiction.

In a few minutes, the train on the opposite platform arrived. The Moslems who were scared and some of them badly injured took a sigh of relief and rushed to get into the train. There was shouting, screaming and crying on the platform. John saw with horror the anarchy on the opposite platform. Some people were lying injured on the platform while others were getting into the train. Some were helping their relatives to the trains. John was not sure what happened to some people who had fallen on the track before the train arrived. Had they got up and moved or they were still under the train! In one corner of the platform John saw a young girl of about two to three years old standing and crying. No one was paying any attention to her. Everyone was busy with their own families and it seemed she was lost.

Some of the mobs were moving away from the platform now, having taken the revenge for the people who arrived from Pakistan. They also took by force with them some of the young Moslem women from their families, their husbands or fathers injured, dead or unable to stop them. Some of the jewellery of women was also snatched from them.

John looked at his wife Alana who seemed to be in a shock with the whole atmosphere at the railway station. He felt his revolver in the pocket. ‘I am going to the other platform for a few minutes.’

‘No, John it is dangerous. You can’t do much in this situation.’

‘I know darling but I won’t be long. Do you think you can wait here for a few minutes?’

‘I don’t know I don’t feel very safe here.’

‘Don’t worry, I will be back shortly.’ John handed her his revolver.

There were only couple of families in the waiting room but they did not do much or said anything just kept quiet as though the situation was very normal. However, they noticed when John gave the revolver to Alana. John looked at the people but no one paid any attention to him. They wanted to get away.

John rushed to the opposite side platform, he had to walk over a small bridge to get there. He saw some of the mobs, coming back from the opposite platform, looking at him but his colour and uniform persuaded them not to bother him. However, he heard one man shouting, ‘go back you stupid white swine; it is you who have done it!’ John heard the person pointing at him and also understood but decided not to retaliate. Soon he arrived at the other platform. He walked towards the little girl who was absolutely scared and crying. She could not speak, only the sound mm……oohn…oohn…ammi…’John wondered why no one was helping her. Everyone was busy with their own things with their baggage or their own relatives. John came close to the girl but she did not pay any attention to him. She continued crying.

A man came close and picked up the little girl. But the girl was not consoled she continued to scream in fact with a little more intensity. John asked the man in broken Hindustani if it was his daughter. The man with the movement of face replied in negative. John extended his hand to take the girl, the man with reluctance, gave him the girl. The girl seemed to be comforted with his loving face in the midst of people either who were crying or worried or shouting. She put her head against John's shoulder. John stayed there with the girl for a while but no one came to him. It seemed that no one, related to the girl, was there any more. After a few minutes, he saw Alana on the opposite platform who was watching him with her hand on the gun. She asked him with a gesture of her hand to bring the girl. John started walking slowly and went over the walking bridge to go to the other platform.

When John reached the bridge, one of the mobs screamed. 'Look this frangi (white man) is taking our child.' John ignored the man he knew to be one of the mobsters. When the man noticed that John was not paying any attention to him, he rushed towards him, and with menace, tried to snatch the girl from his arms. This time John did not have the patience, he put the girl on the ground and punched the man hard on his face, the man fell down on the wooden barrier. If John wanted he could have pushed him over to the rail tracks but he controlled himself. The other people around did not pay much attention to the man who was just beaten. They had more important things to do! John picked up the little girl and walked fast towards the stairs to the other platform.

A minute later, John arrived with the little girl to the other platform. Alana immediately took the little girl into her arms. The little girl seemed even more comfortable in her arms. She immediately put her head against her shoulder and closed her eyes. In her little frightened eyes, she saw her mother in Alana.

About two hours later, while the train was running towards Bombay, John was sitting in the compartment with his wife and the little girl. They had given her some hot milk and some sweets and she had fallen asleep. 'What are we going to do with her?' asked John.

'Nothing, she is our daughter now!' Alana replied with confidence, looking at the pretty girl who was asleep.

'You know one of the mobsters swore at me at the bridge?'

'You should have told him off.'

'I could have broken his jaws, but we are no longer in power here. In old days, they would not dare to swear at a British police officer on his face.'

'But you seemed to be fighting with another man on the bridge. I was ready to come up with the revolver.'

'Yes, he wanted to snatch the girl from my arm. I had to punch him.'

'Thank God they did not attack you; there were still a lot of them on the station.'

They continued to talk for a while.

About three hours later, the train stopped at one of the stations. John went to the platform and bought some snacks. When he came back from the platform he noticed another couple, the man dressed in a smart suit and the woman in a sari, had joined in the compartment, hitherto empty.

After a few minutes, the man asked John, 'Are you going to Bombay?'

'Yes… I and my wife are going there; we are on our way back to England.'

'Hi, I am Jay Kishanlal; I am going back to Bombay where I work. I am from Delhi.'

'Hello, I am John Williams; we lived in Delhi as well for a few years.'

'It must be nice for you to go back to your own country.'

'Yes and no; quite enjoyed the stay in Delhi until the last few days. There are all kinds of riots in the city with mass migration of people between the two countries.'

'Yes, it is sad that the country is partitioned. Until now, in Delhi, in fact all over India, there was no religious hatred, and Hindus and Moslems lived very peacefully together.'

'Yes, I know I never had to deal with a crime based on religion, myself.'

'Is this your daughter?' The man pointed towards the little girl who was sitting now in Alana's lap comfortably. The food and sleep had made her forget her parents for a short while. She was quiet, even though, still showing signs of sadness on her face but not crying any longer.

Before John could reply, Alana interrupted, 'Yes she is. '

'Very pretty.' Jay praised the little girl while noticing her spoiled long shirt and shalwar.

'Thanks... She has been playing at the platform; my wife dressed her in Indian clothes.'

'What do you call her?'

'Alisha.' Alana replied while John looked at his wife with surprise. They had not discussed any names for the girl.

Jay did not believe that it was their daughter but did not question. He knew that at that time, in India, there were a lot of orphans. He changed the subject, 'this is my wife, Sareina,' pointing towards his wife.

Sareina smiled with her folded hands. John smiled back, 'Hello, this is my wife Alana.'

'Hello.' Alana said.

The conversation shifted to why the country was divided when no one was consulted except the political leaders. Why no vote was taken to see if the people of India wanted the country to be partitioned? The train, with a lot of noise of the steam engine and the tracks, continued towards Bombay regardless of what it had seen in Delhi.

After couple of weeks, John Williams and his wife Alana were sitting in the lounge of their home in Highgate (North London). Alana brought a small pouch which contained some precious stones.

'What is this?' asked John.

'I found these sewn inside the shirt of Alisha.'

'Amazing', John looked at the stones: couple of large diamonds, a red ruby and three sapphires.

'These seem quite valuable. Her parents must have considered the worst; in case they were killed or the girl was lost, she would still have something from her family.'

'I must try to find her parents; I think she might be from an important Indian family.' John stated.

'They can't be so important that no one cared for her at the station.' Alana declared.

'No… whatever, I will try to find her parents, send some enquiries to Delhi with the foreign office.'

John Williams was in his late forties while Alana was in her early forties. They had been married for ten years but had no children. In spite of their best efforts, Alana had not conceived. Alana was quite keen to adopt the girl as her own. Alisha was of fair complexion and no one will ever notice that it was not hers. They knew that in North India, some of the people had very fair complexion.

John made some enquiries through the foreign office to find her real parents but it was almost impossible. In those days, with so much anarchy in India, and lack of records, the administration in India was overwhelmed with all kind of enquiries. After couple of months, they gave up. John and Alana Williams adopted little Alisha as their own daughter and named her Alisha Williams.

Alisha was brought up just like an English girl, she went to a private school, and was adored by her adopted parents who did not have any other children. When she grew up, there were some minute traces that she was not of a European origin girl but that of an Indian origin. Because of her fair complexion and the British public school accent, no one noticed. Everybody treated her as though she was the natural daughter of Williams. Alana did not tell anyone that she was their adopted daughter. Alisha in return also loved her 'parents'. In fact, she did not want to marry when she had grown up she wanted to live with her parents and look after them in their old age. But as the youth takes its stride, she did meet one young business man called Albert Noble, and fell in love with him.

Alisha's marriage to Albert was done with a lot of pomp and show. There were church services, dancing parties, main reception in one of the most famous hotels in the West-End and several parties at home. The ceremony was attended by some of the dignitaries from the political and business circle. John William spent a small fortune on the wedding.

About two years later, one day when John Williams was seriously ill and Alisha was visiting them; they were sitting down in the lounge.

'Alisha, my darling I need to tell you something.' John whispered in slow voice.

'No papa, you get better first we can do a lot of talking afterword.' Alisha came close to John and kissed him on his cheek affectionately.

Alana was touched by her love for her papa. 'No darling, this is important; we have been keeping a secret from you.' Alana confided.

Alisha was surprised; after all these years her parents wanted to tell her some important secret. ‘Surely we can talk about it when papa is better.’ She looked at her mother.

‘I might not get better. It is just as well that it is done in front of me.’ John insisted.

‘No papa, please don’t say it. Listen, you are going to get better soon. I know it.’

‘No my love, I won’t feel comfortable if I did not tell you myself.’

‘Okay… but first let me make you a nice cup of tea.’ Alisha got up.

After about half an hour when they had finished the tea, Alisha was sitting next to her papa on the sofa and Alana was sitting in an arm chair next to them.

‘Alisha you are our daughter, and God knows it, we loved you as much as we could.’ John started.

‘Oh papa what’s wrong with you! I have been one of the luckiest girls to have parents like you.’ She looked at John and then at Alana with almost tears in her eyes.

‘We know we feel the same way.’ Alana also felt the emotions.

‘The truth is that you are….you are not our natural daughter.’ John managed to say what has been hidden in his chest for such a long time.

‘What….’ Alisha’s mouth opened in amazement.

‘Yes Alisha… we adopted you.’ Alana added.

‘God….. Is it true….Why you never told me?’ Alisha almost shouted. Then realising that it will hurt her parents she immediately apologised.’ Sorry papa, I did not mean to shout please forgive me.’

‘No we understand but we can assure you it was never with any bad intentions.’ Alana said it seriously.

‘I am sorry again mama, I did not mean to …it was just a stupid reaction.’

‘Don’t worry… we understand.’

‘Please papa, tell me a little more.’ Alisha begged.

John told her the story; how they were coming back from India and how they found her at Delhi Railway station. Alisha listened to the story with utmost concentration.

‘You know something, in school, the other girls used to tease me about my name they used to say that it does not sound English and all kind of speculation.’ Alisha said.

‘You never told me, what did you say to them?’ Alana asked.

‘I used to tell them that my mom was living in India and she chose a name from there.’

‘This is exactly true; one of our Indian neighbour’s daughters was called Alisha. I liked the name so when someone asked me your name that is the name which came into my mind.’

‘It is a very nice name.’ John added.

They were quiet for a few moments. The story had not yet sunk in. Suddenly, Alisha got up and sat down on the floor in front of John, her hands folded. ‘Papa, I do not know what to say. I will always be grateful to you for saving an innocent little girl in that riot, risking your own life, and bringing me up like a princess….. I do not know how I could ever thank you….you have been absolutely amazing,’ the tears pouring down from Alisha’s eyes.

John got up and put his hands or her arms and pulled her and hugged her affectionately. ’No my darling you do not need to thank me…we did not have any children, and you filled our lives with great joy. We hardly ever thought that you were not our real daughter.’

Alana also got up and joined in the hug. They all stood there close to each other and few more tears fell from their eyes to their cheeks. You are our daughter, maybe more than a natural one.' Alana said it in tears.

After a few minutes, Alana showed Alisha the shirt and the trouser she was wearing when they found her at Delhi railway station. She also showed the precious stones: diamonds, ruby and sapphires to her. Alana had kept all her things intact. Alisha was surprised to see the clothes and the stones. She was surprised that they had never sold the precious stones.

'Would these identify my real parents? I wonder.'

'As I said we did try to find your real parents. But in those days, the chaotic atmosphere, lack of records and the mass migration, it had not been possible.'

'Maybe I will visit India one day and maybe with just a miracle I might find them,' Alisha sighed.

'So this is the story of my life.' Alisha looked at her children who had been listening attentively.

'Now I know why you named me Firoza. The girls in the school also asked me why I was called Firoza.'

'Yes I wanted to keep a little bit of my background, choosing an Indian name for you.'

Alisha got up from her chair and went into her bedroom, and brought a small bag. 'Look these are my clothes when your grandparents found me in Delhi and this is the little fortune I was carrying sewn under my shirt.' Alisha showed her children the precious stones.

'I wonder why grandma never told me about it?' exclaimed Jimmy Noble.

'No they never wanted to disclose to anyone that I was not their natural daughter. They did really love me too much.'

Chapter 8

A few months passed. The construction of the 'New Heaven Project' was well underway. The commodity and stock business was making reasonable amount of money. But due to time lag in getting the major investment in New Heaven, Chezan Investments were looking to make some quick bucks. The bank was patient they saw reasonable cashflow but their eyes were also fixed on the return from the New Heaven project.

One morning, Jimmy Noble had a call from Yasin Kanji from Cairo. He told him that the Egyptian police had arrested the local manager, Omer, and he was flying back that night to London. He was going to explain the whole thing in London. Jimmy immediately spoke to his brother, Pearce but he was also unaware of the position. They waited anxiously for Yasin to come back.

Next day, Yasin was in the office, and explained to both brothers what had happened, Apparently, Egyptian police had charged the company for bribing the officials and charging higher prices for the grains supplied to the army. The government audit department had challenged the prices being charged and that resulted in the arrest of the local manager on the pretext that he had been bribing the officials. The ongoing army contract had been cancelled. Couple of assistants were told that the office was closing and if they were needed they will be contacted. They were pleased that they were not arrested and happy to get away.

'Why suddenly this thing happened? Couldn't you have known it or with so many fuckers being bribed, no one hinted?' Jimmy was furious.

'No one could do anything; apparently the orders came from high up. Our contacts were caught completely off guard.' Yasin muttered.

'Why did you run away from there, man? Why didn't you contact some solicitors?' Pearce also raised his voice.

'I was really scared the way they arrested Omer? I thought I was going to be arrested too, and there would be more problems.' Yasin knew he did not handle the position well.

'So basically our operation in Egypt is finished. I still can't believe, what about that retired general?' Jimmy screamed.

'Our prices are not that high, slightly higher than the market price, but then we have been supplying them without any hitch, on time and reasonable quality. So what does this audit report state?' Pearce added.

'You see, the general has got a young wife, apparently, Omer visited a few times their home…..'

'What…. So it is Omer, who has fucked up the whole thing?' Pearce said.

'Not really, he has been seeing his young wife. Apparently, the general learnt about it. He did not inform us about the police investigation or used his connections to save the contract. Maybe he instigated the whole thing himself.' Yasin finally opened up.

'I don't understand, they used to meet up in a café. Why did Omer visit the general's home?' Pearce calmed down.

'Apparently, he visited once their home to deliver ……'

'So he made a habit of going there?'

'Did you know about it?' Jimmy asked

'No… I swear, if I had known, I would have informed you immediately. Besides, in a public café, no one probably would have noticed but visiting one's home regularly, others will notice.' Yasin looked at the floor.

'I still can't believe an important contract has gone down the drain just because one of our men could not hold his prick!' Jimmy said solemnly.

Yasin felt like laughing at the remark but he did not dare. They were quiet for a minute or so. 'I think we can save the situation, apparently the contract will be put to tender in a few months.' Yasin tried to console them.

'The margins will be cut, and there is no guarantee they have not blacklisted us?' Pearce said thoughtfully.

'We still have some contacts left; I can check with them.' Yasin said.

'No please just stay low, do not contact anybody.' Jimmy ordered. 'I will contact someone I know who is going to explain it to me.'

'Alright, you better settle down, make sure that the accounts department are able to put the right entries in the books.'

'And please do not mention to anybody in the office what had happened. Tell them you are back in the office for a while for consultation and some other work. But no one should know that the Egyptian office has been closed or that we lost the contract.' Jimmy warned Yasin.

Yasin realised that the meeting was over; he got up looking at them, in case, they ask him to stay but both brothers kept quiet.

After Yasin Kanji had left the office, Pearce and Jimmy were talking.

'Shit man... this puts a lot of pressure on us. If the bank knew what has happened they will be upset.' Jimmy looked at his younger brother.

'I know we need to look for some other project to make up for the lost business.' Pearce looked at his brother in the eyes.

'I told you this guy is a piece of shit; we should have fired him a long time ago.'

'Perhaps, we can deal with him later; let's see what needs to be done now. At least, he got rid of the local staff and brought all the laptops and important files back, so no one can look into our books. '

Jimmy was quiet for a while. 'Okay, I will check with a friend of mine, he has recently been transferred to the commercial office in the embassy.'

'Do you think they are going to come after us because of all this?'

'No, none of us are on the board in the local company; Omer and one of his assistants are the only directors.'

'Anyway, I do not think they can implicate us, we have never passed any money ourselves. Yasin's name is not in the company either.'

'We will have to help Omer though?' Pearce asked his brother.

'Let him get a lawyer for himself, he knows better than to implicate us. I am sure he will deny everything. It is not easy to pinpoint cash to any one.'

They continued to discuss the matter for another half an hour.

'So are you going to review the position in Boston?' Pearce asked.

'I do not think it will come through there are too many parties involved.' Jimmy explained.

After a short while, Jimmy left Pearce's office. He had to make some important calls.

Another week passed. Jimmy, Pearce and Vincent were in the meeting at Pearce's office. They have been discussing various matters, New Heaven Project, the Egyptian office and the need to get another project going, now that the chances were that Egyptian contract was never going to materialise.

'I think we should tell everyone that Egyptian office was closed due to reorganisation. We will reopen it with new staff soon.' Vincent suggested.

'No, I do not think we are going to get the new contract. I spoke to a friend of mine and he did some work in Cairo and his contacts say that they have already given the short term contract to another company.' Vincent explained.

'Well the only option is to go for another project. I had a call from one of my contacts. He said that a restaurant with live music and dancing space in the West End is going for sale. Perhaps, we should look at it?' Pearce suggested.

'We can look at it once more information is available. When is he going to provide further information?' Jimmy asked.

'Soon, that's what he said last week. Maybe I will follow it up.'

'What about you? Vincent, any ideas?' Jimmy looked at Vincent.

'It may be a coincidence. But I met a friend of mine at the weekend who has been working In New Delhi for the last three years. He said that there are a lot of expatriate people working in India but lacking recreation facilities.'

'We know India has been developing very fast. There are a number of multi-nationals who have got their offices, particularly in ICT and automotive industry.' Pearce said.

'Well this friend of mine said if we were to get a project like New Heaven in some hill station in India, particularly, catering for the needs of expatriates, it should be a good business opportunity!'

Jimmy and Pearce were quiet for a minute. 'I am sure there are many luxurious hotels, golf courses and then they have some nice beaches.'

'I really do not know much about India but my friend thinks that there is still a very good scope, particularly, if it is geared towards the American and European expats.'

Pearce thought for a moment. 'Look I know a few people; we did some business of buying sugar from them last year and also some spices.'

'Pearce why don't you check it out, maybe we can visit India soon?' Jimmy suddenly felt enthusiastic about it. Vincent you also get some more information.'

'Sure.' Vincent replied.

The meeting was nearly over, Vincent got up. 'Please do not mention about the Egyptian office to any one not even to Yasin that you know about it.' Jimmy cautioned Vincent.

'Sure.' Vincent left the office.

After Vincent had left the office, Jimmy and Noble started discussion. 'There is going to be a lot of pressure on our finances due to this Egyptian loss.' Pearce said. 'The bank will need to be informed; I think we will need to transfer some of the funds from Swiss account.'

'No, we shouldn't touch our reserve funds. I will think about something and will speak to Sam in confidence he should be able to advise us.'

'Okay, but somehow I feel that investing in India can be rewarding, no?'

'Yeah, I think we should put some serious efforts into it. It seems a very good idea to me. The country has become an important international market, and the facilities are probably not adequate to meet the sudden demand.'

'Exactly,' Pearce sounded happy.

'Okay let's put it into action.' Jimmy also got up.

'Are you coming to the dinner at mom's place tonight?'

'Yeah, you?'

'Yes, I will be there.'

'Perhaps, we can speak to mom she seems to know a lot about India.' Jimmy left the office.

Two weeks later, there was a meeting in the offices of Chezan Investments Ltd. In the board room, there were Jimmy Noble, Pearce Noble, Vincent Muller, Dean Rowe, Yasin Kanji and two Indian businessmen named Amar Shastri and Arun Basant. They have been discussing the project in the town of Dherapur, a hilly town with a beautiful river, nice forest and waterfall. It was reasonably popular with the tourist but had not yet made to the international scene. It was about 150 miles from New Delhi. Due to its natural beauty and tranquillity it was the perfect place to relax.

Amar Shastri and Arun Basant owned a hotel close to the river and not far from the forest. The hotel was an old fashioned outfit and was frequented by the middle of the road traffic. The object was to completely refurbish it and use its large grounds to create all kind of amenities like a golf course, lawn tennis courts, and inside heated swimming pool. Its closeness to the river provided swimming facility at the river. Arun was sure that due to the size of investment they could take the permission from the municipal corporation (local council) to have exclusive swimming facilities for the hotel's guests.

They had all been given a small few pages summary, describing the town, the property, possible plans and the amount needed.

'What makes you think that the expats are going to visit this facility as opposed to many others available in India?' Jimmy asked.

'You see, the existing facilities are reasonable, but basically what we want to create is a small Switzerland where after during the long hot weather, the expats can relax just like home environment.' Amar said enthusiastically.

'But surely the expats would be looking more to discover the Taj Mahal, Ajanta and Elora caves, and places like that… real exotic?' Pearce added.

'I think they can see these within the first few months of their arrival, indeed they do. But what we are thinking is more like a place where they will, instead of going to Europe and America, spend their time in India.'

'How about places in Goa and Kashmir, they are the type which the expats go for, no?' Vincent contributed to the discussion.

Amar and Arun looked at each other deciding who was going to reply. 'Goa is very nice but well developed and sometimes crowded; perhaps not so suitable for children also. And Kashmir is really not very stable due to political unrest.' Arun explained.

'And you see Dherapur is really blessed with natural beauty. It is in mountains with forest, river waterfalls; one can easily spend two to three weeks without getting bored.' Amar said.

The discussion was long and serious and lasted couple of hours. Jackie had booked a table for them to go to lunch together in the nearby exclusive restaurant. It was decided to continue the discussion next day after having gone through what was discussed earlier and the paperwork.

Next day, the meeting took place as was agreed. All the participants, as before, had studied the material in more detail. After long discussion, it was decided that the deal was good in principle. A small team needed to visit Dherapur to firm up the plans and agree the final matters. It was also agreed that if the deal was finalised, Amar and Arun will have 25% stake in the project with a provisional exit clause of 250% of their investment in the project, after 4 years to be finalised later. Amar and Arun left the meeting happy.

One week later, Pearce Noble, Vincent Muller, Yasin Kanji, Amar Shastri and Arun Basant were sitting in a restaurant in Dherapur. They had arrived that day in Dherapur from London. The long travel and the drive from New Delhi had made them tired so they took the whole day to recover and meet their hosts in the evening. The restaurant was basically Indian but catered for the international food too. It specialised in the river fish from the local river but also had plenty of seafood.

'What do you think of the fish?' asked Amar looking at Pearce and Vincent.

'It is excellent… fish kebabs, the salad with yogurt, naan. I never had such tasty kebabs in my life.'

'Perhaps a little hot for me but the fish is really excellent.' Vincent said.

'For me, it is just perfect…I don't mind chillies.' Yasin added.

'Yes of course, you must be used to Indian food?' Arun asked.

'Yeah I do eat a lot of Indian food, but this type of fish and kebabs not very often. I think it is the quality of the fish.'

'Yes, the local fish is really good.'

They continued talking and dining, it was decided that the business will be discussed tomorrow. The fine Indian beer was a good complement to the food after the Bombay gin and tonic. They continued to discuss the food, local area and a few personal details.

Next day, Amar was driving his Jeep, next to him was Pearce, and at the back seats were Arun, Vincent and Yasin. They were going to the green land attached with the hotel. Amar had decided to do it in the Geep rather than walking. About a few minutes later when they had completed the round, they came to the area where there were a few hut style residences for security and workers of the estate. The servants brought out in the field some chairs and a wooden table and they all sat down there. For Vincent it was all a repeat of the New Island in Caribbean. They started talking.

'Man, you got quite a bit of land; one can build a small village here?' Pearce started the discussion.

'I think there is ample room here for an expanded hotel, a golf course, tennis courts and an outdoor swimming pool.' Vincent observed.

‘You see the potential is there, we can do literally what we need to. The important thing will be to bring the people here, the rich expats who can afford all these luxuries.’ Amar said.

‘One of our strengths is to do the right PR; we have connections all over the places.’ Pearce boasted.

‘I think if we can bring the expats here instead of them getting expensive holidays in Europe, and provide them with all the amenities, they will be happy to spend couple of weeks here. ’Vincent added.

‘I wouldn’t be surprised if they take their annual holidays here provided we can get the beach atmosphere at the river.’ Yasin said.

‘As I mentioned in London, the local municipal corporation can give us exclusive area at the river to build something for the hotel. They are also very keen to see the town developed. This will provide a lot of jobs for the area.’ Arun said enthusiastically.

‘Perhaps they can be offered some additional incentive!’ Pearce looked into Arun’s eyes.

Amar and Arun were surprised at Pearce’s statement. They were pleased that they did not need to explain it to them. Pearce seemed to know how the government departments worked.

‘That should not be a significant cost in the project, I am sure.’

The discussion continued for couple of hours while the servants brought lunch with cold beers. After lunch, they returned to the hotel.

About two hours later, Pearce Noble, Vincent Muller and Yasin Kanji were in Pearce’s room. The laptops were there.

‘I think tomorrow we will visit the town and waterfall as well as a drive in the countryside.’ Pearce informed them of the plan.

‘Yes, I am starting putting some numbers together while Yasin is putting a rough sketch of the estate.’

'The hotel needs to be seriously refurbished and partly new built to meet the European standards.' Pearce suggested.

'Maybe the whole building needs to be demolished and the hotel rebuilt from the scratch? Vincent was not sure.

'We can check with a structural surveyor to ensure that the building can be substantially rebuilt and other floors can be added.'

'Yeah, that's a good idea.'

'I spoke to my brother a short while ago and I said that we will give him a report tomorrow after visiting the area.'

'I should be able to put some numbers together.'

They continued the discussion and work while a female waiter brought them afternoon tea and some pastries.

'Would you like something else?' she asked smilingly.

Pearce looked at her and appreciated the young woman with broad smile. 'No thanks, we should be okay.'

The waitress left the room while they all resumed their work.

The next day after the breakfast, there was a smart Audi Q7 in front of the hotel. Pearce, Vincent and Yasin entered in the back seats while Arun sat on the driving seat, Amar sat next to him. Vincent had a camera to take some pictures.

'Where do we start?' asked Arun.

'I think we should go to the centre of the town, then to waterfall and then cross one small hill and visit the green forest.' Amar looked at Pearce.

'That's fine by me; you decide what you want to show us.'

Arun started the four wheel drive Audi. After a short while passing through the main roads, they arrived at the centre of the town. The centre of the town was more like London suburbia: a few shops, restaurant and a bit of market stalls. However, there was a new impressive shopping mall under construction.

'The town is expanding and you see this shopping mall, it is going to make a lot of difference, people in nearby villages and small towns are going to visit.' Amar explained.

'Yeah, I can see the town is expanding.'

They got out of the car while Vincent took some pictures of the centre. They entered into a restaurant and ordered some coffee.

'The coffee is good, a real cappuccino!' Vincent remarked.

'This has been a very popular drink for a long time all over India. We have had Italian influence for some time, not to mention our old Fiat.'

They continued to talk and after about an hour they started for the waterfall. It wasn't far. When they arrived there, it gave a very different impression of the area. It seemed like the time had stood still. The waterfall and the surrounding area were untouched by the modern development. Only a few notices in English and Hindi here and there, announced that some human hand has been there.

'You should have told me before I would have brought my swimming trunk with me. I would love to go under the waterfall.' Pearce showed his likeness for the waterfall.

'I have got some towels in the boot but unfortunately no swimming trunks.' Arun replied.

There were not many people around, only an odd couple and one person under the waterfall. How come there are not more people here?' Pearce asked.

'You see it is weekday so the locals are working, maybe there will be more people in the late afternoon.' Amar explained.

They all walked around the waterfall; Vincent taking some pictures for the project. The water was not falling from a big height but the fall was quite large and the speed of the water. It would not be very easy to stay under it when the waterfall was at its peak, but there was no danger since the land after it was flat and one could not float away long distance.

'It is beautiful, something going back centuries, absolutely unspoiled and natural.' Pearce seemed to like the waterfall.

They continued to walk around the waterfall and then climbed the hill. It was a wonderful natural beauty attached to this small piece of land.

About half an hour later, when there was no one around, Pearce asked, 'can we go under the waterfall?'

'Of course, but you said that you did not have the swimming trunk? Shall I run to the town and get you some?'

'Oh no… we don't need any swimming trunks, at least I don't. In this natural environment, let's be true to the nature.' Pearce smiled.

'What..?'

Before anyone could say anything, Pearce started taking his shirt off. And to Arun and Amar's amazement he took off his trousers and the underwear, Pearce ran under the waterfall.

'God if someone walks by?' Arun was amazed.

Amar and Arun spoke in Hindi something, and Arun went to the open space where people normally walked into the waterfall. He stood there as to make sure no women pass by. But there was no one at that time. He saw some men working about a few hundred yards away on the road.

When Vincent saw Pearce enjoying himself under the waterfall, he could not resist, so he also took off his clothes and joined Pearce.

Amar looked at the enquiring face as Yasin who only smiled implying that he was not going to join them. While Amar and Yasin started talking they saw two naked men enjoying themselves under the waterfall.

Near the hill, couple of young female college students who were doing some geographical assignment saw underneath. 'What a fucking treat! Two strong men completely naked and en plus white,' one said to the other.

'Let's get closer and see what they have got!' the other young woman giggled.

'Be careful do not make any noise. Let's make sure no one sees us.' They hid behind the long grass and some plants nearby.

'They are really well endowed!'

'You need to see our hostel guard's……..did you know he once said that when he was very young his parents had the quarter of it cut off because it was too long!'

'He talks nonsense…let's leave him out.'

The two visitors continued to enjoy throwing water at each other under the waterfall oblivious that there were other people around, while the two young women had a free scene from a blue film wondering what it would be like to touch those good looking men.

After lunch in the town, they started to visit the natural beauty of the area. They passed through the hills, the Audi not showing any signs of tiredness or complaining about the steep hill. At different places they stopped and took some pictures from their mobiles while Vincent took carefully the pictures in his camera for inclusion in the project. All three of them were impressed. The area was really beautiful, natural beauty at its best and not much human interference in it. Occasionally, they saw some ordinary cottages in awkward places which did not add to the beauty of the place. 'How come these guys got the permission to build such a trash?' Yasin observed.

'You see these are not probably authorised, even if the local corporation finds out the officials get bribed, and no one does anything. Besides, the whole idea is to develop the place here, and bring in tourists when the corporation will realise that these are real eye sores, they will do something about it.' Amar showed the unpleasantness on his face.

After a while, they arrived in the green forest. They parked the car and walked around for a few minutes.

'How big is this place?' Vincent asked.

'Probably about a square mile'

'Should we have tour of the whole site?'

'Why not, let's get into the car.'

They all got back to the car and they had a tour of the Greenland with high trees, some small rocks, some wild plants with flowers. The place was unspoiled and had tremendous natural beauty. They got down on the other side of the forest where there was a large pond.

'You see this place can be used as a picnic spot, it is unspoiled and full of natural characteristics, and there are some very beautiful species of the birds that have been living here for centuries.'

'I think it is wonderful: picnic, jogging tracks, bicycle tracks, fishing in the pond, God the possibilities are enormous.' Pearce showed his delight.

Amar and Arun looked at each other, feeling happy that the project was in the pocket.

'May be we can ask the local corporation to grant us a licence to develop it?' Amar proposed.

'Is it possible? Aren't we going to ask them too much: the exclusive deal on the river for swimming and the substantial development in the hotel, and now the development of this grassland?'

'The local corporation wants to develop this area and they are very keen to help the employment situation, so any major development which will boost the area and the employment would be welcome.'

They continued to discuss and made plans while Vincent took some more photos from different parts, and Yasin started making some notes and sketches.

In the evening, after dinner when Pearce was alone in his bedroom, he rang Jimmy Noble. Jimmy was still in the office as the time difference between India and Europe meant that it was still office time in London.

'You are working late!' Pearce teased his brother.

'No, I was with Dean and Masood, looking at some numbers.' Jimmy explained.

'I hope they were good?'

'I leave these numbers for you when you get back; I want to go to Switzerland.'

'What's the rush, don't you want to wait till I get back' Pearce said seriously

'No, Dean was wondering how come some of our profitable trades are not reflecting in the management account. So I was having a meeting with both of them.'

'I know Masood has not probably done the right treatment. The amounts we skim off from some of the profitable contracts get deposited….'

'Stop… I don't know how safe it is to talk on telephone, when are you coming back?' Jimmy was cautious.

'Okay, I understand. I should be back within couple of days. Let me fill you in.'

Pearce explained to him what had been happening, and the praise for the place and the great opportunity.

'Right, what about Vincent?' Jimmy asked.

'He is doing well as I said.'

'No... about the insurance?'

'He is doing so well, I really think we should let it go.'

'Do you know how much premium we are paying for his Keyman policy?'

'I know but he is doing fantastic work, and I think we can make a lot of money without sacrificing him.' Pearce had started liking Vincent.

'Careful what you speak!' Jimmy warned him again. 'Look you need to keep the sentiments out, I know you have been together and probably getting along well. But twenty five mille is a lot of dough, how long do you think it will take us to make that kind of money?'

Pearce was quiet for a moment. 'You are right I was getting side tracked.'

'Dherapur is probably the spot where it should happen what should have been in the Caribbean.' Jimmy whispered on the phone.

'Okay, let me revive the plan, I spent quite a lot of time on the project.' Pearce took a deep breath. 'Shall I get any of the A's involved (Arun and Amar)?'

'No, absolutely not ... you need to get some outside help.'

'Okay let me think, I will call you later or tomorrow.' Pearce wanted to concentrate on the plan. 'How is mom by the way?'

'She is fine, as is rest of the family. Only Firoza... she can't make her mind up about this guy (Shan).'

'One day she will meet Mr Right...no need to rush it, is it.'

'Yeah...Okay I will talk to you.'

'Bye,' Pearce clicked the button on the telephone.

About fifteen minutes later, Yasin Kanji was with Pearce Noble in his hotel bedroom. They had been talking.

‘You know Yasin you are showing real expertise here. I am really pleased the way you are handling this project.’

Yasin was pleased it was not often any of the brothers praised his work, especially Jimmy.

‘You know I was speaking to Jimmy and he also was very pleased on some of the points you suggested.’ Pearce lied.

‘I try to do my best I was so disappointed with Egypt mess up.’ Yasin did not get the real motive.

‘You know Vincent does not really like you, he feels you are competing with him.’

Yasin was surprised. He thought Pearce really liked the guy. ’Excellent’ he thought in his mind.

Pearce continued. ‘You see I can see you to be the financial director of the whole group.’

‘But Vincent is already CFO?’

‘Yeah that’s true; in fact, we can make you COO (chief operations officer) and give a seat on the board. We can make him report to you.’ Pearce lowered his voice and whispered. ‘You see Vincent is excellent in many ways but he does not understand the mechanism of our kind of business as you do. You know how we use the funds to give as incentives to the officials, how we skim off some of the funds for it etc etc.’

‘You know me I will do anything for you, I may not be as qualified as Vincent but I try my best. I have always been very loyal.’

‘I know.’ Pearce was quiet for a few moments. ‘Look, if for any reasons if we lose Vincent, say he leaves…I know he is very ambitious….or Heavens forbid, he might get involved in some accident then we will have to rely only on you.’ Pearce lowered his voice.

'You can count on me; I will never let you down.' Yasin said proudly.

'Good… let's continue some other time…. Would you like a drink?'

'No thanks, I am fine.' Yasin knew the meeting was over. 'Good night.' He got up and left the room with all kind of plans and thoughts.

Chapter 9

In the office of Manoher Basi (the hotel manager), Yasin Kanji was sitting with Amar Shastri and Arun Basant. They were almost whispering. They were sitting on the sofa while the manager was sitting on his desk nearby, looking at some invoices.

'You see I am one of you, I really would like this project to be successful so that the investment can be made in 'our' country. Yasin emphasised 'our'.

'That's very nice thought it really is a good opportunity.' Amar did his selling talk.

'I think it is a win-win situation for you guys and us', Arun added.

'Yes, I agree. But there is a slight hick up?'

'What?' Arun and Amar said simultaneously.

'You see this guy Vincent....' Yasin stopped for a few second, 'he is a difficult man!'

'What do you mean?'

'You see Vincent is being difficult. He is very profit orientated. He almost killed our Caribbean project, if it was not for me it would have not been realised.' Yasin lied.

'But he seems to have shown a lot of interest in the project, and we did not have any negative feedback.' Arun showed his surprise.

'These gora (white) people are very good in hiding their emotions.'

'I see, what do you suggest?'

'I think we should please him?'

'You mean some financial incentive?' Amar said seriously, making a gesture with his hand like paying money under the table.

Yasin looked at Arun who also winked. 'Not really, I have not known him to be interested in any of these things.'

'So what do you suggest?'

'I think you should organise a good looking girl for Pearce, after all he is the boss… and maybe someone for Vincent.' Yasin lowered his voice further.

'No problem, I noticed Pearce was looking rather admiringly to one of our waitresses. I can send her with our compliments to him.' Amar looked at Yasin into his eyes. 'I can find a beautiful woman for Vincent. We have some very fair women around, with some make up they would be just like gori memsahib.'

'For Pearce that will be fine, I am sure he would like it', Yasin smiled. 'But for Vincent he is not interested in women…..'

'Really! How about some very dark skin girl from south..., that should give him taste of Caribbean. Once I met a business man in New York, and he used to say, 'I like my women black!' Arun also smiled.

'No, I don't think it is a question of the colour. He is more interested in young boys!' Yasin bowed his face a little down so that they could not see he was lying.

Amar and Arun both were shocked. 'No wonder they (Pearce and Vincent) looked so happy naked together under the waterfall.' Amar recalled.

They were all quiet for a while. After a few moments, Amar called Manoher, the manager who was busy in looking at some of the papers in his desk.

'Yes sir.' Manoher looked at them.

'Look we have got some problems here, and we need your help.' Amar opened.

'We are thinking to ask Fibi (the waitress) to spend 'some time' with our business partner Mr Pearce.'

'No problem sir, she has done that kind of thing a few times before, I will ask her but she will expect a good tip?'

'That's no problem; we have always been generous to her, no?'

'Sorry I did not mean….'

'That's all right, but the problem is our friend Mr Vincent Muller. He is not interested in women; do you think you could arrange some young boy for him?'

The manager was surprised, he was never asked before that kind of service. 'Sir… that would be difficult specially, at such a short notice.'

'No, we need to do it… find someone Manoher. You know lots of people; should not be very difficult? You can pay the double tip to that person.'

'Let me see', Manoher went back to his desk and picked up the phone and he spoke to someone in Hindi.

Manoher came back to them shortly afterward. 'Sir, Fibi has a younger brother about sixteen/seventeen; I think we can arrange it.'

'Excellent man, I knew you are a wonderful person!'

Finally, Yasin who was quiet for a while showed his happiness. 'Well it is done, I will be off,' he got up.

'What about for you, Yasin, can we please you as well?' Amar looked at him.

'No thanks, I can live without a woman for a few days.'

'Okay, once this project is approved maybe we can show our gratitude in some other way.' Amar looked at Arun.

'Of course, we like to return the favour.' Arun grinned.

Yasin did not say anything but smiled, and left the office.

Fibi was a young woman about twenty five years old. Her family came as a refugee to Dherapur about twelve years ago. There were some problems in Indian Kashmir at that time, and the family had fled from there, leaving their modest home and bulk of their possessions. Her father was accused of working for the army as an informer, and once this information was leaked, he feared his safety. He was a poor man and did not have a choice, he claimed some people had forced him to be the informer even though, he never admitted to anyone except to his wife.

About two years later, while Fibi was still in the school, her father died. Her mother was not skilled, a very homely woman, she worked as a household help to a few families, cleaning their houses and washing their dishes. The family could not afford paying the rent and the household expenses, even though the schools were free. About a year later, her mother got ill and Fibi was forced to leave the school and worked in her stead for the families. At young age, she was now the breadwinner of the family.

One day, in the family where she used to go to the household work she found the house mistress was not in, only the master of the house; the children were at the school. After she had finished her work, the master got talking to her, he asked her to clean his bedroom where he had dropped a bottle of make-up belonging to his wife. There he asked her to try some of the make-up of his wife; the young woman without realising did what the master told her. One thing led to the other until she found that with full make up on, she was lying on the bed and the master close to her. His hands exploring inside her shalwar (trousers). Fibi was scared she was not so young not to know what was happening. She resisted, even though, she liked it. The man was persuasive, he said to her, ‘with this (showing her a condom) there is no risk, you will be as good as new after! Besides, if you scream it is not really going to help, no one is going to hear you, the house is empty, and you will not enjoy it.’ That is how Fibi lost her virginity. She got a very large tip and a bottle of perfume for being a ‘good’ girl’.

That night there was a scream in the house of Fibi, the mother was slapping Fibi at her face and her back while the younger brother tried to save his sister from their mother. The mother had found the shalwar of Fibi with blood stains and a thousand rupee note in her purse. She knew exactly what had happened. After some time, mother stopped beating Fibi, and asked the younger brother to go out and fetch some milk from the shop. Then she questioned Fibi again. And after some time, lying about that she had fallen and hurt herself and other feeble excuses she finally admitted to what had happened. Her mother said to her she should not have gone into the bedroom when no one was in the house. She was somewhat relieved that the man had intelligence to use the condom. Her mother stopped her going to any households and tried to do some work again herself but having fallen ill again, Fibi had to start work again, but this time she got the work in the hotel as a chambermaid. She got promoted to waitress when the hotel manager realised that she was far too smart and beautiful to be kept inside the rooms.

There was a knock at the door of Pearce Noble. He opened the room and found Fibi with a tray containing a bottle of champagne and two glasses. Pearce smiled, ‘please come in.’

‘Sir, the manager.’ Fibi pointed to the tray. Fibi cursed herself she could not speak English well. She entered the room and put the tray on the table.

‘Thank you…What’s your name?’

'Sir, Fibi.'

'Good name' Pearce was thinking why there were two glasses?'

'Open?' Fibi pointed to the bottle.

'Yes please.'

Fibi opened the bottle and poured the champagne into one glass. She offered the glass to Pearce.

'Thanks Fibi, please sit down and have it with me.'

'No sir, only for you.'

'Please do sit down and have it with me. Don't worry about the manager. I know the owners.' Pearce reassured her.

Fibi did not play hard she knew well why she was sent to his room late at night. She sat down on the small sofa, next to the coffee table.

Pearce put his glass and poured the champagne from the bottle into the other glass and offered it to her.

Fibi kept her gaze low. 'Thank you sir.'

'My name is Pearce Noble; you can call me Pearce.'

Fibi first time smiled. 'Thank you, Pearce.'

'Cheers.' Pearce bought his glass close to hers. 'It is good, do you like it?' Pearce asked.

'Yes.'

They continued to drink for a while. Pearce realised that she did not speak English fluently and had kept her sentences short. 'You know my mother is of Indian origin! I can speak a few words and also like Indian music.'

'Indian mother…. You are a full gora sahib.'

'My father is English and my mother is of a fair complexion, even fairer than you.'

'White mother, Indian?'

'Yeah.'

After a few moments, realising that conversation was not going to be easy. 'Can you sing an Indian song?'

'Indian song, me? You like?'

'Yes, please I like Indian songs.'

'Okay, no laugh.' She mockingly warned him with her finger.

Fibi started one of her favourite Indian songs in Hindi which she had heard many times on the radio and also seen in the film. In India, most of the popular songs were from the movies where they were sung by the leading actors on screen but by playback singers in real life.

'Mere dil ko aksar behlati hein teri chooriyan,
Sonchoon jab jab thujhe, aatie hein yaad teri chooriyan,
Madhosh hoon mai tere faile mohabbat mein, mere mehboob,
Alla, koi sun laiga, khankhanati hein teri chooriyan.....' ©

'Like, Pearce?' Fibi asked.

'Yeah it's nice but I don't think I understood the meaning completely. It is about bangles… right?'

'Sir, the man likes bangles of his mehbooba. But the noise of bangles….he is….' Fibi could not find the word for 'scared' so she makes a face to make him understand.

'I don't understand what is the issue with the noise?'

Fibi started laughing. Then she made some noise with her own bangles she was wearing. 'They loving!' and with her hand gesture she made him understood that they were in the middle of love making.

'Oh I see.' Pearce also started laughing. 'Then I would have to be very careful, in case, the neighbours know what I am up to!'

Fibi did not understand what Pearce said, she continued smiling.

'Please continue.' Pearce requested.

Fibi got up, tucked her sari's portion which was on her shoulder inside the lower portion of her sari. This exposed her beautiful tummy. She started dancing with the song.

The nice champagne and the proximity to a young woman who was singing, dancing and wearing sexy clothes, showing her beautiful tummy, a low cut blouse showing half of her beautiful breasts, and even more when she bent, and the lower portion of the sari…quite low… showing glimpse of the shaved pubic area…..Pearce also got up and started dancing with her. Fibi did not object.

After a while, having drunk couple of more glasses of champagne Fibi was in the bed with Pearce. She did not pretend or discourage him. In fact, after a few moments, it was her who started kissing him from his eyes to his feet. Pearce loved it. Fibi was also not disappointed, since as opposed to her many previous encounters, she found that Pearce not only took pleasure but also gave pleasure. He made almost as much effort to please her as she did to him.

It was a long night. A very tired Fibi returned home early hours of the morning. She felt sore in between her thighs. Pearce had bitten her thighs a few places which was quite erotic during the time but a little painful now. However, her purse was full of Indian notes and some British pounds notes. Pearce had been really generous with his 'tip'.

The same night, a few rooms away, there was a knock at the door. Vincent Muller got up and opened the door. He was wondering who could be there so late at night. A young man, with a tray in his hand, was at the door.

'Sir, with the manager's compliment.' The young man pointed to the tray with a bottle of Champagne and two glasses.

'Come in please, that's nice, thank you.'

The young man put the tray on the coffee table. But before he could open it, Vincent came close to him, 'you are not a waiter are you?'

'No sir, I do some temporary work here.'

'What is your name?'

'Sir, Tarbeez but they call me Tarbi.'

'You look too young….how old are you?'

'Sir, nearly eighteen years.' Tarbi lied, he was only sixteen.

'You should be studying instead of spending your time doing this type of work.'

'Sir, I study but my family is poor, need some money.'

Vincent opened his purse took out a note of one hundred rupee and gave it to him, 'Thank you Tarbi.'

Tarbi was disappointed, he was told to please Vincent and do whatever he 'asks' him to do. 'Sir, can I spend more time here, serve you the drink? …The manager….'

Vincent looked at the innocent face of Tarbi; he understood exactly what was going on, so it was planned to send the young boy with the drink rather than the normal waiter in the hotel. 'Okay, please sit down.'

Tarbi sat down on the sofa near the coffee table. 'Thank you ,sir.'

'So it is the manager who asked you to bring the bottle here instead of the normal waiter.' Vincent looked at Tarbi who seemed nervous now. 'Don't worry, we are the guests of the owners, the manager cannot touch you.'

'Yes sir.'

'Tell me why do you follow the orders of the manager? You are not employed here.'

'No sir, but if I don't do it he threatens to sack my sister.'

'So it means you have done this before?'

'Yes… just couple of times, you see I am a student, my mother is not well, and it is my sister who supports the family.' Tarbi's face showed sadness, he was feeling ashamed.

'Does your sister know that you are here?'

Tarbi was frightened. 'No sir, please don't tell her.'

'Take it easy, I am not telling anyone. Are you gay?'

Tarbi looked at the floor, and after a little hesitation.' No Sir, I am not. It's the question of money; it helps in my studies. I want to go to a college and study.'

Vincent looked at the boy with sympathy who was almost in tears. He brought a glass of orange juice from the bottle nearby.

'Thank you sir…'

Tarbi told him briefly the family story how they came from Kashmir, his father's death and mother falling ill.

'Look Tarbi, I haven't got any younger brothers, I wish I had one. You seem to me to be a nice young man who can do a lot better. You speak well, you look smart and I am sure you have got a bright future.'

Tarbi listened to him, he felt comfortable.

'You need to do some other work, I am sure you will not be paid well for it but it will be better than what you are doing now. Go to college, I believe in India it is not expensive. Do not let these people blackmail you.

I can assure you if they did not need your sister in here they would have fired her long time ago.'

Vincent and Tarbi continued to talk for a while, Vincent felt he needed to help this young man.

In the corridor of the hotel, one man was sitting watching the door of Vincent's room. He took out his mobile phone and whispered in Hindi 'Sir, Tarbi is still in his room.'

About an hour later, Vincent took out his wallet and gave few notes of Indian rupees and some notes of British pounds. 'Here Tarbi, this should help you, sorry I do not have much Indian currency but there are two hundred pounds and couple of thousand rupees. They won't go very far but should come handy.'

'No sir, you have been very kind with all that advice.' Tarbi hesitated.

'No, please do take it. It would make me happy; consider me like your elder brother.'

Tarbi took the notes and put it in his pocket. 'Thank you sir….you are a devta.' A tear came out of his eye.

Vincent came close and gave him a hug. 'Take care.'

'Goodbye.' Tarbi left Vincent's room.

As he went down the stairs, the concealed man in the corridor took out his mobile again and whispered in Hindi, 'he is coming down.'

When Tarbi came down on the ground floor of the hotel, he wanted to get out without speaking to anyone. He did not care for the additional tip he was promised. As soon as he came near the door he heard, 'Tarbi.'

Tarbi stopped and came back, instead of the receptionist staff, the hotel manager, Manoher was standing there.

'Tarbi, did you do what was expected of you?'

'Yes sir.'

The manager looked into his eyes, and up and down. 'Was the gora sahib happy?'

'Yes sir, he seemed very happy.'

'Good boy, let me give you the tip.'

'It is not necessary; sahib already gave me a good tip.' Tarbi brought out a thousand rupee note.

'You are lucky, normally that kind of work only results in two three hundred rupees.'

'He was generous.'

'Good, you stick around with me soon you will have lots of money.'

'That's very kind of you sir, can I go now, my mother is rather unwell.'

'Okay, give her my regards.' Manoher was happy that he saved the tip and will pocket it himself.

'Bye sir.'

Soon after, the manager picked up phone to inform Arun and Amar.

Amar and Arun were happy that everything has gone down well. The Indian entrepreneur and the British businessmen were all happy. Even Fibi and Tarbi were happy. Not only they had a large amount of Indian rupees but also British pounds which will, at nearly one hundred rupees to a pound, make a large sum for them. Amar and Arun were thinking in millions; Pearce was also thinking in millions but in sterling.

Chapter 10

Next day, in a very ordinary café in the centre of Dherapur, three men were sitting. Shrute Sting had flown from London to India but without the knowledge of Pearce Noble. Jimmy Noble had told him not to contact his younger brother whom he thought was going soft on Vincent Muller. They had some tea cups in front of them and samosas. The conversation was in Hindi. Ghenda did not speak English well.

'This guy is a pervert, I saw Tarbi with my own eyes going to Vincent room late at night with champagne,' the waiter who was spying on behalf of the hotel manager said, making a face of disgust on his face.

'I don't think you guys want to let a bloody foreigner take advantage of your young boys here. How old is the boy?'

'I think he is only sixteen but he is asked to say the age as per the circumstances,' the waiter replied.

'Are you sure they had some sexual relationship?'

'I am sure, Tarbi seemed so happy when he came out of his room. He stayed there nearly two hours… and you know he showed a thousand rupee note to the manager. You don't get that kind of tips, a hundred rupee is more like it.'

The third man who was a local gangster, known as 'Ghenda' (Rhino) due to his habit of using his head butt to hurt his adversaries. He seemed convinced that Vincent was a pervert and that he was taking undue advantage of being rich foreigners going after local young boys. 'Do you want me to clean this guy up?'

Shrute with his hand asked Ghenda to stop. 'I think we have finished with him pointing to the waiter.' He took out a few notes of five hundred rupees and gave to the waiter. 'You have been very helpful, now mum is the word. Not a hint of this meeting or conversation to anyone, not even to the manager.'

'Thank you sir, I will be absolutely discreet about it.' The waiter put one of his hands on his mouth to strengthen what he said, pocketed the money and got up.

'Bye.'

'Bye.'

After the waiter had gone, Shrute ordered some more tea. They started talking in low voice.

'What do you think?' Shrute asked Ghenda.

'You are the boss what do you want?'

'I think it should be easy to get some support from local people claiming that the guy needs to be punished as a lesson so that the others will not dare to do it again.'

'You know this kind of things happen often in our society, Dherapur is not any different. Tell me what the real motive is?' Ghenda looked into the eyes of Shrute.

Shrute looked back straight into his eyes realising that the guy is not an idiot. He understood that there is a different reason to punish Vincent. He quickly considered whether to tell him the real reason. 'You see my boss in London wants him out of the way.'

Ghenda was surprised. 'How come you want one of your loyal executives to be removed, in a foreign country?'

'Back at home it would be very difficult. I think we need to find a reason that Vincent has done something bad, and he was punished or a natural incident which struck him. Once I learnt the story of him getting involved with the local lad, I think it sounded a good reason?'

'You still haven't told me why your boss wants him removed?'

'To tell you the truth even I don't know. He is a kind of guy who would not tell his mom what he had for breakfast in the morning… absolutely tight lipped.'

'Look, in my type of work, we do what we are asked to do or better still, what we are paid for, so if you do not know or do not want to tell me that is fine with me.' Ghenda grinned.

'Please believe me I do not know.' Shrute tried to reassure him.

'Let's talk how it needs to be done?' Genda proposed.

'It clearly needs to be an accident so that the local police or in case British police gets involved, they cannot relate it back to us,' Shrute whispered. 'My boss insisted that this should be a 'perfect accident' you see what I mean.'

Let's work out the details. The two 'hardworking' men started devising the plan. It was agreed that Shrute will stay in complete background.

About half an hour later, they had nearly completed the major details, the fine points will be discussed if necessary, later. Genda had full responsibility for the job. Just about the time meeting was going to be over, Ghenda whispered again, 'this is going to cost you a bit.'

'Of course, I knew it won't come cheap but my boss is willing to put up as much money as needed.'

'I think we are talking about five lakhs at least (five hundred thousand rupees).' Ghenda wanted to know the budget.

'No problem.' Shrute was happy that it will cost quite a lot less than what he had in mind.

As soon as Genda realised that he had under quoted, he raised it. 'Of course, this is only for me; it does not include bribing the police or any other officials or person. I do not know at this stage what that would involve.'

Shrute took a little time to think so that Ghenda does not think that there was no limit. 'Still no problem, but the faultless delivery is needed, otherwise…' Shrute touched the small pistol in his pocket.

'I will try my best, I cannot guarantee but I can assure you I have never failed before….Okay, half now and half at the completion.' Ghenda finalised the deal.

'Right… let's meet in two hours and I would hand over the cash to you.'

Soon they both left the café without dropping any hint to the others what business deal they were conducting.

Shrute went back to his small hotel he was staying, and from his room, he rang Jimmy Noble in London. He told him that the whole operation is likely to cost about one hundred thousand pounds. After explaining to him how many people would need to be involved and how many will need be paid to keep their mouths shut, Jimmy approved it. Shrute had already changed a substantial amount of sterling in Delhi to pay for the operation, the rest he could change in the local money exchange or the major town close by. He was happy that this deal would make him substantial amount of money. This was one business where no receipts were sought or provided.

Next day, Pearce, Vincent, Yasin, Arun, Amar were in the meeting discussing the proposed project. Amar and Arun were confident that the deal will be approved. It was a really good deal for all. They spread the risk; besides, they could not get the finance they needed. With British entrepreneur they will get the necessary funds, prestige in the local community that Dherapur was going to be an international city where foreigners will come in bulk, for holidays. They had local organisations and chamber of commerce backing as well, since everyone was going to benefit. They had also made some good 'gifts' to Pearce and Vincent; Fibi had done a great job and Tarbi also is supposed to have provided an excellent service!

'I think I have got the outline of the project completed, I will just need to polish it up in London,' Vincent explained to them.

'You got the architect rough sketches, photos of the site and the city, I hope you also included some hills and green areas.' Arun asked.

'Yes, I have done it all that: lots of photos, various reports, and the local chamber of commerce blessings. What I need to ensure is that we need to finalise the exit clause,' Vincent said.

Pearce looked at Vincent, 'I think that can be done at London. We can communicate that to them.'

Vincent understood that Pearce wanted to leave a few things unfinished so that if they need to walk out there will be a reason for it. 'Yes, of course…I guess I was jumping the gun.'

'How about your cashflow and the business plan?' Amar also did not wish to discuss the exit clause at this stage. 'I can provide some assistance with my financial knowledge. I am a B.Com from Delhi University.'

'I have got the basic facts, and am going to do the cashflow and the business plan, later today. I wish to finish most of the ground work here so that we do not need to spend a lot of time on emails and on telephone.' Vincent explained. 'I will probably call upon your help when I am putting the numbers together', he added.

'How about the CV's of both Amar and Arun and probably the hotel manager,' Pearce enquired.

'I have given mine to Vincent, Amar's is being updated… as to the hotel manager, I think we will need a more experienced manager, someone a little bit more high-powered. This is going to be a major organisation to run it, and deal with so many rich Indians and the expatriates.'

'Let's put the current manager's CV with an explanation that a senior manager will be recruited.' Yasin said.

'Yeah that's fine, what about the Council's permission for an exclusive area at the river bank?' Vincent asked.

'I am working on it, they need to have a little more specific information but I know the mayor, and in their next meeting, they might give conditional approval.' Amar stated.

The meeting continued for hours. Pearce wanted to go back to London.

In the evening after dinner, Pearce, Yasin and Vincent were sitting at the bar. They have had dinner with Amar and Arun but intentionally not asked them to stay for a drink. They wanted to discuss among themselves. Pearce was tired from the last night. He had got carried away with Fibi, and hardly had any sleep. On the thought of Fibi, he realised that she was not working in the restaurant or bar today. He thought of asking the manger but decided not to do so. Maybe, it will be too much to get involved with a waitress; one night stand was the right course.

'How long is it going to get you guys to complete?' Pearce asked Vincent and Yasin.

'Vincent is doing the business plan; I am getting all kind of reports and assisting him.' Yasin replied.

They both looked at Vincent. 'I think we did discuss most of it in the meeting earlier, I need two more days, and we are good,' Vincent declared.

They continued to discuss the business plan for a while. After about an hour, Pearce left to go to bed, he wanted to have an early night while Vincent and Yasin also went to their rooms.

The same evening Shrute and Ghenda were sitting in a bar. They already had their dinner since the bar also had reasonable dinner service. Pint sized glasses were in front of them. It is D-day minus two. They were speaking in Hindi in low voice.

'What time this guy is going to meet us?' Shrute asked.

'He should be here in any minute.'

'I said to you that I wanted to stay completely in the back ground.' Shrute complained.

Ghenda smiled. 'Don't worry, this is the only person, I wanted you to meet.'

'Who is he anyway?'

'He is an ex-police officer. He was fired from the service for taking bribes and beating up the suspects. He still has a lot of influence in the local police, and we need him to get the desired outcome. But don't worry he is very reliable. I have worked with him in the past.'

A few minutes later, a well-built man called Bahadur Singh arrived and joined them. After ordering the beer for him, they started talking.

'Why you guys have to do it here, why not in your own country?' Bahadur Singh raised the obvious point, after hearing the plot.

Shrute did not reply, he did not like his comment. Ghenda who knew him well, explained. 'Look we do not need to know all the details. Besides, the waiter has confirmed that this guy (Vincent) is a pervert; I think we got some moral justifications too. Our friend's boss in London is willing to pay whatever is necessary for the smooth outcome.'

Bahadur looked at the serious faces of both of them. 'Why don't you just finish him off and bury the body in the forest?'

Shrute looked Bahadur in the eyes. ‘I would not need anybody’s assistance, I could do that myself. You see this scheme will require a police case, post mortem, burial etc etc. I need to have proper proofs and funeral services, maybe, someone from British High Commission from Delhi might visit.’

Bahadur, first time looked at Shrute, he realised that he was not talking to an ordinary person. Shrute had the personality to intimidate others. ‘Okay, I understand, you need a proper case with no loose ends.’

They continued to discuss for a while. ‘I need five lakhs for myself and the officers who will be part of the deal,’ Bahadur declared.

‘I let Ghenda to negotiate the amount; he is in charge of the whole project,’ Shrute replied.

Both men talked while Shrute listened quietly.

‘Alright, the agreement is three lakhs (three hundred thousand rupees).’

Shrute first time smiled. He knew that these kinds of people can negotiate better themselves.

‘Is that yes?’

‘Do you want in writing man!’ Ghenda complained. ’You will get half tomorrow morning and the balance after the completion.’

After a brief conversation, Bahadur Singh left, leaving half of his beer unfinished. Soon afterward, Shrute and Ghenda also left.

At the same day in London, Jimmy Noble and the account manager from the bank, Sam Hollworth were meeting in a bar near the bank’s flat where Sam used to stay when required by his work. They had cocktail glasses in front of them. Jimmy took a big sip from his glass, ’I am feeling restless, Pearce, Vincent and Yasin are all away.’

Sam smiled, ‘so you are very busy standing in for all of them?’

'Not really, I just feel I am missing the action. New Heaven project is going smoothly, and I am just hoping that we can get Dherapur project going.'

'You know the bank's position; even my best efforts won't be able to secure the funding.'

'You see, we know some other people who may be interested in financing.'

Sam laughed. 'I don't know with your balance sheet anyone will venture with you.'

'Don't kid yourself man…you know an elephant is still worth a million, even dead?'

'What do you mean? I never heard that expression before.'

'That's what my mother tells me … I think it has its roots in India. Basically, it means that important people may be down but they are not out. We may be under financial burden but you will see we will be soon a very successful company.' Jimmy said proudly.

'I do hope you guys will pull some good deal, my job is also on the line.' Sam confided.

'Don't worry you stay with us and you will go far.'

'I drink to that.'

They took another big sip from their respective glasses. 'When they (Pearce and team) will be back?' Sam asked.

'I think next week. Pearce said he will call me tonight.'

'How is Jackie, haven't seen her for some time.'

'I see why you wanted to meet; you wanted to know about Jackie.' Jimmy teased him.

'No, I haven't seen her for some time. She came a few times to deliver some papers at the flat…'

'I know… we did not send her to bribe you. I understand you guys had a good time.'

Sam's colour changed, he did not know that Jimmy knew about his indiscretion. 'No…it's just that I helped her some time ago to get the mortgage.'

Jimmy knew Sam well and they were at friendly terms. But Jimmy also knew well that he had to be careful, Sam was their account manager. 'Look, may be next week or so, we will send her with the Dherapur project.'

'Yeah, that would be nice; I am really looking forward to review your new project.'

They continued to talk and drink. After a while, Jimmy came to the real purpose of the meeting. He looked around making sure no one was listening them but everybody was busy in their own conversations/drinks. 'If we were to bank a large sum into the bank, do you think we will be able to draw some funds?'

'Depends where the sum came from and what you need the funds for?'

'Let's say if we were to make a real killing in the market and deposit all the funds then do you think we will be able to get the funding for this new project?'

'I can't guarantee but I am sure if the project is viable then bank's exposure which would have been reduced, can be increased.'

'That is good enough for me.' Jimmy was pleased with his answer.

After half an hour, the 'two friends' parted.

Next day in Dherapur, Pearce, Vincent and Yasin were in Pearce's room with their laptops and some files. They started working and discussing the project.

After an hour, Pearce told them that the two A's were going to meet them after lunch, and later in the evening, there was a party, basically, to introduce them to the local dignitaries.

'Aren't we jumping the gun here? It seems that they are assuming that the deal will be made.' Vincent exclaimed.

'No… the deal will be made I am sure we might need to twist some arms over percentages and exit clauses.' Pearce was confident.

They continued with the business plan, and had a working lunch in the room.

That evening, the restaurant was converted into a party mode. The restaurant was closed to the public. Only the guests living in the hotel were allowed therein, and Amar and Arun had invited a few important people. The meeting room close to the restaurant was opened and provided additional space; some of the tables were moved to make room in the middle for the guests to stand, and later for dancing.

Around nine in the evening, guests started coming to the party. Arun Basant and Amar Shastri were there to receive the first guests which were Pearce Noble, Vincent Muller and Yasin kanji. They introduced them to their wives who were all very reserved and dressed in beautiful party gowns. Pearce, Vincent and Yasin were all in smart suits. They started talking while other guests started arriving. Amar introduced Pearce, Vincent and Yasin to a local exporter who had a lot of dealings in the UK. They moved with him to another corner while Amar and Arun received other guests. About ten minutes later, the local president of the Chamber of Commerce arrived, and Amar brought him to Pearce. They talked and Pearce realised that Indian businessmen were really smart, well educated and absolutely on the ball. The globalisation had its real impact on India.

About an hour later, while the guests were enjoying the drinks and canapes, there was the noise of a spoon striking against a glass.

'Ladies and Gentlemen, thank you very much for coming', Arun announced in a slightly loud voice. 'It is our pleasure to introduce you our new business partners from London, Mr Pearce Noble and his team. Pearce is the joint CEO of Chezan Investments Ltd, an international investment company. We are very proud to welcome him in Dherapur, and Amar and I, are really looking forward to working with him. He has got his CFO Mr Vincent Muller and an executive Mr Yasin Kanji.' Everyone looked at Pearce, Vincent and Yasin. 'Among the distinguished guests tonight there are Mr RK Rana, the president of the chamber of commerce, Mr Zakir Ali Khan, the mayor of Dherapur, and of course, some of our successful businessmen and … and …not to forget their beautiful wives!' Arun stopped there while everyone clapped.

The party continued. There was some background soft music while people talked and drank. Pearce, now separated from Vincent, was mingling with the guests who were all eager to meet him. He spent some time with RK Rana and Zakir Khan, both in their late fifties with their heavy make-up wives in equally heavy jewellery. He noticed Fibi serving drinks, he discreetly looked at her, she was busy. Vincent talked to some of the couples and their wives. He was sure if he stayed long enough in Dherapur, he would definitely be involved with one of the local wives.

About an hour later, they all sat down, and the dinner was served. It was a seated dinner. Arun his wife, Pearce and the mayor and his wife and one more couple were seated together while on the next table, Amar, RK Rana and their wives, Vincent, Yasin. The rest of the guests were seated in tables around the middle area where they were standing before. The dinner was a mixture of European and Indian dishes. There was fine wine from France and Australia.

All the guests seemed to like the food, specially butter chicken, it was very popular and a lot of people praised the chef in their conversation. Fibi was serving the food and drinks along with three other waiters. The manager was there supervising that the party was a success, and that all the guests got due attention. Fibi came close to Pearce serving him one of the dishes, she came rather too close and her breast slightly brushed Pearce's shoulder. Pearce smiled but did not say anything. 'Would you like some more?' Fibi looked into Pearce's eyes meaningfully. 'Yes please just a little, thanks.' Pearce replied. Arun who knew about Pearce and Fibi a couple of nights ago, also smiled discreetly. She looked very beautiful even in her waitress clothes. He was wondering why he never paid attention to her. He should have tried her before offering her to others, but then in the small town, it was difficult to keep secrets, his wife could have known and the hell would have broken loose. Let me keep these things when I travel, he said to himself. 'Sir, some for you?' he heard Fibi close to him.

'Yes please, Thanks.'

About an hour later, the dinner was nearly finished. There was a spoon and cup ritual again to gain the attention. Everybody quietened. Amar stood up 'Ladies and Gentlemen, sorry to disturb you in your dinner but I think the mayor has some important thing to say. Ladies and gentlemen Mr Zakir Ali Khan, the mayor of Dherapur.'

Zakir Khan stood up. 'Ladies and gentlemen, it is a great pleasure to be here, and let me start by saying thanks to Amar sahib and Arun sahib who have increased the importance of our town by bringing it to the international stage. Now we have international entrepreneurs investing in our key industry, soon we will have a lot of tourists from all over India and from other countries. From the town of Dherapur and its people we welcome you Mr Pearce Noble, and we hope that you will find our friendly and hardworking people a pleasure to work with. We also hope the investment in our town will bring you great rewards both financially and morally. The investment is going to help a lot of other businesses and the infra structure of our town. We are already building some new roads and flyovers. This programme is going to get accelerated. Once again, thank you and welcome.' Zakir finished his small speech. Everybody clapped. Zakir was well liked in Dherapur due to his long time services to the town and its people.

About half an hour later, some people were sitting on their seats and drinking coffees or liquors. There was a live local pop group who were playing music. Some people got up and started dancing. Pearce got up and asked Mrs Amar to join him, and they moved on the floor along with some other couples. Yasin sat on his table thinking what he was going to do; Vincent was as unscratched from the earlier episode. Vincent asked Mrs Arun to dance with him and they went to the floor. The group playing the music sang some Indian disco numbers and some Western music. Soon, Arun was with Mrs Khan and most of the people were on the dance floor. The party continued.

About half an hour later, Fibi also came, after changing her clothes. She was now wearing a modest long dress; she was no longer serving drinks. Some waiters will pick up the used glasses; otherwise, it was now self-service from the bar where a number of glasses were ready of different drinks to be picked up along with some snacks. Fibi stood on one corner. Vincent noticed her and came to her, 'may I..' Fibi did not reply but with a smile took his hand and they were on the floor. While dancing Vincent realised that he had never slept with an Indian woman before, even though, in the college time he was friendly with some, but the matter had never progressed to the bedroom. While dancing on a slow rhythm song he found Fibi warm and sensuous. She came close to him and he felt her breast and thighs close to his body. He also realised that he did not have any women for some time. He held her tight, and she felt his body, his hands getting warm, her blood running a little faster. Fibi noticed, from distance, Pearce was now with Mrs Khan.

A little later, the hotel manager, Manoher was dancing with Fibi. He held her close. His hands moving from her shoulder to her bottom. She tried to politely move his hands. He brought his mouth too close to hers. 'Sir, not here, people around.' She whispered in his ears. The manager was not very happy with her lack of response she always tried to keep her body away from him. When the manager noticed she was looking at Vincent often. He whispered in her ears, 'that guy is not interested in women.'

Fibi was surprised and spoke in Hindi. 'What do you mean?'

'He likes young boys,' the manager replied with a mischievous face.

Fibi was quiet; she could not understand while she was dancing with Vincent, she felt him all over her. That can't be a gay person. Maybe he likes both men and women, some people were like that. Soon the song was finished, and she excused herself and went to the bar to fetch a drink. When she came back she noticed the manager was sitting on the table. She sat next to him. 'What were you saying about Vincent?'

'I know he likes young boys, the other day, we sent him one young boy to his room.' Manoher slipped.

'Nonsense…I don't believe you, maybe you are jealous; look, Mrs Amar is falling all over him.'

'No...That is a facade. These gora people hide their intentions well.'

'What boy did you send him? I did not see anyone going to his room.'

Manoher, having had quite a few drinks and good food, was slightly tipsy. 'We sent Tarbi a few nights ago to his room.'

Fibi was shocked. 'Are you serious?'

Manoher suddenly realised what he had done. 'No… no…I am not sure what happened, I know the other night Tarbi was working temporarily in the hotel.'

Fibi knew he was trying to avoid saying what she feared. She could not believe his younger brother was being used by this bastard, and for Vincent, she was furious inside. She took a big sip of the drink in front of her. How long it has been going on? Is her brother also gay? She was wondering.

'Hey, where have you gone, would you like to dance?' the manager asked.

'No, I don't feel like it; I am a little tired.'

Manoher got up and went to look for another woman. Fibi was sitting there, still in a bit of shock; she was so disappointed about her younger brother. After the death of their father, she was working hard to bring him up and did everything for the family to have a reasonable life. She paid for all of his studies. I think maybe the manager is drunk, she consoled herself. She saw Vincent coming towards the table. 'May I,' Vincent said smilingly. Fibi did not really wish to dance any more she was too upset inside. In order to know him a little better, and not to upset the two A's she got up.

The group was singing an old Indian song with Cha Cha music. A few people started dancing Cha Cha while others remained on the disco dancing.

'Can you do Cha Cha?' asked Vincent.

Fibi did not reply but immediately changed her steps to Cha Cha. Vincent was a good dancer: both ballroom and Latin. He was pleasantly surprised and started dancing with her.

'Are you alright, you don't seem to be enjoying?' Vincent exclaimed.

'No, little tired…little.'

After the song finished, Vincent walked with Fibi to a table nearby. 'Let me get some drink for you, what would you like?' He asked.

'No, please I...'

'Nonsense…how can I let a lady get me the drink?'

Fibi was still reluctant but before she could reply, he went. In a few minutes, Vincent returned with two glasses of cold white wine. He offered one glass to her and sat next to her. Fibi looked at the glass, 'thank you, what is it?'

'Some cold white wine? In London, they say, it makes the women cool down. You seem to be on some sort of edge.'

'Thank you…but I no drink wine.' Fibi lied; she had drunk a few times in modest quantity.

'It's too late my dear lady… I want to see you smile.' Vincent played his charm.

Fibi looked at him, how can such a gallant man be a homosexual? 'Alright, I drink…. for you.' She pointed to him with a finger.

'Thank you, Cheers.'

They started talking again. Vincent told her that he was married, no children so far. He was of German origin, his family migrating to England just after the Second World War. He was born in London. He was more like an Englishman now. Fibi gave a brief account of herself, how she stopped her education after her father's death, and was now responsible for the family. Vincent realised that she struggled with her English. So he did not ask many questions. Fibi discreetly looked at Pearce who was sitting with Arun and his wife on a table nearby. Vincent realised, 'he is my boss, Pearce.'

'I know.' The wine started affecting her mood, and she began to relax. After a little while, Fibi asked him, 'like boys...'

Vincent thought she meant children. 'I love children.'

'No …not children...the boys…you know Tarbi, my brother.'

Vincent was not sure what she was trying to say 'Yes, I know, he told me.'

'Meet my brother?'

'Yes, the other day he was in the hotel and brought some refreshment to my room.'

Fibi became quiet again; her coolness, before coming, had gone quickly. She was now sure that he was a bisexual who had misused her innocent brother. She immediately got up. She wanted to talk to Tarbi.

'Hello… what's the matter? Don't you like this wine?'

'No, I go home…tired.' She started walking.

Vincent also got up and walked a few steps with her. 'Toilet', she said and disappeared in the ladies' room. A disappointed Vincent came back to his table. Yasin, who had been observing everybody instead of dancing, came to his table. 'What's the matter…Fibi left you.'

'No she was tired, I hardly know her.'

Yasin looked at him to read his mood. 'There are plenty of other women around?'

Vincent got up, 'sorry but I think I am tired too. I am going to hit the bed.'

Before Yasin could say anything, Vincent said 'good night', and walked towards the table where Pearce and Arun were sitting, Amar and his wife also had joined them. He shook hands with Amar and Arun. 'It is a wonderful party, thank you.'

Pearce looked at him, 'would you like to stay for a drink with us?'

'Sorry Pearce, I am a little tired.'

'I see you are a good dancer,' Arun's wife complimented.

Vincent smiled, 'thank you…good night.'

Fibi did not live very far from the hotel. Her mother had rented a small modest house. The driver/concierge of the hotel used to give her a lift when she was working late at the hotel; otherwise she used to walk back to her home. He was an elderly man called Ram Lal who knew Fibi's family and also knew how she managed her family. She was doing a man's job looking after her mother and bringing up her younger brother. His only child, a daughter was married and lived in the USA. He missed her that was another reason for him to be kind to Fibi; it reminded him of his own daughter. It was past midnight, her mother was awake she never slept before her daughter got back at home. The house only had two bedrooms; she shared one bedroom with her mom while the brother, Tarbi used the other bedroom.

‘You are back, my darling’, her mother asked.

‘Yes mom.’

‘How was it?’

‘A good party, Arun sahib and Amar sahib were there with their wives.’

‘You should have said hello on my behalf; they are very kind to us.’

‘I did, mom.’

‘Alright, I was waiting for you, I am going to sleep. You must be tired too.’

‘Yes I am, good night.’

Fibi changed her clothes, and after a few minutes, she went quietly to her brother’s room. Tarbi had heard the door and knew his sister was back, she did not like him to stay awake late; otherwise, he had difficulty in getting up in the morning. So he did not greet her. As soon as he realised that she was close to his room, he immediately switched off his mobile with which he was texting his friends. Fibi entered the room. Tarbi pretended that he was asleep. ‘Are you awake?’ Fibi asked in a low voice.

‘Not really.’ Tarbi replied then started laughing.

‘So you were pretending to be asleep.’ Fibi said seriously.

Tarbi looked at her, she was not smiling. ‘What’s the matter? Didn’t you enjoy the party?’

‘Tarbi, I need to talk to you.’

Tarbi got up and sat down on his bed. Before he said anything Fibi said angrily, ‘did you go to Mr Vincent’s room at the hotel?’

Tarbi was surprised. He did not know that apart from the hotel manager, anyone else knew that he went to Vincent’s room, and what was the purpose of his visit. His face sank, ‘ I….I…’

'What I…I ? What were you doing there?' Fibi slapped him hard on his face.

'Baji…what's the matter with you? I am not a little boy anymore.' Tarbi looked at her angrily. (He called his elder sister Baji).

'Do you know I have been humiliated in the hotel, the manager told me that he sent you with the drinks to Vincent room.' She started crying.

Tarbi immediately got up from bed and made her sit on his bed. 'Please Baji, what are you talking about?'

'Look, tell me straight, I have gone through a lot of things in my life. I can bear it as well, but tell me the truth why did you go to his room and what did you do there?' She looked at him disappointingly.

Tarbi looked at the sad face of his sister. He felt ashamed for what he had done in the hotel, a few times.

'I am waiting.' Fibi kept her voice low so that her mom does not come there too.

Tarbi made a quick decision to tell her the partial truth. 'You know when the other day I was working temporarily at the hotel, the manger sahib asked me to bring some bottle of wine to Vincent's room; he also told me that I should do whatever he asks me to do.' He lowered his voice as well as his eyes. Tarbi felt ashamed.

'So what did you do there? Are you homosexual? Why did you not tell me? Have I not been looking after you?' Fibi bombarded him with the questions.

'Relax I am going to tell you all.' Tarbi kept his cool.

Tarbi told her in detail how he went to Vincent's room, what was expected of him, what happened and what was the reaction of Vincent. He got up from his bed, and from one of his trousers he brought out the pound notes which Vincent had given to him. 'Here, these are the notes he gave me.'

'But for God sake, why did you accept to go to his room in the first place?' Fibi instead of being touched by the story was still very angry.

'The manager sahib threatened that if I do not do it, he would fire you.'

'I see…. that son of a bitch…for that bastard my services are not enough, he also had to use my brother.' Fibi fumed, she and Tarbi did not know that it was devta sahibs (Amar and Arun) who had asked the manager to arrange it.

Tarbi was still holding out pound notes in his hand. Fibi took the pound notes from Tarbi. 'I am sorry. I feel really ashamed.'

'Do you know if mom knows about it; the people around what would they think of us. We are from a respectable family.' Fibi started crying again.

Tarbi was now genuinely sorry to make his sister cry. She was everything to him: father, elder brother, sister, friend and a lot more. 'Look I am really sorry, I won't do it again.' Tarbi put his fingers on his ears.

Fibi looked at his brother; she felt he was genuinely sorry. She grabbed his hand and put it on her head, 'Look if you ever do it again, I swear I will kill myself. You swear to me that you will never do it again.'

Tarbi looked at her face, he noticed the seriousness on her face, he knew she wasn't joking; otherwise she will not put his hand on her head. He thought for a few moments, the manager had made him do it, threatening to sack my sister, he was not a gay person; he was far too interested in the girls at school. I will have to settle my score with him, he thought.

'Where have you gone? Do you want to say something?' Fibi shouted.

'No Baji, I will kill myself before you do any such thing. I swear to you I won't do it again.'

'Even if anyone threatens to sack me, rape me or do anything.'

'I think I will break his head off if anyone tries to rape you.' Tarbi said it with a firm resolution.

Fibi released his hand from her head. 'Now sleep, this money will come handy for your next year, to pay for the books and fees. You might need some private tuition in maths.' She looked at him; he seemed very upset but she knew that she had to be strict with him.

'Okay Baji, once again I am sorry. Good night.'

Fibi left his room. After a few minutes, Tarbi took out his mobile phone and texted to his friend, 'Received a slap from my sister, off to bed.'

Fibi came to her room, her mother was sleeping. She quietly put the sterling notes along with other pound notes she had got. She will change them in rupees when needed, she thought. It was quite late, she went to bed. She was convinced that her brother would not do such a stupid thing again. He seemed genuinely sorry. The effect of white wine seems to be coming back. Soon she was thinking of Vincent and Pearce. On the thought of Pearce, she felt a strange feeling; her hand touched her below her tummy. He was such a lover; no one ever had made her so happy. Then she felt sorry for Vincent who was so gallant and nice with her but she misbehaved with him. He was equally attractive, physically even more so than Pearce. I could have had a wonderful night, either Pearce or Vincent. God that would have been great. Perhaps, a night like before with Pearce. She regretted that she did not know the facts before, otherwise; she would have been very nice to Vincent and may be……and just maybe.

The busy night continued seven seas away in London. Jimmy was meeting Marc Kohnvich in his office; most of the staff had left. Jimmy told him briefly that Pearce and Vincent were in India on a project. Jimmy got up and brought out from the drawer an instrument which he kept on the desk.

'What is it for?' Marc asked.

'This is just to ensure that our conversation is not heard or recorded.'

'I see.'

'Look I know Pearce and you are well aware about the Keyman insurance policies.' Jimmy gradually came to the real purpose of the meeting.

'Yeah I know.'

'Tell me, if say there was an accident, Pearce or Vincent was to suffer some handicap or even die…?'

'Heavens forbid if Pearce were to die, you only have a small policy for him. The main policy is that of Vincent.'

'Well, Vincent is the really keyperson, this company is going to be turned around by him.'

Marc smiled. 'You do not need to play with me. You know Pearce and I have already discussed it. I am told that I will get ten percent.'

'Okay tell me what would happen.' Jimmy was thinking ten percent was too much to pay to this idiot.

'The insurance company will have to pay up.'

'What is the position if it happens overseas?'

'India is fairly well developed; there are lots of expatriates working over there. So if something happens there, you just want to make sure that similar procedures are followed as in the UK.'

'What procedures?' Jimmy was not sure.

'I mean, if it is an accident, then police report, post mortem, death certificate etc etc.' Marc looked into his eyes.

'I see.' Jimmy was quiet for a few moments. 'You know Pearce has agreed too much for you. Ten percent is really high.'

'But I shall be putting my neck on the line, I will have to fill all the forms, make sure I do it in such a way that no suspicions arise. I might have to pay some other people under the table…I have an important role still to play. The insurance companies do not open their wallets just like that.'

Both were quiet for a few moments. ‘Besides, I may need to advise you what to do, in case, something goes wrong or your plans misfire.’ Marc tried to justify his ten percent.

They continued to discuss the details for a few more minutes. After about half an hour, Marc left Chezan Investments offices, a happy man. Finally, there was a chance to make some serious money. As soon as Marc left, Jimmy rang Shrute in India.

Chapter 11

The next day, Pearce Noble, Vincent Muller and Yasin Kanji worked throughout the day. In the evening, Vincent decided to stay in his room and work there to finish off. Pearce was to leave for London next day, and he wanted to do some basic business plan before he leaves. After couple of days, he and Yasin were also to return to London. Pearce and Yasin went with Amar and Arun to meet the chamber of commerce president RK Rana.

There was a knock at the door. Vincent opened the door, Manoher Basi was outside. He rushed inside the room. 'Vincent, you know they are meeting with Mr Rana in the town. They need you to join them urgently.'

'Why suddenly, Pearce did not mention it.'

'I was speaking to Mr Rana's assistant and he mentioned that they need you over there. Apparently, Mr Rana has pointed out that the government is willing to give some grants for the project, and you know Mr Pearce Noble is leaving tomorrow so they all want you to participate in the discussion.'

'Let me ring Pearce.' Vincent took his mobile. He dialled the number twice but it did not work.

'What's the matter?' Manoher asked.

'My mobile does not seem to work, can I borrow yours?'

'I haven't got mine with me, sorry. Maybe you can ring from the hotel telephone.'

Vincent thought for a moment. It was already late. 'Is there anyone who can drive me there?'

'I wanted to go home early today, so I can drop you in the hotel car.'

'Okay… give me a second.'

Vincent went to the bathroom, looked himself in the mirror, brushed his hair and came out. He put on his Jacket, 'Okay I am ready.'

About ten minutes later, the hotel manager, Manoher was driving the car and next to him sat Vincent. They were on the main road. 'Shit, the road is closed. They are doing some work over there.' He complained.

Vincent saw the sign of the road closure. 'Is there no other way?'

'No, I have to turn back and take the small road, it is not very good and it's quite hilly.'

'Is it going to take longer?'

'No only a few minutes, in fact, it is a short cut but I avoided it.'

Soon they were on the small hilly road, there was hardly any traffic; occasionally, there was an odd car or scooter pass by. When they were going downhill they saw a large truck broken down. The manager who was driving rather fast saw it, he knew the area well and was a good driver. He applied the brakes. Suddenly, another van from the dark appeared; hit them hard from the back. The small car could not take the impact, rolled over and fell from the hill to the slope below. Due to heavy impact, the car kept on rolling on the slope until it went into the field full of trees and bushes.

The van stopped, and a smiling Ghenda got out of the van with the driver. 'God it's lot easier than I had thought. Tell the truck to move.'

The driver immediately took out his mobile and spoke to someone on it.

'Let's go down.'

In a few minutes, Ghenda and the driver were near the car which was substantially damaged. It was lying upside down. They looked inside with the mobile phone's torch. They found the manager dead. They noticed the passenger side, the broken glass window.

'Where is the gora sahib?' asked the driver.

'His name is Vincent. He must have been thrown somewhere here. Let's find him.' Ghenda ordered the driver.

They searched for Vincent for a few minutes but could not find him. They noticed that from the road someone was walking downhill. In the dark, they could not make out. 'Let's hide man,' said Ghenda. They both hid in the trees behind the long bushes. Ghenda felt his knife he knew he might have to use it.

In couple of minutes, they saw a woman and an elderly man coming down. They went over the car.

'God it is the hotel car and this is our manager, Manoher sahib.' The woman's voice full of shock and horror.

The elderly man, whose name was Ram Lal, was the concierge of the hotel, and the woman was Fibi. He was dropping her at home nearby when they heard the sound of a falling car from the road above, and decided to drive there. 'Let me have a look', he used the torch of his mobile to see inside. 'Yes it is manager sahib.'

Ram Lal immediately rang the hotel and talked to the assistant manager. 'They are going to ring the police. Maybe someone from the hotel will also come here.'

'Can we do something to help him, Chachaji (uncle)?'

'No, he is definitely dead. Let the police handle it.'

‘Was he alone?’

‘No they did not say it. I think he must have been alone.’

Fibi thought for a minute, ’but Chachaji, I seem to remember that Manoher sahib and Mr Vincent were going together out of the hotel.’

They looked around for another minute or so. Fibi suggested, ‘let’s wait for the police.’

‘No dear, if we hang around here they will ask all kinds of questions, and then you, as a young woman, will be bothered by the police all the time.’

Fibi reluctantly agreed with him, and they walked back to the road where their car was parked.

As soon as they were slightly far away, Ghenda and the driver came out. ‘Look, the door is locked; he must have gone out of the window, it is unlikely that he could be thrown out from the window.’ Ghenda observed.

The driver was impressed he knew Ghenda had brain as well as muscles. ‘Yes you are right, he must be somewhere around.’

Ghenda took out his knife and they went further near the river. About a few meters away, Vincent who had after the accident, crept out of the window, was lying behind a small rock; he heard the voices. He was not able to walk much and badly injured. He immediately worked out that the accident was planned and these people were after him. They had not tried to do anything to help the manager but they were searching for him. It was dark, but the glimpse of the knife in the hand of Ghenda confirmed his doubts. He covered himself with the long bushes.

After about ten minutes, Ghenda declared ‘It is enough; I am going to come back with more men and the dog. Maybe he is drowned.’

‘No let’s look a little more.’ The driver suggested. They came close to the bank of the river and looked around carefully but could not find any signs or clues.

In a few minutes, they heard some noises again. It seemed some people were coming. 'Let's go man.' Ghenda whispered.

The two men rushed to their van.

Fibi and Tarbi saw the two men getting into the van and driving off with a speed. They both wondered who they were. The manager was dead, and it did not look like Vincent.

'Who were they Baji?' asked Tarbi.

'I have no idea. Let's go to the car.'

When they arrived near the car, Fibi found the car still in the same position, and the manger's body therein. She put her hand inside the window to see if the manager was breathing. She realised that Ram Lal was right; he was dead like a stone. There had to be someone with the manager, the hotel said they were not sure.

'Let's look around to see if there is someone else.' Fibi felt that there must be someone in the car; she knew Pearce, Yasin and both A's were in the meeting with Rana sahib. Fibi felt it was Vincent, why the hotel claimed that they did not know? Why the two men ran away as soon as they were around? What were they looking for? A lot of questions came into her mind. They both looked around and came close to the bank of the river. Vincent heard some noise, and he barely managed to move the bush from his face and looked, his vision was blurred but he heard some voices. He tried to make some noise but could not. With a lot of efforts he moved his unbroken leg. It made some noise on the ground and Tarbi heard.

'Look Baji, there is someone', he exclaimed.

They both rushed towards the rock under which Vincent had hidden himself. They moved the bushes.

'God.... it is Vincent sahib.' They both said simultaneously.

Fibi touched Vincent, 'Can you speak?'

Vincent was too injured, he could not speak, and he barely could open his eyes, with blood all over his face. With the blurred vision he noticed it was a woman. With the hand he made a gesture that he could not speak. Fibi rushed to the river and immediately put her dupatta (long scarf) into the water. She rushed back and put a few drops of water in his mouth. Then she wiped his face with the scarf, Vincent felt a little better. They heard the sound of the police siren from distance. Brother and his elder sister made the quick decision to take him to their home.

Fibi was not sure but she worked out quickly that it was not just an accident. She felt that there was definitely something fishy about it. She took Vincent's torn jacket off, took out his wallet and gave it to Tarbi. She took the jacket to the river and picked up a stone and put the jacket around the stone and threw it in the river. She came back quickly. Both tried to lift him but could not, so they made him stand and each one of them on both sides, Vincent limped.

After walking with difficulty for a few minutes, the path to her home appeared. They saw one of the neighbours and called him. The man came quickly, he knew Fibi.

'What happened, who is this man?' asked the neighbour anxiously.

'It is my cousin from Kashmir; he fell down hill near the river.' Fibi's quick mind helped.

The neighbour looked at the man whose white face was still with a bit of mud and blood; he knew Kashmiris were of a very fair complexion. But he did not understand why they were so late at the hill and why they did not call the ambulance. He was thinking she is a young woman and this man looks also reasonably young. Maybe, they were 'enjoying' themselves near the river in the dark night, where they could not be seen. He decided not to ask any further questions. He was a strong man. He and Tarbi lifted Vincent and walked to their home.

When the police arrived at the scene, Bahadur Singh was in the police uniform. His accomplice in the plot was the police Inspector. They put their torches on, came near the damaged car and looked inside, and found the manager's body. The inspector immediately rang for the ambulance. They started looking around. One of the police officers started taking photographs of the scene and around. 'Where is the second body?' Bahadur Singh asked.

'What makes you think that the other person has died?'

'Ghenda rang me and told me that they searched all over, could not find him dead or alive.'

'Let's look around.'

They both looked around for a few minutes before the ambulance and another police car, with two more police officers and in the Audi Q7 both A's, Pearce and Yasin, arrived. The medical staff immediately, with the help of the police, turned the car around and took out the manager's body. They tried to resuscitate to see if they could revive him but the manager had gone permanently. They waited to see if another injured passenger or body could be found.

There were discussions between small groups of them. Everyone was giving their own opinion as to what had happened. The consensus was, in the end, that it was an accident; the hotel car driven by the manager was hit at the back and fell over from the small hill road to down in the bushy and rocky land near the river. Nobody was sure why the manager took the small road late at night rather than taking the normal road which was well lit and used by most people.

'We must find Vincent or his body?' A serious looking Pearce said in a sombre voice.

'We have been looking for him before you came', the inspector replied.

They all tried again, some with torches and others with their mobile phones' torches lit on. After half an hour, walking all around, they could not find Vincent dead or alive.

'Look there are some footsteps, not very clear but someone seems to have passed here', remarked one of the police officers.

'Do you think he swam?'

'I don't know, maybe, he wanted to drink water or clean his wounds.'

After a few minutes, walking near the river, they decided that it was too dark and they needed the divers with special equipment to see if he had drowned. Leaving the two police officers on the scene, everyone left.

That night, there was a fanatic activity over the phone. Ghenda speaking to Shrute and informing him what had happened. Ghenda was not happy that the wrong person had died and they could not find Vincent dead or alive. Bahadur Singh was not happy that his police training was not of much help. The cancellation of the plan B of Ghenda, in case, the accident did not happen, one of his men with a gun near the corner of the road was waiting. Shrute immediately rang Jimmy in London to update him but he found his phone engaged.

In the hotel, Arun, Amar, Pearce and Yasin were sitting on a table with cup of teas. They were discussing, and it was decided to call it the day and start the matter after the police have found something. Pearce and Yasin went to their rooms.

From the room of the hotel, Pearce rang his brother Jimmy and informed him what had happened. Jimmy's reaction was strange; he did not jump or showed his amazement. 'What are you going to do about Vincent?'

Pearce who had started liking Vincent quite a lot, 'we are going to search for him, I hope he is alright.'

'Nonsense man, you should be thinking of twenty five mil. If you find him it might be an idea to finish the whole thing off.'

'What are you saying, he has been such a useful person, you know he was joining us to discuss the government grants which Mr Rana informed us.'

'I knew I will have to deal with it, I will ask Shrute to take care of it.' Jimmy showed his displeasure.

'You mean he is in India?' Pearce said in amazement.

'No ... no I mean.. I will have to send him there.'

'No please don't; I hope he is alive and we find him.' There was the silence on the phone for a few moments. 'Do you think we should inform Greta Muller about it?' Pearce wondered.

'No I think let's wait till tomorrow; you said the police is going to search the area, and also divers in the river.'

'Yes.'

'Okay, let's talk tomorrow; I guess you are not flying back tomorrow.'

'No I will cancel my flight tomorrow and wait for a few days till the matter is sorted.' Pearce said.

'Alright then I will talk to you tomorrow.'

'Okay… give my love to mom.'

'Will do... bye', Jimmy replied, and disconnected the phone.

Pearce also disconnected his phone and went to the bathroom; he wanted to take a shower before sleeping. The day had been too hectic.

Arun Basant rang the wife of the hotel manager, Manoher Basi who had been ringing the hotel to find out why he was late. The hotel staff did not tell her what had happened. Arun told her about the accident, she started crying over the phone, she wanted to know where he was. Arun said that his body was with the police in the hospital; they were going to do a post mortem, and only after some time, they will release his body to her. The shocked woman continued crying loudly over the phone, she did not listen when Arun told her that he will visit her tomorrow. Amar Shastri and the hotel staff saw Arun's eyes wet, he seemed to be a lot affected by the manager's wife crying. He felt really sorry; Manoher had been working for them for several years.

When Fibi and Tarbi arrived home carrying Vincent with the help of the neighbour, Fibi's mom rushed to the door. She could not work out who was being carried. She took a sigh of relief when she noticed that her daughter and son were safe.

'Who is it, my dear?' she asked.

'Mom, I am going to explain all in a minute.' Fibi put a finger discreetly on her mouth for her mother not to speak. They put unconscious Vincent who had lost his consciousness, in Tarbi's room.

Before the neighbour could realise why her mom did not recognise her 'cousin', Fibi looked at the neighbour. 'Thank you sir, most grateful for your help.'

'It was my duty; I think he needs urgent medical attention. Do you want me to call the ambulance?' The neighbour looked worried seeing Vincent's condition.

'No please, you have already helped us a lot. Tarbi is going to the doctor and bring him here.' Fibi folded her hands (Indian way of thanking).

The neighbour left.

'Mom, this is Vincent Sahib, he has been very kind to Tarbi. Today, he was involved in an accident. I think some people were trying to kill him....' She told her the brief story adding that they needed to be very careful, in case, someone knew that he was here.

'But what happens if they find out he is here. We would all be in trouble.'

'No mom, no one is going to find out that he is here. We just need to be careful and repay his kindness to our family.'

They continued to talk. Tarbi went to fetch the doctor. Fibi and her mom cleaned Vincent and changed his clothes. The trouser was torn a few places, there was mud and blood. Fibi's mom used her late husband's clothes; Tarbi's clothes were too small. Fibi, after cleaning Vincent face, brought a foundation tube from her makeup box and put it on Vincent's face. This made his face less red.

In a few minutes, the doctor arrived. Fibi gave him the story that it was her cousin who was visiting from Kashmir, that they both were in the hills near the river, and that he fell down. Doctor did not quite buy the story. 'You see he is my fiancé.' Fibi said it shyly. The doctor seemed more satisfied that they were probably having a 'good time' in the hills.

In the meantime, Vincent became conscious. He tried to speak. 'No dear, no speak.' Fibi put her finger on her mouth. Then she said something in Pashtu (Kashmir language).

Vincent understood that she did not want him to speak; besides, his face was so hurt he could not really speak.

The doctor examined him carefully all over and then looked at his leg. 'I think it may be fractured but I will bandage it, but in the morning, take him to the hospital and get an X-ray to be sure.'

'Sure.'

The doctor put the bandage on his leg after putting some lotion. He looked at the wounds on his face and hands. 'These are not serious wounds they should heal themselves.' Fibi just listened to the doctor. He gave Vincent an injection, put some lotion on the wounds and gave a prescription of the medicine they needed.

The doctor got up and picked up his bag. Fibi paid him his fees. 'Thank you doctor, you have been most kind coming late at night.'

'No, that's nothing; we do it all the time.'

'Take care.'

'Bye.'

The doctor left after putting the money in his pocket. Tarbi went to fetch the medicine.

Fibi explained to Vincent that they had brought him from the accident place, and she has told everyone that he is her cousin from Kashmir. Vincent tried to speak but found it difficult. He looked at his clothes. 'Don't worry, Kashmiri man you are now ', she joked with him. Vincent feeling slightly better but still in a lot of pain, decided to sleep it off. He knew he was in safe hands. Fibi served him some soup and in a few minutes, Tarbi was back with the medicine. Fibi gave Vincent the medicine and he fell asleep.

The next morning, there was a lot of activity near the river. The police had cordoned off the area and a number of policemen were searching for Vincent Muller. Two police dogs were there to help. They could not find him or his body. Finally, they rang for the divers who came quickly as they were expecting. With their sharkskin suits and oxygen cylinders they dived into the river. As it was bright morning, they did not need any light. After a lot of effort and search, the only thing they recovered was a torn jacket. They all looked at it and found there was nothing inside except a mobile phone. A discussion took place and it was considered that the jacket must be that of Vincent. The Inspector rang Arun Basant at the hotel.

About ten minutes later, Arun Basant and Amar Shastri arrived together with Pearce Noble. Pearce looked at the jacket and confirmed that it was Vincent's jacket; the mobile was wet with muddy water and did not work.

'What do you think?' Pearce asked the inspector.

'Sir, I do not know I think he probably walked to the river and slipped or went intentionally.'

'But they have not found his body?'

‘Yes that is strange…’ Arun said. ‘If someone has picked him up or he has walked to somewhere, why his jacket was in the water?’ he added.

‘Maybe the body has floated away quite far with the flow of the river.’ Amar sighed.

‘Yes…it is possible… I do not know how much of the area we can cover’, the inspector said.

Finally, it was decided that the divers will go in a motor boat and cover an area of a few kilometres. Where they suspect his body could be, they will dive and search that area.

Pearce, and two A’s returned to the hotel after waiting for an hour.

In the hotel, Pearce rang Jimmy Noble and explained that Vincent’s body was not found. Jimmy was unhappy with Shrute Sting that he had not done his job properly but he did not mention it to Pearce. They discussed the action plan.

‘Look I am going to tell Greta that her husband was involved in accident and he is presumed dead.’ Jimmy said.

‘She would want to fly to India straight away. Maybe we should wait couple of days, tell her that they are still searching for him.’

‘Okay… what about the project?’

‘I think the business plan and cashflow etc are all done by Vincent, Yasin can pick it up and finalise in London.’

‘Alright, you should get all the necessary reports and certificates before you leave.’

‘What do you mean?’

‘I mean if he is not found or his body is found then we must make sure we have the police report, post mortem report, death certificate etc etc. We will need all of it for the insurance claim.’

'I hope he is well and let's just wait.' Pearce did not like his brother's hastiness.

'Don't lose the sight of the main objective. Listen we got this opportunity without we doing anything wrong, so our conscious is clear.' Jimmy encouraged his younger brother.

After a few minutes, the conversation was over.

About a few miles away in the afternoon, Shrute Sting was meeting Ghenda. Shrute was not happy with Ghenda that the job was not done properly.

'Don't worry man I am sure he is dead. Bahadur Singh said that the police have not found his body after searching quite a large area in the river.'

'You see my boss is not happy. There is uncertainty, and maybe Vincent is still alive.'

'He would not have known the plan, you and I are the only ones who knew it.'

'We need to have his body; I know you said that the police have found his jacket and phone. Why his wallet was not there?'

'It might have been in the car which is in police custody but they have not found anything in it.'

'Maybe it fell in the ground, go there and search again.'

'The police have been very thorough in their search, important people involved. They are doing their job very efficiently.' Ghenda whispered.

'Okay let's suppose he is dead, drowned or whatever. We still need another body for my purposes to show that he died of the accident and that there is no uncertainty.'

'I can kill Pearce and then you have another body!' Ghenda said it calmly.

Shrute looked at his face to see if he was joking or serious. He could not make out. 'Don't be mad, he is the brother of my boss. Look I can provide you another body right now.' He took out his small pistol and put it under the table on Ghenda's tummy.

Ghenda was shocked he did not expect that reaction. 'Sorry, I did not mean it but I can find a body for you and then we can claim it is Vincent's body.'

'Okay, let's discuss it again this evening or tomorrow.' Schrute passed him an envelope. 'Here you are.'

The two men got up, shook hands and left as though they were good friends.

The same afternoon in a hospital in Dherapur, Fibi was there with Vincent and Tarbi. Vincent was still in a lot of pain. At the reception, she gave false information about Vincent who was dressed like a Kashmiri man; Indian trouser, long shirt to the knee and a small turban on his head. Fibi explained that her cousin from Kashmir had a speech impediment, could not speak well. Besides, he only spoke Pashtu and few words of English. And due to the pain and the wounds on the face, he hardly could speak. The hospital had always too many patients; they did not need to know more than it was necessary for their official records.

There was an X-ray and the doctor confirmed that it was a small fracture, and he needed plaster, and for walking, crutches. Vincent got plaster from his ankle to just underneath his knee. Bibi pretended to speak to him in Pashtu translating from the doctor, even though the doctor and nurses spoke mostly In English. Vincent thought Fibi was a good actress.

Before they were ready to leave, the nurse observed. 'Your cousin is really handsome.'

'Yes, isn't he; he is also my fiancé.' Fibi said happily, giving her a good tip.

'No, please it is not necessary.'

'No, please I insist; you guys have done a good job, thank you.'

'Thank you and good luck.' The nurse was also happy now.

A few minutes later, they returned home in a taxi.

About an hour later, Vincent Muller was talking to Fibi in her home. After the plaster on his leg, and the medicine, he was feeling a lot better. They discussed the event from the time of the accident to the hospital. When Fibi learnt: that the main road which they were supposed to take was blocked, that they were obliged to take the hilly small road at night; the fact that there was a car broken down and someone hitting it at the back; the search of him by a man carrying a knife etc; it was clear to them that is was a pre-planned scheme. Vincent started wondering why someone wanted to hurt him or even kill him. He couldn't work out. He did not have any enemies in India, he was doing a good job for his employers and both A's were very happy, Pearce was also pleased with his work.

'Could you please give me your phone; I need to speak to my wife in London.' Vincent had not rung his wife since the incident.

'Not good; not know who attacked? Maybe London connection.' Fibi said thoughtfully.

Vincent thought for a minute; it is true it has to be connected to London. It was not an accident. If they knew he was alive she could be in danger as well. He decided to wait till the next day. 'You go to the hotel and find out whatever you can, please.'

'Okay. You rest. Tarbi at home.'

'Thank you Fibi, you saved my life.' Vincent looked at her.

'You rest.' Fibi smiled.

Later that evening, about five miles away from the scene of the accident, a body was found in the river by the divers in their motor boat. It was a man's body; the face was bitten by fish, so unrecognisable. The divers thought that they had found the body they were looking for.

'But his body does not look like a European man', observed one of the divers.

'Look, we have spent hours looking for it, now we have found the body, let's call it a day. In the muddy water it must have changed its colour. And look it does not have the jacket.'

The two divers thought carefully. It has to be him they concluded; it would have been too much of a coincidence.

Behind the bushes, Ghenda and his man were hiding and seeing the reaction of the divers when they found the body. They smiled at each other when they saw them stopping the search and carrying the body to the bank.

The inspector, who was accomplice of Ghenda, arrived at the scene immediately with two police officers in the police van. Soon Bahadur Singh also arrived. The police officer started taking the photographs while the inspector and Bahadur Singh started talking in the corner. It was decided that the inspector will take the body for the post mortem, and then ring the hotel to inform Arun Basant and Amar Shastri. They both knew that it was not Vincent's body.

About couple of hours later, Arun Basant, Amar Shastri and Pearce Noble were in the police station. The inspector explained to them that their mission was successful, and that they had found the body of Vincent. Pearce felt almost sick to hear when the inspector told him that the fish had bitten his face, even though, the body was reasonably intact.

'Can we go to the hospital to identify?' Pearce asked.

'Sir, what is there to identify… you don't get two European bodies in the river in one day. Besides, it might hinder in the post mortem. The doctors earlier being completely satisfied started the post mortem.' The inspector showed their efficiency.

'Yes, we would like this matter to be closed quickly.' Arun said. They knew this accident was not good for their project and would certainly generate bad publicity. Amar also nodded.

Pearce thought for a minute. There was really no point. Vincent was gone. He genuinely felt sorry for the poor man.

'Did you find anything in his clothes?' Amar asked.

'No sir, there was nothing except a pen with the name of your hotel in one of the pockets. That's all.'

'I see.'

They were quiet for a few moments. 'Can I get some tea or coffee for you, Sir', the inspector said politely. The two A's were influential people in the town.

'No thank you Inspector, you guys have been very efficient.'

After a few minutes, the police clerk did the official entries and other paperwork, both A's and Pearce Noble returned to the hotel.

In the hotel, Fibi was working in the restaurant. She saw Amar, Arun and Pearce entering into the hotel. They sat in the restaurant. Fibi immediately went to them.

'Sir, can I get you something?'

'Yes please… can you get us some cold beer we are rather thirsty and tired.' Amar Shastri looked at others.

No one objected to the beer. Fibi brought the drinks quickly and overheard. 'Poor man… how am I going to tell his wife?' she heard Pearce saying.

'I know it is really unfortunate to lose one of your loyal employees.' Amar remembered Manoher Basi.

Pearce kept quiet. 'Let me tell you, we are willing to work hard to complete all your paperwork if you need to.' Arun sympathised with Pearce.

Amar thanked Fibi who was standing there. 'Perhaps you could ask Mr Yasin to join us.'

'Okay, sir.' Fibi went to the restaurant counter where the telephones were, to ring him on internal phones.

'No, I think Yasin should be able to handle it. We got the password of Vincent's laptop. Besides, he copied me and Yasin on the draft as we went along.' Pearce was still thinking of Vincent.

Soon Yasin Kanji joined the group. When he learnt about Vincent he was really sorry, he wanted him out of his way but not dead. Fibi from distance saw them talking.

After a few minutes, Fibi noticed that their beer glasses were empty. She went to the table again.

She heard Pearce saying 'The body was found in the river, we just got back from the police station.'

'Sir, can I get you another drink?'

'No thanks, we will have dinner in the restaurant in about an hour. Amar replied. 'Yasin, would you like something?' He asked.

'No thanks, nothing for me, maybe with the meal.' Yasin replied.

Fibi went to serve other customers.

About half an hour later, Pearce was speaking with Jimmy in his room. When Pearce told him that Vincent was definitely dead and that his body was found, Jimmy did not show any surprise. Since he had already learnt from Shrute that a body was found in the river, presuming to be of Vincent. He had already given him the details of the face being disfigured etc.

'I am going to ring Greta and tell her.' Jimmy asked Pearce.

'Yes, now it has to be done, Poor Greta she would be in shock.' Pearce felt sorry for the lady. 'Perhaps you can meet her instead of telling her on the telephone?'

'Yes that's better. It does not look nice to break this sad news on the phone. She is going to ask me why I did not tell her yesterday.'

Pearce was quiet for a few moments. 'Well, you can say that yesterday we were hoping to find him. There was a massive search operation and we did not wish to cause her unnecessary pain.'

Jimmy was pleased with Pearce's answer. 'You are clever; no wonder you are my brother.'

'How is the business?' Pearce ignored his compliment.

'Okay, yes I remember there is another bad news.'

'What's that?' Pearce asked quickly.

'One of the traders is being accused of putting the profitable trades in the name of the clients who were close to him or giving better commission.'

'But that is the industry practice…I knew about it.'

'But what you did not know that it is not allowed. Dean Rowe said we received FCA complaint and they are going to investigate it.'

'I will deal with it when I get back.'

'No, Dean is checking with the solicitors, we might have to fire the trader. But don't worry about it; the main job is to clean up the position in India.'

'I think it is going to take a few more days; I want to make sure that there are no loose ends and that the insurance company is well satisfied.'

Jimmy was pleased with his brother. 'Well done, you know what you are doing.'

The two brothers continued over the telephone for a few more minutes.

Fibi could not wait to finish the shift in the hotel. She wanted to update Vincent what was happening immediately. Patiently, she waited and gathered some more information by talking to the assistant manager and over hearing the conversation in the dinner time when she was serving two A's and the company. Chachaji dropped her at her home. Vincent was feeling better; her mother had served him some pilau and shorba (Indian soup). She went to Tarbi's room where Vincent was resting. Tarbi was also with him.

Fibi came close to Vincent and touched him on his face then on his shoulder. 'Bhoot, bhoot (ghost)', she screamed.

Vincent could not understand and Tarbi looked at his sister as if she had gone mad. 'What's the matter?' Vincent said angrily

'Your body in river!' Fibi laughed.

Vincent pulled her hand and made her sit next to him. 'Tell me what are you talking about?'

'A body in the river… Everybody, the police says you.'

Vincent looked at Tarbi impatiently, 'look you ask her to explain in your language and then translate it to me in English.'

Fibi explained to him through Tarbi that they had found a body in the river. Everybody including the police considered that it was that of Vincent. The body had gone for post mortem. When Vincent asked how a European man can be confused with a local body, Fibi explained that the face was bitten by fish so unrecognisable, the body in size was close, and that the colour of body has turned bluish due to having remained in the water. Besides, they also found a pen, with hotel name on it, in the pocket. She continued to answer his questions through Tarbi for a few minutes.

'I think I should ring Pearce and tell him what has happened', Vincent said.

'One more thing, Pearce said that he did not ask you to join them that evening. No, I don't think it is a good idea. Don't you see that they are determined to prove that you are dead? It is not a coincidence that there was an accident and conveniently they found a body claiming to be yours.' Fibi explained to him through Tarbi.

Vincent thought for a minute: all the incidents came back to his mind like a flashback: the main road closed, the broken down vehicle then other van hitting their car at the back, the man with a knife looking for him. He realised that it was a plot to kill him. 'God', he put his head in his hands.

Tarbi was also shocked. 'Why anyone wants to kill Vincent sahib?' he said softly.

'Let me think…. Let's wait for another day or so and see what happens.' Vincent said in desperation.

'Tomorrow, funeral of Manoher Basi, the manager.'

'I see; are you going to attend?'

'No Tarbi would go, women not attend.'

Fibi got up and also looked at his brother; he also got up. 'You rest, tomorrow we talk.'

Vincent looked at Fibi. ‘Thank you Fibi, I don’t know what would have happened to me without you.’

Fibi smiled. ’Good man, you.’

They both left Vincent in the room confused and worried.

Chapter 12

In Dherapur, there is a Shamshan Ghat (Indian crematorium) where they cremated the bodies. Arun Basant, Amar Shastri, Pearce Noble, Yasin, Tarbi, the assistant manager and few other people from the hotel all were there along with the relatives of Manoher Basi. Two police officers in plain clothes were also there. Arun had told the widow of Manoher that Pearce Noble had offered to pay all the funeral cost, in good quality wood including some sandal wood, pure ghee, and services of the top pundit. He had also offered a sum of five hundred thousand rupee as a gift to the widow since he felt Manoher had died because of the work he was doing for them. Manoher‘s young son was there with shaved head and wearing a white colour dhoti.

The occasion was sombre, just to see Manoher's young son in white dhoti and shaved head would have made anyone think how mortal they were. In one corner, there was the body on a wooden panel covered with yellow flowers while the mourners were standing in a crescent. The pundit chanted bhajan in Sanskrit language. The pundit and his assistants had prepared a small 'bed' of wood logs; Manoher's body was placed on it. His son was crying along with a few other relatives. Amar Shastri and Arun Basant were trying to control the tears in their eyes. Everybody was quiet and still as though they were synchronised with the dead man. In quietness, only chanting of the prayers by the pundit and his assistants could be heard. Some more wood, including a few logs of sandal wood, were placed on top of the body. The body was now almost hidden inside the timber logs. Then the young son made a few circle around the pyre carrying a wooden log fire in his hand. His tears were more visible than the flame of the burning log in his hand. Finally, he set fire to the pyre. Pundit came forward and he poured some more ghee from a can. This immediately set the fire alight.

Soon the body of Manoher could not be seen, it was engulfed in the flames. The pyre was burning with ferocity while the Pundit kept on putting some more ghee on it. After about half an hour, Pundit came close to the son of Manoher and said something. He moved back. Then he came to the brother of Manoher and said something into his ears. After a few minutes, most people returned to their respective places to wash themselves as it was part of the ceremony to wash one's body after attending the funeral, to cleanse. The next day, the son and the brother would come to collect the ashes to be thrown in River Ganges.

During the funeral ceremony, Pearce Noble kept on thinking who called Manoher to bring Vincent to the meeting with RK Rana. He did not ask for it, Yasin also did not. The question kept on creeping into his mind. He decided not to ask Amar or Arun. He assumed that they might have asked. The whole thing did not make any sense. However, in a way, he was relieved that they did not have to kill Vincent, that was done by God and their conscious was clear. Poor Manoher, he had nothing to do with it. Was he the collateral damage? He wondered.

Two A's and the staff who attended the funeral returned their homes, and the day was declared a day of mourning. Those who attended the funeral had the rest of the day off while Amar and Arun were also not to return to the hotel that day. Pearce Noble and Yasin Kanji came back to the hotel. After lunch, they started looking at the project again. Yasin Kanji had to understand all the numbers and complete where Vincent had left. When they opened the laptop of Vincent Muller they saw the picture of Greta. Suddenly, Pearce thought about Vincent, the funeral of Manoher had overtaken his thoughts. He was wondering what would have been the reaction of Greta.

In the police station, the police had recovered the van which presumably hit Manoher's car. It came by accident. One of the informers had alerted the police when the car was given to the garage for repair. The owner of the van was arrested. He claimed he had no idea when the van was stolen and returned to the street where he normally parked it. He had informed the insurance company. The inspector, who was the accomplice of Ghenda, was leading the investigation himself. He asked why the van was not reported stolen? The owner had claimed that the van was already there and it did not suffer any serious damage. The inspector took the statement of the owner of the van and then released him on the condition that he will stay in Dherapur until the enquiry was concluded.

Ghenda, Bahadur Singh and Shrute Sting were sitting in a café discussing the development. Ghenda was updating Shrute. He told him that the funeral of Manoher had taken place. Their accomplice inspector was doing the enquiry to make sure the matter is closed in proper way. Bahadur Singh had visited the post mortem hospital and had agreed with the coroner what kind of report they were going to give. They will definitely mention that even though the face was bitten by the fish, the body looked very much of a European origin person; the DNA was not Asian.

'Look Vincent's wife is going to be here. I am not sure if they are going to take the body to London for funeral.' Shrute said worriedly.

'We are sure that is the body of Vincent. Even the English doctors would not be able to prove otherwise.' Ghenda reassured him.

'No, there might be some of his old medical records which might not match. It is too much of a risk.'

'Maybe you can convince your bosses that Vincent's body should be cremated or buried in Dherapur. Near the old church, there is a small graveyard, I can arrange (he makes a gesture with his hand implying money) to get permission for it to be buried there.' Ghenda said confidently.

Bahadur nodded. 'I think you should tell them that due to the weather conditions in India, the body would rot, and what are they going to achieve by taking the poor man to London, who had already suffered so much.' Bahadur Singh contributed to the discussion.

'I will try my best. From tomorrow I am going to be staying in the hotel with the London team including Mrs Vincent Muller. You guys go out and look for him. If he is still alive and escapes, we are all going to be… (He makes a gesture with his hand towards his neck implying that their heads will be cut off.)

Ghenda laughed. He thought it was a joke. With the police in their pocket and everybody being paid for their 'services', there was a little chance.

Shrute looked angrily at Ghenda. 'Don't be over confident, you don't know my boss. He can find the guy who could finish all of us. He has got the means.'

Bahadur Singh looked at Ghenda unpleasantly. 'I am sure Ghenda wanted to make the conversation lighter. We are spreading the word to see if anyone of the police informers or any other person finds out that a white man is hiding or lying somewhere in the hospital. We are going to visit all the hospitals close by.'

'You do whatever it takes. Search again in the river, and do all that is necessary. If you find him, make sure the job is completed without any trace; we do not want another body of Vincent.' Shrute warned them. 'Also from tomorrow, if you see me in the hotel with Pearce Noble or anybody else, ignore me.' He added.

After a few more minutes, a ritual packet containing cash was passed by Shrute to Ghenda, and the meeting was over.

In the evening, Fibi was working in the hotel. There were a few people in the restaurant and fewer staff on duty due to Manoher's funeral that day. She entered the room of Pearce Noble with a trolley containing pizza, some chicken wings, salad and red wine. Pearce and Yasin Kanji were busy discussing the project. When Pearce saw Fibi, his mood lightened up. 'Thank you Fibi.' Pearce looked at her pleasantly.

'Something else, Sir? Fibi asked. Pearce looked at her and with a head gesture asked her to wait.

'Would you like to join me for the pizza?' Pearce looked at Yasin.

Yasin knew him well. He understood that Pearce wanted to be alone. 'No, Pearce, we are nearly finished. I am a little tired. I will go for a curry later on.' Yasin got up and left the room.

'I haven't talked to you for a long time. Have a seat Fibi.' Pearce pointed to the sofa.

'Sir, not much staff today.'

'I know, I will ring downstairs, they will find someone. Besides, there can't be many people in the restaurant.'

Fibi sat on the sofa. Pearce came to the tray, picked up the wine bottle and poured it into two glasses (the meal was for two people). He offered one glass to Fibi and sat next to her on the sofa.

'Thank you, sir.'

'What is this sir, sir, just call me Pearce.... cheers.'

'Cheers.' Fibi did not show much enthusiasm.

After a few moments, Pearce noticed that she lacked the sparkle which was part of her personality. 'What's the matter; why are you so quiet?'

'Vincent sahib.' Fibi's voice showed sadness.

'Oh yes, of course, we are very sorry for Vincent. Such a marvellous person, a brilliant accountant.' Pearce took a slice of the pizza. 'Would you like some?'

'No...thanks. His family?'

'Oh they are well off; besides, his wife is going to get some insurance money. All our employees are covered for the life assurance.'

'Insurance?'

'Yes, his wife will get life insurance payment, she will be okay…young woman.' Pearce did not mention the large sum under the Keyman insurance policy they will get.

Fibi was quiet for a few moments; she was thinking that these people are really good, how they gave money to the wife of Manoher, paid for his funeral, and now they were going to give money to Vincent's wife. 'Where have you gone?' Pearce asked her when he saw her quiet again.

'You are good man…. care for people.'

Pearce put her hand on her shoulder and brought her mouth close to his. 'Oh yes, I am a good man.' He kissed her on her lips.

Fibi did not want to encourage him too much but knew that he was a nice person who cared for people. She kept the kiss a little longer than necessary.

Pearce picked up the bottle and filled both glasses again, taking a slice of pizza. 'Here you are, my dear.'

'Thanks.'

'Look, can you stay with me tonight?' Pearce came to the point.

'Sorry Pearce…maybe another day.'

'Tomorrow Greta would be here? I am going to be busy.'

'Mrs Vincent?'

'Yeah, Mrs Vincent Muller.'

Fibi was pleased she had collected a lot of information. Pearce put her hand on her shoulder which moved to her breast. Fibi wanted to go home, and tell the whole thing to Vincent but she thought she might get some more information.

'She…. friend of you?'

'No, I know her. She is beautiful.'

Fibi's mind worked quickly… did he want Vincent to be killed due to her? 'You love her?'

'No silly… she is also a friend of mine… if I love every woman I am friendly or slept with. ..There are going to be dozens of them.'

'Sorry, not understand.'

'No, I do not love her.' He increased his hand pressure on her breast.

Fibi felt the handsome man's hand on her breast. She already had two glasses of wine. She knew if she stayed there any longer … it would be like the last time, for days she was sore. 'What Mrs Vincent do here?'

'I think she probably wants to take his body to London, or maybe she would agree to his funeral in Dherapur.' Pearce brought his mouth to hers again. Fibi did a quick kiss and got up.

'Sorry Pearce, another day…tonight too tired.'

Pearce was disappointed; he thought she was really good in bed. But he also knew that he was going to be very busy next few days.

'Okay my dear, another day.' Pearce got up and took out a note from his wallet.

'No Pearce… thanks….. Good night.' Fibi left the room. She already had a large tip!

At the same time, in the offices of Chezan Investments Ltd in London where the offices were opened due to timing difference, Masood Panji, the accounting manager, was in the office of Jimmy Noble. He had been pointing out to Jimmy about the large sums of money taken out by Shrute Sting in India.

'But Jimmy, he has been withdrawing large sums of cash.'

‘He is on the company’s business there’, Jimmy did not like the bean counters to interfere with the company’s business.

‘He has withdrawn well over fifty thousand pounds there; what is he spending on? I cannot put it in travel expenses?’ Masood persisted.

‘Maybe he is giving cash to Pearce or Vincent for their work over there. Look in our kind of business, specially, in foreign countries; cash is used to facilitate business.’ Jimmy tried to be patient and explained to him.

‘Okay…I will check with Pearce when he gets back.’

‘You don’t need to check anything Masood, put it in the bloody director’s current account, okay.’ Jimmy snapped.

Masood did not like the tone of Jimmy’s voice. He put forward some papers on the desk. ‘These are the expense claims for your approval.’ He got up and left his office.

Jimmy gave an unpleasant look when Masood left but his mind was too busy with the Keyman insurance policy and how it needed to be monitored. He decided to sort out Masood, in future.

A few minutes later, Jimmy pressed the intercom button and called Jackie Breton. She came quickly with a cup of coffee.

‘Thanks, Jackie, please sit down.’ Jimmy took the sip of coffee.

‘It is good; you make such a good coffee.’

‘It is from the machine…I haven’t done anything.’ Jackie was surprised with sudden compliment.

‘No it must be your touch.’ Jimmy looked into her eyes.

Jackie was amazed. He had never paid any attention to her before. Why suddenly those looks. She was experienced enough to understand men. They are all bloody the same whether Sam, Pearce, Tom and many others. ‘Yeah I have that kind of touch,’ she played with him.

'I am a bit tired and worried, Pearce and Vincent not being there, too many things happening (Jackie did not know about Vincent).'

'I am sure the coffee will relax you. Do you want me to get you some paracetamol?'

'No I need to relax… this stress is too much for me.' Jimmy looked again into her eyes.

Jackie was quiet for a few moments, thinking what he was after? Jimmy was getting impatient hinting her, what he wanted. 'You know Jackie, Pearce and I are very close. We share our secrets too. I know you make him relax sometimes….'

Jackie suddenly realised what he was after. She cursed Pearce in her mind not keeping the secret. If Jimmy knew, God knows how many other people know. Then she considered that they both own the business. Pearce was also away for quite a few days, and Tom had been as drunk as ever. She could oblige him, it will strengthen her position. She got up, locked the office door and came close to him, turned his chair and put her hand on his shoulder. 'I can give you a massage.'

Jimmy took her hand gently in his hands and kissed it. He led her hand to his thigh. Jackie sat down on the floor moved his chair to face her. And her hands went to his zip. Jimmy put his hands on her head gently, rubbing her hair.

In a few minutes, Jimmy was relaxed just like his younger brother used to be. Jackie had performed her 'service' with the same great expertise.

Later that night, Fibi was anxious to give all the useful information she had collected at the hotel. Vincent was feeling better; Tarbi and his mother really looked after him. With rich Kashmiri food, he was getting better. His leg was also not hurting as much. As soon as Fibi arrived home, after greeting her mother, she went to see Vincent in Tarbi's room. Tarbi was with him.

‘Good evening, feeling better?’ Fibi asked Vincent.

‘Yes, thank you, and you?’

‘Good…your wife coming tomorrow.’

‘Really, what for?’

‘Your body, she takes.’

‘She is going to take my body to London?’

Tarbi interrupted, ‘Baji you tell me and I will translate before he loses his patience again.’

Through Tarbi, Fibi explained to Vincent that his wife was arriving, either there will be his funeral in Dherapur or she will take his body to London for funeral. She also told him that the owner of the van which had hit Manoher’s car was arrested by the police and released on bail. The police were investigating the whole accident. His wife was going to get the company’s insurance policy for all the employees. At that point, Vincent shook his head. ‘I am a fucking idiot’, he murmured.

‘Sorry, Vincent sahib what’s the matter?’ Fibi asked quickly.

‘You see the company has probably got some important Keyman insurance policy on me and on the two brothers. I never knew myself the amount but the amounts are substantial and it is the company which is going to get the large sum under that policy.’

‘But Pearce said, your wife.’

‘No that is the small amount for all the employees based on their salaries but the Keyman insurance is substantial. It is only for two three people, and it is the company which will get that money.’

Tarbi explained to Fibi exactly what Vincent had said. Everybody was quiet for a few moments. Vincent was thinking Pearce had been very nice with him and they were getting along well. They were the only people who were going to benefit. Maybe it is a mere coincidence, but then he remembered the man near the accident with the knife. He was definitely looking to hurt him. Fibi agreed with Vincent that someone has been definitely trying to kill him.

Fibi looked at his worried face. 'Tomorrow your wife comes, see.'

'Yes, you are right, let's see what happens tomorrow when she arrives. She must want to see the body and she will recognise that it is not mine.'

They continued to discuss for a while and it was decided that Fibi will do some more spying next day in the hotel to see what happens when Mrs Greta Muller arrives.

Later that night, when Vincent Muller was alone in the room, he felt really sorry for himself. What was really going on? Were the brothers gone mad after the money? I was trying to make a lot more money for them. He was not sure if Greta loved him, why she did not come before. Of course, she could not contact him his mobile was not with him. It did not work from the time of the evening of the accident. Had someone screwed it up? All kind of questions came into his mind. He had to control himself for not asking Fibi's phone to ring Greta. A very confused and upset Vincent finally fell asleep.

Chapter 13

Next day, Greta Muller arrived at New Delhi International airport. She had not booked the connecting flight to Dherapur which would have entailed a long waiting since the flights were so infrequent. Jimmy Noble had told him that Shrute Sting would be there to receive her. She also had the full address of Dherapur hotel where she was supposed to stay with Pearce Noble and Yasin Kanji. She knew Shrute, and had met him in a few of the office parties and the Xmas dinner. Greta walked out of the arrival gate of the airport with her small suitcase on the wheels. She looked around but before she had time to look properly, she heard 'Mrs Muller.'

'Hello Mr Sting; have you been waiting for long?'

'No, I arrived a few minutes ago.' Shrute took the suitcase from her. 'Did you have a good flight?'

'Yes, thank you. You came last night?'

'Yeah, I stayed in the hotel near the airport.' Shrute was told by Jimmy not to mention to anyone that he had been in Dherapur for some time. 'Would you like to have something? We have to drive for a few hours to Dherapur.' Shrute pointed to the airport restaurant.

'No thanks, I am fine, perhaps on the way we can have a coffee.' Greta wanted to be in Dherapur as quickly as possible.

'Yeah, there are a few cafes and restaurant on the way, we can stop there.'

They came outside where a driver was waiting in the car. As soon as he saw Shrute, he came out of the car. 'Hello Sir, Ma'am.' He took the suitcase from the hand of Shrute and opened the door of the car.

In a few minutes, the car was speeding up in the busy roads of Delhi to take the grand road towards Dherapur.

'How long it is going to take?' Greta asked after an hour.

'It would take nearly four to five hours. The car would have to slow down near the mountainous roads.'

Shrute and Greta were sitting at the back seats in the car. Shrute saw her closing her eyes. 'Snooty bitch' he thought, she did not talk to him very much. He remembered how she used to laugh and chat with the bosses. She also kept her distance in the seat, sat quite away from him. Then he realised the situation, her husband was dead and she had a long flight. Was he really dead? His body so far was not found. He was sure that the body they had found was not of Vincent. He thought of the money he was going to make? At least, thirty thousand? That's a lot of money for couple of weeks. Then there will be yearly bonus which should be substantial for his work. He smiled and looked at Greta who still had her eyes closed. He also dozed off.

A few hours later, Shrute Sting and Greta Muller arrived at the hotel in Dherapur. The acting manager who knew about their arrival, received them warmly, and rang Pearce Noble. Pearce arrived immediately at the reception. He kissed her on her cheeks and then shook hands with Shrute. A waiter came quickly to take their suitcases to their rooms. Due to police restrictions, the room of Vincent Muller, where his clothes, brief case etc. were still there, was not available. The hotel forms were filled quickly and they both signed. Another waiter escorted Shrute to his room while Pearce Noble walked with Greta towards her room. When they arrived at the room, Greta started crying.

'I am so sorry Greta; I don't know what to say. You know since the accident I have not slept one night properly.'

Greta looked at him she believed that Pearce was really sorry. She came close to him and put her head on his shoulder. Pearce put his hand on her head. 'Don't worry, it is God's will.'

In the meantime, the waiter brought the suitcase of Greta. Pearce told him from his hand to put the suitcase on the side, and he left the room without waiting for his tip.

'Look you better take rest; you must be tired of the long drive. I will see you for the dinner in an hour or so.'

Greta took out the handkerchief to wipe her tears. 'Thanks Pearce.'

Pearce left the sad Greta in her room.

About two hours later, Amar Shastri, Arum Basant, Pearce Noble, Yasin Kanji and Greta Muller were having dinner in the restaurant of the hotel. Fibi had made sure that she served them so that she could eavesdrop their conversation. Fibi thought Greta was a beautiful woman; no wonder, Vincent did not care much about other women. She remembered a famous Hollywood actor's quote: "When you have got the steak at home why go for hamburgers outside."

'Can I visit the hospital to see Vincent?' Greta asked.

'Gretaji, it is late in the evening, they would not allow in the hospital this time. Tomorrow we can go there.' Amar replied.

'I think we should consider the next step.' Pearce added.

'What do you mean?' Greta said anxiously.

'I mean what do you want to do; do you want to take his body to London or do a funeral over here?'

'I think I want to take it to London and do the funeral there. I rang his uncle in Frankfurt.'

'Does he not have a family?' Arun asked.

'No, he is the only child and both of his parents have passed away, only his uncle and his family in Germany.'

'In that case, it might be an idea to have the funeral here.' Arun looked at her and the others around.

Greta was quiet; she was not sure what to do. 'I will think about it. What are the facilities here?'

'We have got an old church here from the time of the British rule, and there is a small graveyard. We can arrange the burial there. Or if you like a cremation Indian style.' Arun replied.

Fibi and other waiter continued serving them the meal and the drinks. Greta was quiet. 'There is definitely a case for the funeral here. The poor man not to be jerked around in box, let him rest in peace here.' Pearce tried to convince Greta.

'Maybe I should ring his uncle in Frankfurt, what do they think?'

'Well you can decide overnight, we will provide all the support you need. Vincent sahib was a fantastic man. He impressed us immensely.' Amar Shastri who was sitting next to her slightly tapped on her shoulder.

'In our religion, we do not keep the bodies for long time; in fact, we bury them within twenty four hours.' Yasin Kanji said.

They continued to discuss and continue with their dinner.

About two hours later, Pearce Noble was in Greta Muller's room. They were talking.

'I rang Uncle Hans, he said he is in Africa, he was expecting me to bring his body to London, he cannot attend the funeral in Dherapur in time but he said to go ahead if it is convenient to do it there.' Greta explained to Pearce.

'Look Greta, Vincent is gone, make things easy for you, and let the poor man rest in peace here.' Pearce looked into her eyes.

'I would like to visit his grave some time.'

'India is not very far, in eight hours you are here. You can fly back the same day literally.'

'Okay, you tell me how it is going to be arranged.' Greta was more or less convinced with the idea.

'Let me order some drink, and I will explain it to you.' Pearce picked up the phone and ordered a bottle of wine.

They started talking again and in a few minutes Fibi arrived in the room with the chilled bottle of wine and glasses. 'She opened the bottle and served them with two glasses.'

'Thanks, Fibi.' Pearce smiled at her.

'Would there be anything else, Sir.'

'No thanks Fibi.'

After Fibi had gone, Greta remarked. 'She is beautiful, do you know her?'

'No she is just a waitress in the hotel.'

'No, it is just the way she looked at you.'

'No, this is the way all the beautiful women look at me. Cheers to my friend Vincent.' Pearce took the sip from the glass.

Greta was wondering, how this man is so carefree, Even in such a tragic situation, he does not forget his sense of humour. She also took the sip from the glass without saying anything.

They started talking, what could be arranged in Dherapur. About half an hour later, when the bottle was nearly finished, Greta had made up her mind. She knew no one will join from London from her own family. And Pearce's arguments were convincing.

'I am feeling tired. Maybe I will just hit the bed.' Greta looked at Pearce. 'The white wine was good I feel a lot more relaxed now.'

'I know … do you know if I stay tonight with you, you will feel even better. 'Pearce looked back into her eyes.

Greta was tired but after speaking with Pearce and the effect of half a bottle of wine in her she was feeling a lot more relaxed. She did not have to think much about Pearce's new proposal.

'Alright, you can stay here tonight on the condition that you will let me sleep in peace. I am rather tired.'

'I just want to give you company in this situation. So that you don't feel too uncomfortable.'

'Thanks.' Greta opened her suitcase and took out a nightie and went to the bathroom.

In a few minutes, she was back. She sat on the bed. 'Don't you want to fetch your pyjamas?'

'No, I am okay.' I am not going to spend the whole night here. When I see you are settled and sleepy I will go to my room. Anyway, it is only a few doors away.'

'Okay.'

Pearce came and sat next to her on the bed. "Did you know your brother is not like you at all?' Greta said. 'When he met me, he was so clumsy. He did not make any effort to come close.'

'I know he is not so confident with women. Besides, the situation was also not quite right. You know we both liked your husband.' Pearce knew how to handle a woman.

'You are great. We really had a good time a few months ago.'

They continued to talk, and in a few minutes, Greta had forgotten that she came to Dherapur for her late husband; she did not know if it was Pearce's charm or the wine.

'You know you are such a beautiful woman. I kept on thinking about you after our last meeting.' Pearce came close to her and took her face in his hand then delicately he kissed her lightly on her lips. Greta who had not had sex for some time, and the combination of close proximity to a handsome man, half a bottle of wine in her tummy, she brought her mouth forward and kissed Pearce. Pearce felt the warmth of her kiss and then his hands moved on her shoulder and within a few seconds they were on her breast. Greta did not object she did not want him either to take his lips or hands away from her breast. She moved her hands to his thighs. Pearce responded in kind and his hands moved under her tummy. It wasn't long before her nightie was off and her legs spread wide open, and a naked Pearce thrusting in her with passion. Neither Greta nor Pearce had the slightest regard that she was a widow now who had come to collect her husband's body.

Fibi was serving in the restaurant. It was nearly the time for her to finish her duty and go home. But she kept on thinking what was going on in Greta Muller's room. Was Pearce still with her or had he gone back to his room. He seemed too friendly with her. She decided to ring him in his hotel's telephone. There was no answer. So without any reason, she picked up a tray, put some smoked salmon sandwiches in it, and on the pretext of serving them she went to Greta's room.

When she arrived there she wanted to knock at the door then she heard the sound of deep breathing and moaning. Fibi had been herself in that situation many times, she knew Greta was moaning. Pearce was making her as happy as he had made her just a few days ago. She could not believe that a woman, who had just arrived in such tragic circumstances and who should be crying the night long, was having steamy sex with 'her' Pearce. Poor Fibi had a crush on Pearce. Fibi stood in front of Greta's room for a couple of minutes, listening to the voices inside which seemed to die down.

Another waiter saw her standing in front of the room. Fibi turned back pretending to be annoyed that Greta was not answering the knock at the door. Fibi realised that she did not like Pearce sahib anymore. Inside the room, two bodies were still clinching to each other.

Ram Lal, the hotel concierge dropped Fibi at her home after finishing his duty. Fibi rushed to the house and even without greeting her mother, she went to Vincent room who was sitting there talking with Tarbi. 'So what's the news at the hotel?' Vincent could not wait to know what was happening. Fibi looked at him sympathetically. 'Sorry, your wife no good.'

'What do you mean, my wife no good?'

'She is friend with Pearce sahib.'

Vincent looked at Tarbi who again translated Fibi's English to him.

Fibi told him that Greta Muller had arrived. There was a talk that the funeral should take place in the old small church in Dherapur. Everyone was advocating that argument. No one was coming from London or Germany. There was a new man who escorted Greta Muller from New Delhi airport. And that Greta was far too friendly with Pearce Noble.

'What do you mean far too friendly?' Vincent insisted.

'She ….she…' Fibi was not sure what she should say.

'Please tell me clearly…you can't hide things from a dead man!'

'She sleeping with Pearce sahib.'

'How do you know?' Vincent said angrily. 'How can you accuse her of such a thing?'

Again Tarbi came to the rescue of his sister and explained to him that she took the bottle of wine in Greta's room where Pearce was there with her. She also went to serve them some sandwiches but she did not open the door and she heard the voices of love making inside. She was hundred percent sure it was Pearce who was in her room. She also found that Pearce was not in his room.

Vincent was shocked. She did not have any reasons to lie to him. His face sank once again. So this is my beloved faithful wife who stays lonely when I am travelling. He almost felt like crying. What is more in store for him? He was attacked, they found his body, insurance scam and now his beloved wife was also unfaithful but probably part of the conspiracy.

Fibi came close to him and put her hands around him sympathetically. She wanted to hug him and comfort him. This is the first time she felt such a strong desire to comfort this man. She was sure it had nothing to do with Pearce sleeping with Greta. Vincent's eyes were filled with tears, he hugged her. Tarbi had never seen his sister close to any man. He was wondering if he should stick around or leave them alone. But what if he sleeps with her? He could not let this married foreigner sleep with his sister. While he was thinking he saw Fibi pointing him to go out. He left the room reluctantly.

First time Vincent also realised that Fibi was an attractive woman. Her closeness to him, in spite of he being very upset did make his blood run faster. He kissed on her lips lightly. Fibi did not object to it. But she was disappointed as the kiss was very light and lacking any passion. She got up from the bed, 'I need cold water; you like some?'

'Yes please.'

Fibi went to the kitchen, she saw her mother praying in the other room. She drank some water and brought some water for Vincent.

'Thanks, Fibi…you really are a very kind woman.'

'No mention.'

After drinking the water, he put the glass on the side table. 'Fibi, I do not know what I would have done without your family. My leg is better now. But please do tell me how did you know all these things?'

'No problem, good spy.' Fibi laughed, she did not go into details.

'Who was the person who escorted Greta, was it Jimmy Noble, the brother of Pearce?'

'Not know…a middle aged man…. like Yasin.'

'Oh I see it must be Shrute.'

They continued to talk for a while before Fibi decided that he would rather be alone. She got up, 'good night.'

'Thanks again Fibi, and Good night.'

The next day, Greta was visiting the local coroner's office where they had kept the body of Vincent Muller after the post mortem. Pearce Noble and Amar Shastri were with her. Ghenda and Bahadur Singh had already arranged with the coroner that the body should be shown in such a way that no suspicions arises that it was not that of Vincent Muller. They had painted the face of the body pink and tried to do make up in such a way that it came as close as possible. Some fish bitten marks and accident marks were left on the face intentionally.

When Greta looked at her husband's body, she felt almost fainting. The handsome young man was reduced to such a state, she could not believe. She looked at him again. But he does not look like Vincent she thought in her mind. After a few moments, she spoke to Pearce, 'Vincent was taller than this and look at the colour of his body. Are you sure it is Vincent's body?'

Amar wanted to say something but he noticed Pearce replying. 'Dear, this is the body which has been in the river for some time it has changed its colour. And don't forget he had suffered injuries in the accident as well as the fish marks.'

Greta started crying. She could not identify that body with her handsome husband. Pearce looked at Amar who looked at the Doctor who immediately covered the body with the blanket. 'Come my dear, more you see him, more you will feel hurt. The poor man has gone through a bad time. Let's leave him in peace.' Pearce took the hand of Greta to go to other room.

No one tried to answer the question why the body was shorter. They all moved to the office. Greta took out her handkerchief, and wiped her eyes and nose with it. In the office, some forms were produced and Greta signed these. These confirmed that the body had been identified by the nearest of kin. Pearce Noble signed as the witness along with Amar Shastri.

In the evening, Fibi briefed Vincent Muller what had happened during the day. Tarbi was the translator as usual since Vincent wanted to know the exact details. Fibi told him that Greta had identified his body. The funeral would take place next day at the Old Church, as it was known. Vincent had another shock he could not believe that his wife of several years would not recognise that it was not his body. He began to believe that she is probably part of the conspiracy, that she had joined Nobles.

'Shall I go to the police?' or ring the British High Commission in New Delhi?' he thought loud.

'Not good… they kill you.' Fibi advised

Vincent learnt another shocking news. Tarbi told him that someone was enquiring at the hospital if there was any non-local person being treated. The brother of the nurse at the hospital was a friend of Tarbi and had told him that his sister (the nurse) had not mentioned their names, but sooner or later they will realise, if they check the hospital records. He said the people who came to enquire in the hospital looked like 'gundas' (bad men).

Vincent Muller thought for a minute. 'Look if these people are after me, you guys are going to be in danger too.'

Fibi said something in her language to Tarbi. 'Baji is saying that she will go to the nurse and ask her to remove the records, you don't need to worry, we have stood by you we cannot leave you now.'

'No darling, you are too kind you should not endanger your family.' Vincent was touched by Fibi's resolve.

Fibi looked at him for a few moments. 'Good man Vincent sahib, we love.'

Vincent wanted to take her in his arms and kiss her but he knew she did not like to be close to him in the presence of her younger brother. That was against their culture.

'Look, can you get my passport from the hotel room; I am going to New Delhi and fly to Europe. I will deal with the situation in London.'

'Your leg?'

'No, it is fine, I am able to walk… slight limp.'

They discussed how the passport can be taken from the hotel room which was sealed by the police till the completion of the investigation. After a few minutes' consultation, it was decided that Fibi and Tarbi would get it from the room. Fibi will get the key and make sure that no one is around and Tarbi will sneak into the hotel room and steal the passport. Vincent told them to be extra careful.

Next day, there was a grand ceremony in the Old Church. It was the funeral of Vincent Muller. The attendees were numerous: Mrs Greta Muller was in a dark dress with dark light coat. Pearce Noble, Yasin Kanji, Shrute Sting were all in dark suits, Amar Shastri, Arun Basant, local mayor Zakir Ali Khan, the president of the chamber of commerce RK Rana and their wives. A number of hotel staff including Fibi and local dignitaries was there. Tarbi had decided to stay at home since he heard that some people were looking for Vincent. Bahadur Singh was also there, Ghenda had decided that Bahadur Singh would watch for the ceremony. The inspector of police was there in plain clothes, and two police officers in their uniforms. A representative of the British consulate was also there. Pearce wanted to make sure that the whole thing was formally done with all kind of photographs and the certificates. After all, twenty five million pounds were at stake.

In the church, in front seat Greta Muller was sitting with Pearce Noble. The rest of the people were seated according to their importance in the front seats and behind. The body of Vincent Muller was in a good quality coffin dressed in one of his own suits, which was opened. For the ceremony additional make up was done by the expert make up people who made him look like real Vincent as much as possible. Greta looked many times at her husband's body; more she looked at him more it looked to her that it was real Vincent. She was a figure of sorrow in her dark clothes.

After a few minutes, everybody had settled, no one was there to see Vincent's face; only a round of walk by Greta and Pearce was made. She put a kiss on him through her hand on his face lightly. Amar Shastri got up and went in front of the seats where there was a small platform to address. He spoke through the microphone and gave a small speech.

'Ladies and gentlemen, we are gathered here to pay our respects to Mr Vincent Muller, a learned man…a wonderful man who was so loyal and duty bound to his employer. We remember his contribution to our town, the big project we are planning would change the face of Dherapur. His dedication to work was unparalleled; he died while performing his work. We also remember his great personality, his sense of humour and his helping attitude.' He paused for a few moments then he looked towards the coffin of Vincent Muller. 'On behalf of my partner, Arun and the people of Dherapur we thank you and remember you Vincent sahib, May God bless you.'

Amar finished his little speech which was well received by the audience. Greta had decided she was not going to say anything. Pearce got up and went to the microphone where the priest of the church was standing.

'Ladies and gentlemen, thank you for attending the funeral of our dear colleague Vincent Muller. I think Amar has already highlighted his personality and the contribution he has been making to Dherapur. What I would say is that Vincent was a man dedicated to his work. He had enormous sense of responsibility. Besides, being a hardworking man, he was loyal to his employer and friendly with people he worked with. I also remember the tragic way he died. I am sure the local police will catch the people responsible for this accident. (He pauses) Chezan Investment Ltd would always remember him and miss him as a very capable executive; he was the key man in our company and a driving force in the diversification and the development of the company. But I personally will also miss him as a friend; I worked with him so close here and in London. He was like a brother and a friend to me.' He paused and looked at the coffin of Vincent, 'On behalf of my family who unfortunately could not attend, Chezan Investments Ltd, the management and the employees of the company and especially from my brother Jimmy Noble, I salute you Vincent. We will all miss you. … (then looking at Greta), and of course, our heartfelt sympathies to his beloved wife Greta Muller.'

Pearce walked back to his seat. The priest, in his decorative dress, started the prayers. In about half an hour, the ceremony was finished, and the actual burial took place in the grounds of the old church. Vincent Muller's body was buried in the grounds where some important officers of the British army and the bureaucrats of the Indian Raj were buried. He was not even invited to be there himself. The real Vincent Muller was waiting anxiously for Fibi to come back.

Chapter 14

The same day of the funeral, in the evening, Pearce Noble was in his room in the hotel in Dherapur. He informed his brother Jimmy Noble in London that the funeral of Vincent Muller had taken place and that he had all the necessary certificates.

'So when are you returning to London? I can't wait to get my hands on the insurance money.' Jimmy said happily on the phone.

'We are nearly finished here, Yasin and I have looked at the numbers and the rest of the work can be done in London. Due to Vincent's death, even both A's are lot more flexible… I think we should be able to tidy up the rest in London.'

'Good, how is Greta?'

'She is okay… of course, she has been upset but I have consoled her quite a lot and made sure she does not stay alone.'

'How many other women have you consoled in this stay?!'

Pearce laughed, 'you know me….'

'Yeah, yeah, I do… Are you planning to leave Yasin there?'

'No, I think we will all come back together, maybe tomorrow.'

Pearce and Jimmy continued for a few minutes more. Both were satisfied that everything was working well. Pearce thought it was sheer luck that they did not have to do anything. Poor Vincent made his way out of this world without any help!

While Pearce was in his room, Fibi was working in the restaurant. There were a few customers. She saw near the front desk, the acting manager was sitting on his desk, busy looking at the computer screen. Fibi walked to the front desk where the keys of the guest rooms were kept. She discreetly looked at the key of Vincent Muller's room which was locked by the police; the room key was not there. She came to the steel safe where inside the other locked drawer, cash was kept, the important books, the petty cash box and a few other valuables.

'Are you looking for something?' the acting manager asked.

'Sir, I am looking for the petty cash, I need a stamp, it is too much to walk to the post office.' Fibi said smilingly.

'It will be closed now anyway.'

'Yeah, I had forgotten.'

'It is still there.' The acting manager also smiled. He always thought that Fibi, indeed all the female staff, came as a benefit in kinds with the job. He has been waiting for a suitable opportunity. At present, with death, police and funeral etc it was not the right time.

Fibi pretended to look inside the safe and take out the petty cash box; with a very delicate touch, she grabbed the master key from the drawer along with the petty cash box. She brought the box on the front desk, opened it and took out a stamp from it. She closed the box and put it back in the safe again while hiding the master key in her blouse.

'Thank you, sir.' Fibi said in a charming voice.

'You are welcome my dear, any time.' The acting manager was happy to oblige her.

In a few minutes, Tarbi walked into the hotel. Fibi went to him to talk; he was not on the temporary duty in the hotel that day. They pretended to talk and Fibi discreetly handed over the master key to him. Fibi went to fetch a soft drink for her brother while he sat on the chair near the front desk. The acting manager saw him and smiled.

‘Good evening, Sir,’ Tarbi said in English.

The acting manager, who knew him, did not reply but smiled back at him, and got back to his computer screen. Fibi came back and gave the drink to her brother. The acting manager continued with his work. In a few moments, when he saw the time was right Tarbi got up, but instead of going out, he walked towards the guests' rooms. Shortly afterward, Fibi also walked towards the guests' rooms, taking a tray with a drink on it. No one around thought anything unusual, it was a typical hotel evening. No other waiters or guests knew if Tarbi should or should not be going towards the guests’ rooms since occasionally he worked therein.

Fibi walked towards the room of Vincent Muller, and saw her brother opening the door and enter in it quickly. She stood outside pretending to be knocking at the opposite room. A guest came by and saw Fibi but moved on, Fibi greeted him by smiling. In a few moments, Tarbi, who knew exactly where the passport was, came out. He signalled his sister that the work was done. She took back the master key from him and hid it in her blouse again. Tarbi quickly walked towards the restaurant and without waiting for his sister, got out of the hotel.

When Fibi got back to her home at night, she saw Vincent waiting for him anxiously. Tarbi was also there. He smiled when he saw her.

‘You and Tarbi are great, the way you got my passport.’

‘We love you, Vincent sahib.’

‘Thank you. I am really grateful.’

Through Tarbi, he explained to her that he intended to leave for New Delhi next day. Fibi did not like the idea she wanted to see Pearce Noble and company depart, so that there is no risk. Vincent explained the risk of goondas looking for him and the potential risk to her family. Reluctantly she agreed.

'How go to New Delhi?' she asked.

'Train or maybe there is coach service. I think plane may be too dangerous because these culprits would be looking at the airport closely.'

'Yes, the police always look more closely at the airport passengers, and the foreigner will be picked up too quickly.' Tarbi added.

After discussion, it was decided that Vincent would go to New Delhi in the coach service. Railway was also considered but there will be too many people in the railway and at the railway station. The fares were cheaper in the coach, and people looking for economy preferred to travel in it. Besides, they will be able to see the passengers before departing and if there was any risk, can leave the coach; train was too much to vouch for.

'I come with you.' Fibi declared.

'No I should be alright, you just need to buy the ticket and drop me at the coach station.'

'You will need to stay in New Delhi overnight because there might not be service back the same day.' Tarbi was worried about his sister.

Fibi explained to both of them that her presence will ensure that she can communicate with the people around. Tarbi had to look after the mother and stay at home.

The next day, a private plane was chartered by Pearce Noble to fly him and the rest of the party to New Delhi for their flight to London. Arun said it was waste of money to hire a private plane when the domestic airline could do it. But Pearce wanted the flexibility. At the airport, it was not very busy because the commercial flight time was in several hours. Amar Shastri, Arun Basant were there to see them off.

Greta came close to both A's. 'I am really grateful the way you have helped me and Vincent.'

'No ma'am it was our duty. We feel still very sorry for Vincent Muller, what a splendid man. I wish he was going with you.' Arun replied in a warm voice. Amar nodded. Both A's truly believed in what they said. 'Bon Voyage.' They said simultaneously.

'Thank you.'

Pearce, who was standing next to Greta, shook hand warmly with Amar and Arun. 'Thank you, I will be in touch.'

'Yes thank you and good journey.'

Yasin Kanji and Shrute also shook hands with Amar and Arun. And after a few minutes, Pearce Noble and the party went to the boarding gate.

They entered the private plane chartered for them. The air hostess and the captain greeted them. Greta from the door of the plane, looked back at Dherapur 'Goodbye my darling Vincent, rest in peace.' She could not control her tears.

Around the same time, at Dherapur coach station, Vincent Muller was dressed like a Kashmiri Pathan with long shalwar, long dress and a turban. His beard had grown in the last weeks. With a little brown cream used for sun tan, he looked very much like a true Kashmiri. He still had a plaster underneath the shalwar but the leg was no longer painful. Fibi was dressed in a modest sari. She had intentionally kept her make up to minimum. They both looked like a poor couple. Vincent carried a bag with his wallet and passport. Nobody paid any attention to them. The coach was filled with noisy passengers. Just before the departure, Fibi pretended to go out to buy a bottle of water and looked around carefully who were the passengers. She came back quickly with a bottle of water.

Vincent wanted to say something but Fibi asked him not to speak. He had to play dumb, in case, someone tried to speak to him. They could not pretend to speak in Pashtu because people around will catch English words and there might just be someone with the knowledge of Pashtu.

About an hour later, the coach was passing hilly areas, the scenery outside was magnificent. Beautiful hills and the valleys and the greenery all round. Vincent was happy just to watch the scenery outside. Fibi found it difficult to keep quiet. She was not used to stay silent for a long time. When she noticed that in the nearby seats people were dozing off she spoke to Vincent. 'How are you?'

'Okay, beautiful scenery.'

'No bad people in the coach.'

'It seems like that.'

Fibi opened her purse and showed it to him. Vincent was surprised there was a knife inside. He looked at her with a surprise.

'Protection', she smiled.

'Okay, he brought his arm around her to pull her towards him.'

'No please…people', she whispered.

The journey to New Delhi continued slowly but without any events.

In Dherapur, there was a knock at the door of Fibi's home. Tarbi went to see who it was, he saw Bahadur Singh. He recognised him, having seen him a few times at the hotel and at the funeral of the manager.

'Can I help you?'

Before he could say anything further, Bahadur Singh forced the door open and pushed him inside. 'You certainly can.'

Tarbi did not like to be pushed like that, he looked angrily at him. 'What do you want?'

'Where is your relative from Kashmir?' Bahadur Singh demanded in a menacing voice.

'He is not here, he left for Kashmir.' Tarbi replied abruptly.

'Let's get inside.' They walked inside the house to their lounge which was also used as bedroom by the mother. She was resting on the bed.

'Who is this gentleman?' Fibi's mother asked.

'Mom, this is the man looking for our cousin from Kashmir.' Tarbi emphasised the word cousin.

'Oh beta, he has gone back to his home.'

Bahadur was ashamed when she addressed him as 'son'. 'Sorry, can I just see the house?'

'Sure, beta. It is a small house, we are poor people.'

Bahadur looked at Tarbi and asked him to move with him to the other room. When they entered Tarbi's room, Bahadur looked around but did not see anything unusual. 'Why was he going to the hospital?'

'He had fallen down and hurt his leg, so I and Fibi took him to the hospital.'

'I see, and where is your dear sister?' Bahadur asked sarcastically.

'She went with him to Kashmir he was not well so she was escorting him.'

'How did she go?'

'Through the coach, you can check at the coach station.' Tarbi held his nerve.

'Okay, give me the mobile number of your cousin.'

'I don't know.'

Bahadur Singh slapped him hard on his face. 'Don't try to be too smart with me.'

Tarbi looked at him; Bahadur Singh was a lot stronger than him and probably armed. 'Okay, let me check, he took out his mobile and read out his own number to him, and at the same time put his phone on the voice mail.

Bahadur Singh tried the number on his mobile but kept on receiving the voice mail. 'Try your sister', he barked.

Tarbi pressed the number of his friend and claimed that it was also engaged.

'Okay you give me your sister's number I will speak to her later.'

Tarbi picked up a pen, and on a piece of paper he wrote his friend's number. Bahadur Singh was not a fool. He dialled the number from his phone and without speaking to the person, he slapped again hard Tarbi. 'You son of a bitch; trying to be too clever with me.'

'Sorry, maybe I gave you the wrong number.'

Bahadur grabbed the phone from his hand and saw Fibi's name and pressed it.

'Hello Tarbi.' Fibi answered the telephone.

Bahadur Singh heard the sound of the coach; he was convinced that she was in a vehicle. He did not say anything, 'ask her where she is?' Bahadur gave the phone to Tarbi.

Tarbi took the phone, he discreetly disconnected the phone. 'Hello Baji, where are you?'

'Sorry the signal is bad she is in the coach, it is disconnected.'

'Bahadur was convinced that she was travelling. 'Okay', he grabbed Tarbi's phone and put it in his own pocket.

'When is your sister coming back?'

'I think she will be back in two days. You see they are engaged.'

Bahadur looked at him menacingly again. 'I will be back in two days, okay.'

Tarbi did not reply. Bahadur Singh marched out of the house.

In the coach when Fibi received the call but there was no reply she was surprised why he did not speak to her. Her sixth sense told her that something was not quite right. Vincent looked at her. 'Tarbi, no answer.'

In a few minutes, Fibi rang her brother but instead of him another voice replied, 'hello.'

Fibi could not work out whose voice was it? She sensed something wrong. She said a few times hello, hello, like she could not hear the other side, and disconnected the phone.

Vincent looked at her with an enquiring face. 'Some other person, not Tarbi.' She said.

Vincent grabbed the phone from her hand, and threw it out from the window. A passenger looked at Vincent as though he had gone mad. Who, in their right mind, will throw the phone? But he did not say anything. Fibi was also quiet. She knew why Vincent had thrown the phone away.

In a few hours, Fibi and Vincent arrived in New Delhi. They took a taxi to Connaught Place (a central area of New Delhi); there, Vincent went to a British bank and drew some cash, luckily neither his account nor credit card was blocked since Greta never bothered to inform the bank that he had died. They walked to a clothes shop nearby; Vincent bought a new suit and a shirt. He took off his Kashmiri clothes and put it in his bag. He bought Fibi a business suit: a dark trouser and the matching jacket. They walked into the travel agent office nearby. They learnt that there was no flight available that evening but a flight late at 3.30 in the morning. Vincent was tired he decided that it would be better to wait till tomorrow and booked for himself a flight early in the afternoon. Besides, he wanted Fibi to return back to Dherapur.

Few minutes later, they checked into Deluxe hotel. At the reception, Vincent Muller gave his passport and his own credit card (he did not use the company credit card intentionally). Fibi presented her identification card. The receptionist looked at Fibi and thought that they do chose the beautiful women, these foreigners are no fool. There was no problem in the double room.

When they were in the room, Fibi took a sigh of relief. She was always worried that someone was going to catch them or something was going to happen. When Vincent went to take an overdue shower, she rang her home at the landline. Tarbi was relieved that his sister and Vincent were safe. He explained to her that a rough looking man had forced himself at their home and has threatened him. He wanted to know where Fibi was and who the cousin was, and why they were in the hospital. He also took his mobile. Tarbi had been trying to ring Fibi at her mobile without success. He also threatened to come back in two days. Fibi explained that her mobile phone had been thrown away once she heard the voice of some stranger on the phone. She told him that she will be back next day and that in case of any emergencies he should contact Chachaji (Ram Lal) who was always helpful to their family. Fibi knew that she will be able to handle the situation once she got back to Dherapur. Little they knew that Bahadur Singh along with Ghenda had their home phone tapped with the help of the accomplice inspector of police.

About an hour later, when Fibi also had taken a shower, they ordered the dinner in their room. Vincent felt comfortable after a long time; his flight was booked, he had proper clothes and cash. Fibi was also relaxed. The hotel was a quality hotel and they both felt comfortable.

After dinner, they were talking. Fibi wanted to drop Vincent at the airport while Vincent wanted to drop her at the railway station so that she goes home safely. Finally, it was decided that Fibi will see him off at the airport and then take a taxi to the railway station from there. They watched TV for a while and it was the time to go to bed.

'No two beds?' Fibi suddenly noticed that there was only one double bed.

'Sorry, I forgot to ask them the twin beds, but I can sleep on the sofa, you can sleep on the bed.' Vincent said innocently.

'No, you gentleman, I trust.' Fibi looked into his eyes.

Fibi changed from her smart new suit to the sari she was wearing before and Vincent decided to sleep in his underwear. In the bed, after a few minutes, Vincent realised that he had never been so close to her. Fibi was thinking if Vincent was going to be the same as Pearce who had kept going for hours without break. After a few awkward side changes, Vincent looked at her who was looking the other side. He put his hand on her shoulder, Fibi did not object. In a few moments, she turned to his side. Two young persons, one in a thin sari, and the other in underwear; their bodies were heated up quickly. Vincent had not slept since he left his wife in London, and Fibi could only remember the beautiful time she has had with Pearce a few days ago. Vincent brought her mouth to her lips and kissed her. Fibi did not show much passion; maybe it was goodnight kiss she thought. Vincent took his mouth away when he noticed that Fibi did not respond with passion. He put his hand on her cheeks. Fibi closed her eyes. Vincent had no intention to let the opportunity go, he needed to try a little harder. His hands moved from her cheeks to her back and he pulled her towards him. Their bodies touched, Fibi felt the warmth of his body all over hers.

In a few minutes, Fibi felt that Pearce had come back in the shape of Vincent. Her legs were apart and an energetic Vincent was thrusting in her with passion. Fibi felt the heat going inside her, and the thought of Pearce went away, she opened her eyes and kissed him, her hands massaging his back. As the time passed her moaning became louder. It wasn't long before Fibi struck her nails in his back and screamed with delight. She was not a difficult woman to please.

About half an hour later, Fibi got up from the bed, she wanted to go to the bathroom. Vincent first time noticed the complete naked body of Fibi. He was amazed how beautiful she looked, a very shapely body, firm breasts and beautiful shaped hips would turn any man on. He felt his erection. He was wondering why he had never noticed her before. Soon Fibi returned from the bathroom, Vincent was all ready for the second round.

'Not much gentleman.' Fibi teased him while entering in the bed.

'It is impossible to be next to such a beautiful woman and be gentleman.' Vincent immediately put his hands on her body and jumped over her. He kissed her on her lips and then on her breast, and then he moved to her tummy, finally below her tummy. It wasn't long before Fibi was screaming with delight when Vincent entered in her the second time. In a few moments, Fibi realised that Vincent was a better lover than Pearce. She knew she had fallen in love with him. Their lovemaking continued for hours. Fibi did not remember how many times they made love. But she remembered how tasty his body was, she did not want to leave an inch untouched.

After a few hours, when Fibi and Vincent had fallen asleep, Ghenda and Bahadur Singh entered into the hotel and walked towards the hotel reception. The night receptionist and the concierge looked at them carefully from their respective desks. The hotel was a luxurious hotel and the type of the two men did not correspond with their clientele.

'Good evening, sir', the receptionist forced a smile.

'We are looking for our friend Mr Vincent Muller; we believe he is staying in this hotel.' Bahadur Singh replied.

'Sorry we cannot disclose that information, we cannot disclose our guests.' The receptionist looked at the concierge who was already on guard, not liking the two men.

The concierge pressed a button underneath his desk, and immediately a well-built security guard walked in there. Bahadur Singh was still arguing with the receptionist. 'Can I help you, sir?' The security guard asked, looking at them in their eyes.

'Yes, we have our friend Mr Muller staying here. We are from Dherapur. He left something there and we want to give it to him.' Bahadur Singh replied while Ghenda looked at them angrily feeling his knife in his pocket.

'You can give that thing to us we will pass it to him tomorrow morning. It is very late, and we cannot disturb our guests.' The security guard stared at Ghenda while replying to Bahadur Singh.

'No, we cannot give it to you. We wish to see him ourselves, call your manager.'

'The manager is not here at present, the night manager is busy, but I have told you the position.' The security guard said it firmly, increasing the volume of his voice.

'Okay, tell us his room number, and you don't need to do anything.' Ghenda demanded.

'Have you tried his mobile?'

'No we haven't got his mobile number.'

The security guard was in no mood of arguing. 'Please come back in the morning.'

Ghenda suddenly brought out the knife from his pocket. It was late at night, and there was no one around in the reception area. Seeing the knife in the hand of Ghenda, the concierge immediately rang the police discreetly. He walked towards the reception.

The security guard was not frightened at all; he was an ex-army officer, warned Ghenda in an intimidating tone. 'Please put your knife back, you can be in serious trouble.'

Bahadur came to Ghenda and held his hand and asked him to put the knife back in his pocket. He whispered something in his ears. They spoke for a few moments themselves while the security guard looked at the concierge. At the same time, he changed his position ready to attack them.

'Okay, we will be back in the morning.' Ghenda put the knife back in his pocket, and they walked towards the coffee shop which was opened twenty four hours, to decide their next move.

The security guard admired their self-confidence; they did not try to run away.

A few minutes later, two armed police officers arrived. New Delhi Police was extra careful around that area, as a number of important foreigners stayed in the hotels therein, and the diplomatic enclave was adjoining. The security guard spoke to the officers briefly, and took them to the coffee shop. Before they could finish their coffee, Bahadur Singh and Ghenda were arrested and taken to the local police station. Vincent Muller and Fibi were fast asleep in their room after their 'hard work'. They had no idea what was going on in the hotel.

Next morning, Fibi got up before Vincent; she looked admiringly at Vincent and felt that she was definitely in love with this handsome man. With that thought she carefully, without making noise, went to the bathroom.

About an hour later, Vincent and Fibi were taking the breakfast in their room. Fibi had not stayed in such a luxurious hotel before; she was impressed with the breakfast.

'It is really like a meal.' Fibi said while eating scrambled eggs with mushroom, grilled tomato.'

'Yes it is nice, taste this French cheese.'

Fibi got up from her chair and came close to Vincent, 'I want taste you.' Fibi was wearing the dressing gown of the hotel; she put her hands around him.

Vincent took her hand and kissed them. She bent down, her breast touching his head. Vincent got up and put his hands inside her dressing gown, moving them on her body. They started kissing, the time passed and they realised that it was nearly time to go to the airport. Vincent took his mouth and hands off, and sat down.

'Let's finish the breakfast.'

'I had mine.' Fibi smiled and went to the bathroom.

Vincent was thinking what a wonderful woman. As soon as you touch her you want to make love to her. He finished his breakfast and started to get ready for the airport. A few minutes later, Fibi arrived dressed in the new suit which Vincent had bought her. She looked quite ravishing in that outfit, an executive right inside the boardroom.

'You look …'

'Yes, I look at you my dear, you look absolutely stunning.' Vincent smiled. 'You need to be careful if I don't take you with me.'

'Ready.' Fibi raised her arms with an innocent smile.

Vincent came close and gave her a kiss on her cheek. 'Thank you my dear.'

About an hour later, Fibi and Vincent Muller were at Indira Gandhi International Airport, New Delhi. Vincent was in the queue of Lufthansa desk. He was flying to Frankfurt instead of London. Fibi was standing with him. No one noticed them; they were like many other passengers, all busy in their own things. In a few minutes, the check-in was completed; it was a lot quicker for the business class travellers. They walked towards the passport control. Fibi looked sad, at the same time; she was worried; she looked around nervously.

‘What’s the matter Fibi, you look worried.’

‘Checking, no bad men.’

‘No don’t worry, this is a very secure area, no one can hurt you or me here.’

‘You remember me…. Europe?’ Fibi’s eyes were almost wet.

‘Of course, my darling.’ Vincent hugged her and then kissed her on her lips. ‘How can I ever forget you, you saved my life. In such a short time, you have given me so much love and affection.’

Their hug was long, first time, someone noticed them. While they were hugging, not very far from there, Pearce Noble, Greta Muller, Yasin Kanji and Shrute Sting were checking in for a flight to London. While they were in the queue, Greta looked around, but she could not see far enough in the crowd, where her husband and his new friend were hugging themselves. Vincent did not want to look anywhere other than in Fibi’s eyes. First time, he realised that he had developed strong feelings for her, he felt like taking Fibi with her.

‘I really feel like taking you with me.’

‘Truth?’ Fibi asked, not sure if he meant it.

‘Of course, I swear at my life.’

‘Believe you.’

Vincent took out from his wallet the Indian rupees he had withdrawn the day before. He gave her the small bundle.

’Keep, you need.’ Fibi refused to take.

‘No silly, I don’t need Indian rupees anymore.’ Vincent insisted. ‘Take taxi to the railway station and buy the train ticket to Dherapur. Not in a coach or plane.’

'Not worry, I have…' She showed him her bag where she still had the knife. Reluctantly, Fibi took the small bundle of the notes from Vincent, 'Thanks, Vincent sahib.'

'For you I am just Vincent, no sahib.'

There was an announcement for the passengers to go to the gate for Frankfurt flight. Vincent took out his passport from the pocket and they moved towards the gate of the passport control.

'Goodbye, Fibi, Thank you.'

Fibi did not reply she came again to him and hugged him close, she could no longer hold her tears and started crying.

'Sorry Fibi got to go.'

'God protect ……' before she could finish, Vincent walked towards the gate.

Fibi waited there until Vincent finished in the passport control, moving towards the security scan, waving his hand towards her. Fibi waved back.

Fibi waited there until she was sure that Vincent had cleared the security and gone inside the departure lounge. When she turned back to go out of the airport she saw, from distance, Pearce Noble and the party coming towards the passport control. She immediately turned her face the other side, and started walking towards another direction. From the distance, Greta Muller saw Fibi but did not recognise her. A hotel waitress and a smart looking business woman had no connection, besides, she hardly knew her. Pearce Noble was still probably counting millions in his pocket. Fibi went out and took a taxi to the railway station, Greta Muller flew to London with Pearce Noble and her 'dead husband' flew to Frankfurt. They could have met at the airport, but didn't.

Chapter 15

The same night, Lufthansa flight arrived at Frankfurt international airport. Vincent Muller was the first few passengers who came out of the arrival gate. He did not have any baggage. He still had a slight limp on his leg. He looked around, and of course, there was no one to receive him. He immediately took a taxi and went to his uncle's house who lived in Frankfurt. The taxi arrived at one of the detached houses in Schweizer Platz, a quality area of Frankfurt. Vincent Muller got out of the taxi and asked him to wait there. He did not have any Euros to pay him. He rang the bell of the house, and his aunt Mrs Johanna Muller came to the door. Her eyes opened widely when she saw Vincent. They greeted in German and kissed each other on the cheeks. Vincent did not speak German fluently so they spoke in English.

'I need some cash to pay the taxi, auntie.'

Johannah rushed into the house and came back with her purse. She took out a few notes of Euro and gave to Vincent who paid the taxi man with a tip. The taxi man departed quickly thanking him for the generous tip.

They sat down in the lounge. 'Where is uncle?'

'He was taking a shower, should not be long…can I get you something?'

'Yes please, some juice will be fine.'

Johannah went to the kitchen. Vincent looked around in the lounge. How many times he had been there. All old memories came into his mind. He used to come to Frankfurt after his father's death frequently, at young age, with his mother, then occasionally alone. He was very close to his uncle. While Vincent was thinking of his childhood memories, his uncle Hans Muller walked in. Vincent immediately got up and hugged his uncle. He could not hold his tears, and the uncle noticed him crying.

'What's the matter son, we were told that you had died in an accident in India?'

'Let's sit down and I will tell you all about it.'

Hans who loved him like his own son, being the only thing to remind him of his beloved elder brother. He hugged him again and wiped his tears. 'Don't worry my son you are in a safe place.'

They sat down. In the meantime, Johannah came back with a tray with three glasses of orange juice.

'Thank you auntie' Vincent took the glass and took a few big sips.

'Take your time, relax.' Hans Muller told his nephew.

'No Uncle, I have to get it out of my system.' Vincent started telling them that he was in India for a project, the accident, the man with the knife, Greta's arrival, his phoney funeral and the help of an Indian family who literally saved his life.

'I wish I would have been there, you will not have to go through all these. Greta was in a rush to do the funeral and I was in Africa at that time.' Hans Muller looked sympathetically at his nephew. 'Why did you not face Greta in India?' the expressions on his face changed.

'I am not sure if she is not part of the conspiracy,' suddenly Vincent remembered the Keyman insurance policy' you see uncle my employers want to cash in on the Keyman insurance policy and that's what I have understood.'

'How Greta is going to benefit from it?'

'I think there is a general policy for all the employees as well which will be given to their next of kin, in case of death in duty, especially more if it was an accident.'

'I see.' Hans went into some thoughts.

'I told you Greta was no good for you.' Johannah, who did not really get along with Greta, let her view known.

'So everyone in London thinks that you are dead.' Hans looked at his nephew.

'Yes, apparently they got all kinds of certificates, accident report from the police, photographs of the funeral etc etc. even I understood an officer of the British High Commission attended the funeral.

'I can't believe that Greta would not recognise your body.'

'They claimed that the body had been in the river and that fish had bitten the face.'

'It seems to me that it is a well premeditated plan, not so many people including the police can be so easily fooled.'

Vincent took another big sip of the orange juice, feeling a lot better after explaining his story to his dear ones.

They continued to talk for another half an hour or so.

'Don't worry my son; everything is going to be okay. I will settle all the scores.' Hans Muller assured his nephew with a resolute voice. Johannah announced that they had already eaten but she had put some thing for him in the oven and it would be ready in a few minutes. Vincent went to the spare room where he had stayed many times before, he found a clean pyjama and a gown on the bed; he went into the ensuite bathroom to take a shower.

After dinner, Vincent Muller slept well in his uncle's house without any fear, first time in weeks.

In London, next day, there was a lot of activity in the offices of Chezan Investments Ltd. Jimmy Noble, Pearce Noble and Marc Kohnvich were in the locked board room. They were discussing the Keyman insurance and the general insurance. There were a number of papers and photographs on the table along with the coffee cups. Marc Kohnvich explained to them that he had already advised the insurance company when he learnt from Jimmy Noble that Vincent Muller had died in an accident.

‘So what do you think, Marc?’ Jimmy asked impatiently.

‘I think the paperwork seems adequate, I am going to do some form filling and advise the underwriters so that it can be processed.’ Marc seemed pretty confident.

‘This death certificate, is it okay? Pearce said.

‘Yeah, it seems fine but you could have got it certified by the British High Commission in India.’ Marc pointed out.

‘We had a guy from the High commission in the funeral, this is him.’ Pearce pointed his finger to a figure in one of the photographs.

‘Look, I think everything is fine.’ Marc smiled. The thought of ten percent commission was making him, minute by minute, happier.

‘The fact that this was an accident is not going to cause any issues?’ Jimmy set aside Marc’s optimism.

‘We are the main beneficiaries, I mean Chezan Investments’, Pearce said.

‘Yeah, I know, I might have to take a few people out for the dinner; you see it is not just the form filling I will have to answer many questions on your behalf and advise you what to say.’ Marc justified his ten percent commission.

Jimmy and Pearce looked at each other, they knew for ten percent, Marc is never going to jeopardise the claim.

'What about the 'Employees Policy'?' Pearce asked.

'That should be pretty straight forward; you told me that his widow is Greta Muller.'

'Yeah, it is not a major sum; they should not be asking too many questions.'

'Yes, indeed.'

'Okay, let's get on with it.' Jimmy wanted to conclude the meeting.

'I haven't touched my coffee in the excitement.' Marc complained.

'We are going to have a lot of bubblies soon!' Jimmy assured him.

'I drink to that.' Marc made a gesture of raising the glass with his hand and got up.

A few meters away, Yasin Kanji was holding another meeting with the accounting staff in Vincent Muller's office. Masood Panji and the other staff were listening to their new boss. Although, no final decision was made, Yasin knew that his bosses were going to honour their promise and would make him the CFO. Yasin Kanji explained to them the tragic death of Vincent Muller, and how he managed to get the project going after his death. Masood updated Yasin about the department activities and the forthcoming audit. About an hour later, the meeting was finished, only Yasin and Masood were in the room.

'So what about my promotion, you promised to make me the financial controller?' Masood felt jealous of Yasin.

'It is not in my hands, I can only propose to them (Jimmy and Pearce).'

'What do you mean? You should make a strong recommendation.' Masood made a face.

'I understand that you have not been quite cooperative, upsetting Jimmy about the petty cash withdrawals.'

'This guy Shrute has been withdrawing large amounts in cash, he had already taken large sum for travel before he left. It was my duty to bring it to the attention of the bosses.'

'But you should have not argued with them, you see they are under a lot of pressure at the moment: the new project and the untimely death of Vincent.' Yasin took a sip from his coffee.' Besides, Shrute is going to give his expense claim form, right?'

'I wonder what was he spending such a large sum for in India. Did you see anything?'

Yasin gave it some thought. He remembered that Shrute had arrived only a few days before. He also started wondering about the large cash withdrawals. 'No, I am not aware of any major expenditure but wait till he gives his expense claim form. Jimmy or Pearce would need to approve it, anyway. Maybe, he bought something for the brothers, once Jimmy had mentioned that they were planning to buy some emeralds from Jaipur.'

'Sorry, I suppose they do not have to confide something like that to a junior man.' Masood showed his sarcasm.

'Now don't be stupid. Before the promotion you are working towards a demotion.' Yasin warned him.

Their meeting lasted for another few minutes.

Later that evening, a few hundred miles away, in Frankfurt, Vincent Muller was having coffee with this uncle and aunt after dinner. They were sitting in the lounge. Johannah, who had seen her young son die at an early age, treated him like her own son. She did not want to see another 'son' dead. He was the person who was going to carry Muller's name. She listened very carefully to the conversation between her husband and her nephew.

'You tell me everything about these two brothers, who are their friends and their enemies.' Hans Muller asked his nephew.

'I have told you about their business. The project in Caribbean is going well and soon should be productive, Indian project you already know, they have got large sums borrowed from the bank.' Vincent took a sip of the coffee.

They continued talking for an hour, in which Hans Muller learnt a lot about the Nobles, their business which was discontinued in Egypt, the Caribbean and now the new venture in India.

'Greta has not rung.' Johannah pointed out.

'Shall I ring her?' Vincent was not sure what he should do.

'No, absolutely not, we want to make sure if she is part of this plan or innocent.'

'My friend Fibi told me that she was sleeping with Pearce in India.' Vincent said in a low voice showing his sadness.

'Women can't keep their legs close.' Hans forgotten that Johannah was sitting there. 'You should not consider that her culpability.'

'I did not hear it.' Johannah smiled, she knew her husband was very angry.

'Sorry darling, you are special.' Hans quickly made amends with his wife.

In a few minutes, it was decided that Johannah Muller will ring Greta Muller to ascertain a little more. She picked up her mobile and rang Greta in London.

'Hello Auntie Johannah.' Greta replied. 'I was going to ring you tonight.'

'Don't worry darling, how are you?' Johannah played ignorant.

'I am so lonely, since the return from India I keep on thinking only about Vincent. I have not even gone out of the house.' Greta said in a sad voice.

'You should come to Frankfurt for a few days and tell us all about it.'

'Yeah, I wish you and Uncle could have come to India. I really felt lonely there.'

'You know Hans was in Africa that time and you were in such a rush to do the funeral.'

'In India, they do not keep the bodies long, it is their custom, besides, there was no point. Everyone advised that it is not worth delaying or bringing the body to London.'

'Yes I understand.' Johannah stopped. 'Is there someone with you?'

'No auntie, it is the TV, shall I put it off?'

'No darling, you take care, and let me know about your plans. Hans is also missing you.'

'Sure….Bye Auntie.'

'Bye dear.' Johannah disconnected the phone.

In the house of Vincent Muller Greta looked at Pearce angrily. 'Why were you making such a noise, my auntie heard you.'

'You are not a little girl, you have your life.' Pearce ignored her anger.

'I did not want her to know that immediately after my husband's death I am inviting friends for dinner.'

'I am not here for dinner, darling…. You know what I am here for?' Pearce said in a naughty tone.

'Yeah, I know what you are after, but we have to have dinner first.'

Pearce came close to her and held her tight in his arm and kissed her. Apart from their own Keyman insurance money, Greta was also going to be liquid with the money she was going to receive from employees' insurance, it increased her charm. 'Whatever you say.'

The next two days passed. Vincent showed his leg to the doctors in Frankfurt and after x-ray they gave him some medicine and a gel. In London, Greta Muller received the funds from the insurance company from the employee policy. Marc Kohnvich submitted the claim form and related certificates, photos etc to the insurance company for the Keyman insurance policy. The insurance company told him it is going to take a little time to process the claim and their own verification of the information supplied.

In the evening, Greta Muller was by herself at home. She decided to check her bank account online. She had received a substantial sum under the employee insurance. She had in the past, left all the banking and financial affairs in the hands of Vincent. She only took care of her debit and credit cards. But now it was her duty to manage the financial affairs. She knew that she should transfer the funds received in the account to the deposit account. When she logged in she felt happy, a large sum was sitting in the current account. She transferred most of it to the deposit account. She also decided to look at the credit card. She had a shock when she saw some airline ticket purchased in India and also withdrawals of big amounts in cash. She checked the date. It was days after Vincent's death… who was it? She decided to ring the bank next day during the business hours. However, she could not wait and rang Pearce Noble. She explained to him.

'Don't worry darling this must be some imposter, you tell the bank and they will have to refund the money. Besides, you should cancel his credit card.'

'I feel strange, how could anyone so easily use his credit card?' Greta showed her nervousness.

'You know we never found his wallet. It seems to me that someone has got his wallet and using the credit card.'

Greta felt a little comfortable after speaking to Pearce. She rang the credit card company and requested them to cancel Vincent's credit card. They immediately put a stop to it and confirmed that they will investigate the ticket purchase and the money withdrawals in India.

A few more days passed. Jimmy Noble and Pearce Noble were getting impatient about the Keyman insurance funds which were not yet received. They had been following it up with Marc Kohnvich, who told them to be patient since it was going to take its course.

One usual morning in the offices of Chezan Investments Ltd, four officers from Fraud squad arrived and it changed the very fabric of Chezan Investments Ltd for ever. The officers questioned about the death of Vincent Muller. Both brothers took the officers to the board room and explained the whole saga of Dherapur. They produced the copies of the death certificate, photographs of the funeral, Indian police report etc. The officers told them that Vincent Muller was alive and well. Jimmy asked Yasin Kanji to join them who confirmed that Vincent Muller had died in Dherapur. Police officers would not disclose when and where they met Vincent Muller. They also had the Keyman insurance claim copy with them. Both brothers were arrested and taken to the local police station, accused of conspiracy to murder Vincent Muller and cash in the Keyman insurance policy. However, both of them were released quickly on substantial bail since they used some of the best lawyers in London.

In the office, it was quite a scandal, all the staff, the whole day long, were wondering what had happened. Only Yasin Kanji knew what had happened. He decided to keep his mouth shut.

After releasing from the bail, Jimmy Noble came to the office, he wanted to shoot Shrute Sting who had assured him that everything was executed according to the plan and that Vincent Muller had been killed. He never mentioned that there was any doubt. When Jimmy was told that Shrute had not shown up in the office since the day the police arrived, Jimmy got suspicious. He rang on his mobile but the mobile company stated that the phone was not in service. Jackie rang his home but no answer. Shrute

Sting had disappeared without a trace. One of the staff visited his flat and found it to be locked. No one could give any information about his whereabouts.

A few more days passed, Greta Muller was questioned by the police. They asked her to stay in London until they finished their investigation. She had to return the insurance money she had received from the insurance company. Greta Muller tried to find her husband; she rang Frankfurt but learnt from Auntie Johannah Muller that Uncle Hans was away on travel to Africa again, and that she was not contacted by Vincent. Johannah showed her surprise that Vincent was alive. She was as good an actress as Greta.

One night, Jimmy Noble was in a restaurant with one of the detectives he had hired to find out what exactly was going on about Vincent: where was he, what had happened to Shrute? How could the Indian police, the church, the funeral etc. had gone so horribly wrong? While they were sitting in the restaurant discussing discreetly, two men had been observing them very carefully. When Jimmy Noble finished with the detective, he stayed at the table and rang someone.

After a few minutes, Jimmy left the restaurant and came to his car which was parked in the street nearby. It was late at night and there was hardly anyone around. As soon as he sat in his car, before he could turn the ignition key on, a knife went into his neck from the back. He screamed but in the closed car no one could hear. A gloved strong hand came on his mouth and he could not breathe or scream any more while the blood went all over the car. Jimmy was a strong man six feet tall, he struggled but the gloved hand and the pressure on the knife in his neck, made him helpless.

About two minutes later, a man, wearing a dark leather jacket, dark trousers, dark gloves and a dark hat which nearly hid his face, got out of the car. He closed the door and looked around. No one was close by. A car came with a speed and stopped near him; he entered in the car without making any noise. And the car picked up the speed immediately. Once inside the car, the man in the dark clothes changed his gloves and picked up his mobile and rang overseas in Africa. He told the receiver of the call that his holiday was finished and asked him to inform his family. He did not wait to hear other person's response and disconnected the phone. The man changed his jacket inside the car which had some blood stains on it. The dark car disappeared in the dark night with the increased speed.

After a few minutes, Jimmy regained his consciousness; a lot of blood was all over him. He tried to open the door but found he had no strength. With a lot of efforts, he opened the door of the car but could not manage to walk out, his body shifted towards the open door, and a nearby passing car noticed him. In a few minutes, the ambulance and the police cars rushed to the scene, and he was brought to the A&E unit of the hospital.

Jimmy Noble died early in the morning in spite of the best efforts of the doctors. Noble family went into mourning. Albert Noble, Alisha Noble, Firoza Noble and Pearce Noble were absolutely in grief. Pearce was obliged to tell his parents what has been happening. He told them about Vincent Muller, his death which was not real, and his reappearance, disappearance of Shrute Sting. Albert Noble was angry with his son. He felt that maybe they were responsible for the accident of Vincent. But then Vincent was not a kind of a person who would resort to the violence like that. The way Jimmy was attacked and killed could only have been a professional hitman. Could it have anything to do with Egyptian business where the local manager was arrested by the police, maybe he wanted to settle the score since Nobles did not really help him. Or was it Shrute, he was a rough type but he was always very loyal to them. Alisha thought that someone was after his sons and advised Pearce to leave the country and disappear for a while until the situation calmed down.

Police investigation was continuing. Marc Kohnvich was also interviewed but there was no proof that he was part of the conspiracy, indeed after Jimmy's death and Shrute's disappearance there was no proof that there was any conspiracy at all. The lawyers assured Pearce that there was no case. In fact, Pearce had not been involved in any of the scheme of Vincent's 'death'. The Scotland Yard investigation officer contacted New Delhi police for assistance.

Colonel Vinod Khanna, a senior experienced police detective, was handling the case of Vincent Muller. He was advised by the Police commissioner that there was some pressure from the foreign office to resolve this case where they suspected that some local gangsters had been working with the foreigners. For Colonel Vinod it was a piece of cake. He had solved a lot more difficult cases in the past. He immediately interviewed Ghenda and Bahadur Singh. Their account was inconsistent. They could not explain why they were looking for Vincent Muller when he was certified dead by Dherapur police.

In a few days, Colonel Vinod sorted the whole thing out and reported to the Scotland Yard officer in charge of the case. He had dug the phoney grave of Vincent Muller and did a DNA test. He also found some masks which were placed on the face to make it look like Vincent Muller. The fish marks proved to be a metal instrument used to make it look like fish bites. From the hotel CCTV he managed to get the pictures of Shrute Sting. Finally, Ghenda and Bahadur Singh (after some physical force was used) conceded and admitted that they had been working on the instructions of Shrute Sting who was an employee of Chezan Investments Ltd. Colonel Vinod also sorted out the disappearance of another local man who had been reported missing and was never found.

The justice was swift. Ghenda and Bahadur Singh remained in the jail in New Delhi pending the full prosecution for the murder of hotel manager, Manoher Basi, attempted murder of Vincent Muller and the murder of a local man. The local accomplice inspector was sacked and he was happy that he was not arrested. The coroner was given a stern warning to be more careful in future. Fibi never heard from Bahadur Singh even though, she continued to be very worried and careful. Tarbi always stayed home in the evenings until they heard that Ghenda and Bahadur Singh were jailed.

The police had now quite a strong case that Nobles were involved in the conspiracy to murder Vincent Muller, as the statement of Ghenda clearly identified Shrute Sting who was an employee of Chezan Investments Ltd. Nobles were the main beneficiaries of that death. Possibly, to a certain degree Greta Muller, since she was also the beneficiary of the insurance money. The police was also searching for Shrute Sting but there was no trace of him. There was very little on the record in Chezan Investments Ltd about his background or previous employments.

The lawyers continued arguing. For Jimmy's death the investigating officer visited Frankfurt to see if Mullers were responsible for his death but he could not find any evidence. They had not travelled to the UK and his enquiries showed that all their movements were accounted for. The local police was very helpful and vouched for Hans Muller who was an important person and known to them.

The days passed. One morning, Sam Hollworth was summoned into the new CEO of the New Country Bank's office and was told that he no longer had a job and asked him to resign with immediate effect. He was told that the bank had been reviewing their corporate loan portfolio, and he was found to be negligent in a few cases, particularly, in case of Chezan Investments Ltd. He rendered his resignation and moved with his wife to Scotland immediately. He had also not forgotten Jimmy Noble's brutal murder.

The New Country Bank, learning after the scandal of the Chezan Investments Ltd, and from the pressure of its own board of directors, called in the loan due from Chezan Investments Ltd. Of course, they could not repay the loan and an official receiver was appointed to sell the business as a going concern. Pearce Noble, one after another, kept on receiving the shocks. They had a lot of funds hidden in Switzerland but his brain told him to keep that in reserve and let the company go. Of course, Jimmy Noble was not there to advise him. They tended to make the decision jointly. Albert Noble did not want the company to go but could not afford to repay the loan by himself; he was not a party to the 'reserve funds' in Switzerland.

In Frankfurt, Vincent Muller was keeping pace with what was happening in London through his Uncle's contact. His leg had healed and his fitness was also back. He had not made any effort to contact Greta Muller. His uncle and aunt wanted him to wait and see what happens. In London, Greta was getting more and more upset with Vincent that he had not tried to contact her even though, the police had confirmed that he was alive. She did not know where he was? According to auntie Johannah and Uncle Hans, no one knew his whereabouts. Finally, she was convinced that Vincent was in Frankfurt and that his uncle and auntie were not telling her the truth. Greta was depressed.

One evening, Pearce Noble came to see her. They had some light meal. Pearce did not look like the cocky joyful person he was. Greta was also not in a good form either.

'You don't reply to my phones?' Greta complained.

'No darling, I am frightened and worried. You know they did not want to kill Jimmy they wanted to torture him as well; it must have been a very painful death for my brother.' Pearce tried to hold his tears.

'But who is doing that? Do you think it is Vincent?' Greta was horrified.

'No I don't think so, he is a professional person but you don't know these days.'

Greta Muller looked at him sympathetically. She came close and kissed him but the passion was missing.

In a few moments, Pearce made up his mind to tell her the main reason for his visit. He took a big sip from the glass of wine. 'Listen carefully Greta. I am going to ask you something.'

Greta looked at his serious face. 'Go on, I am all ears.'

'They have a strong case against me. The police are definitely going to prosecute me. The insurance company had also suspended the Keyman insurance policy all together. They might be suing me as well for fraud. I am absolutely fucked … sorry for the bad language.'

'Would you like some water?'

'No thanks, 'Pearce took another big sip from his glass. 'I am thinking of leaving the country for a while, until things cool down.'

Greta looked at him. 'But you are on bail, no?'

'Yes I am…, I am thinking to jump the bail and fly to Venezuela where there is no extradition treaty. I am surely going to be prosecuted here. The business is being sold; the official receiver has already received interest from a number of parties.'

Greta was shocked, in such a short time the life had changed so much. She felt sorry for Pearce. 'Can't you just fight it off? Maybe you can put the blame on Jimmy he is no longer there to defend himself.'

'No Greta. It will not work. It would be impossible to prove that I did not know or was not involved. Shrute has disappeared; God knows if he is still alive.' Pearce paused for a few moments. 'You know what I am not sure if I am not going to be the next one to follow Jimmy; that is my biggest concern.'

Greta Muller was quiet. 'I have got some funds in Switzerland and I think I can live comfortably with it. After some time, I plan to move to the USA.' Pearce took another big sip and emptied the glass. 'You know I want you to come with me.' Finally, Pearce told her the main reason for his visit.

Greta was not shocked but surprised. 'Do you know what you are asking me?'

'Yes, I do…. Look Vincent is avoiding you, he has not contacted you; surely he thinks you are also part of this so called conspiracy, otherwise, why is he staying away from you?' Pearce got up and came close to her and put his hand on her shoulder affectionately. 'You know I have fallen for you…you will probably think that I am in deep shit and looking for someone to give me the support which is partially true.'

Greta looked at him trying to work out whether he was genuine in his feelings but she could not read his face. 'The thought of leaving Vincent is too much for me. I may mess around a little but I am still very much in love with him.'

'Don't you see, Greta darling, it is me that is in love with you. Vincent, no longer, cares for you.'

They continued discussing it for a while until Pearce hands slipped from her shoulder to her breasts, and about an hour later in the bedroom, Greta finally realised that he was an adequate alternative for Vincent.

Later that night, Greta Muller sat down on the desk in the study. She wrote a letter to Vincent Muller.

"My darling Vincent,

It has been a long time since I saw you. You probably do not realise what I went through when I heard about your accident and resulting death. I know you probably think that perhaps I was involved in the conspiracy which I am sure was conceived by Jimmy Noble. I swear to you on my life that I had nothing to do with it.

Yes, I have been unfaithful to you, and wanted to apologise to you and promise not to do it ever again. But you never gave me the chance. I know you are alive and well (thank God) but I fail to see the reasons why you do not wish to contact me. Has your love completely died down? At least, your current attitude proves it. Uncle Hans and Auntie Johannah have not been honest with me I am sure you are living with them in Frankfurt. So that proves your family does not care about me either.

I am not going to bore you with all the details. When you come back to London, you will find your house and everything in it. I have returned the insurance money and your bank accounts etc are all in order. You know I am reasonably well off so I can look after myself. I am not asking anything from you. I hereby agree to the divorce so that you do not feel bound to me. I enclose the keys of the house.

I know I will never be able to forget you or stop loving you. But it is impossible for me to live with a man who no longer loves me or cares for me.

Adieu.

Greta"

Greta read the letter and signed it. Before putting it in the envelope she read the letter again. She opened the drawer and put the house keys set belonging to Vincent in it.

Chapter 16

A few months passed. Pearce Noble had fled the country to Venezuela with Greta Muller. The business and assets of Chezan Investments Ltd were sold as a going concern by the official receiver, and later, that company was put into liquidation. Hans Muller and Johannah Muller, along with their nephew Vincent Muller, bought the business from the official receiver with the help of an equity stake by a venture capital company. The name of Chezan Investments Ltd had lost bulk of its goodwill due to the tabloid making a meal out of Jimmy Noble's death and the appointment of the official receiver. Hans Muller who was a shrewd businessman, and of course, Vincent Muller who had a great financial brain bought the business at a substantial discount. For Hans Muller it was putting all eggs into one basket, but then that basket was to carry his family name.

The new trimmed down business was given a new name, Hans Muller Investments Ltd. Most of the staff continued as though nothing had happened, the business was the same, the premises were the same and the staffs were also the same. Only Yasin Kanji did not want to join the new company. The 'New Heaven' project came as part of the deal, and Vincent immediately had contacted 2A's to confirm that Dherapur proposed project will be continuing and that Hans Muller Investments Ltd will replace Chezan Investments Ltd. The 2A's had no objection to it. All the terms were the same only the names had changed. Hans Muller was the chairman of the company and Vincent Muller became the CEO of the company. Johannah Muller was a director of the company and

Dean Rowe was promoted to be the director of the company in charge of the hedge fund business.

By jumping the bail, Pearce Noble had more or less conceded his guilt and the case continued in the court. The police had issued an arrest warrant for him but he was nowhere to be found. The police learnt that he was in Venezuela after some time but they could not extradite him from there. They were considering their next move to bring him to the justice. So far Jimmy Noble's murderer was at large and no progress was made in that direction. The police had already cleared Mullers but Egyptian link was still needed to be pursued but there was hardly any ground or support from overseas.

There was a party in one of the exclusive hotels in Park Lane of London, an area well known for the quality hotels and events. The occasion was to celebrate the start of the construction project in Dherapur, India and the completion of the first phase of New Heaven project in Caribbean. The guest list was long: Amar Shastri and Arun Basant were there with their respective wives, Bradley Connors and Baxter Connors, Josh Kunta and Thema Kunta, most of the senior staff of Hans Muller Investments Ltd, Dean Rowe and newly promoted financial controller Masood Panji; the account manager from the venture capital company, a few hedge fund clients with or without their partners, and surprisingly Firoza Noble and Shan Reza.

Hans Muller and Johannah Muller were standing with Vincent Muller and Fibi.

Vincent Muller, soon after settling back in London, had contacted Fibi and brought her to London to be an executive of the company and coordinate the Dherapur Project. She was to spend half of her time in London and half in Dherapur. Eventually, she will take the place of Greta Muller, something which was not a common knowledge but speculated.

With the noise of the champagne corks, all kind of food and canapes, and the hustle bustle of the place, the atmosphere was jolly. It was a long time since the staff of Ex-Chezan Investments Ltd had a real party and celebrate something. Most of them were fed up with the police, reporters, and cameramen in the past few months. In one corner, Firoza and Shan Reza were talking. 'Doesn't she look beautiful?' Shan remarked looking at Fibi who was in an expensive evening gown.

'Yeah, it is a Pygmalion, didn't you tell me that she has been having English lessons in the company's time.' Firoza made a face.

'To me it seems that she has passed all the tests. Look at the way she is speaking to Baxter; what a confidence and what a style.'

'And who is that young man who is floating around as though he owns the place.' Firoza discreetly pointed to one young man.

'I think he is Tarbi, probably related to Amar or Arun, he came with them.'

'I see.' Firoza looked at Vincent Muller and Fibi walking towards them.

'Hello Firoza, delighted to see you here.' Vincent meant it since he never expected that anyone from the Nobles family will join in the celebration.

'Hello, a marvellous party.' Firoza did not show her emotions. How she wished that instead of Vincent there was Jimmy or Pearce heading the function.

Vincent wanted to show that his heart was clean, he genuinely felt that Firoza had nothing to do with his past problems and that the brother's guilt should not affect the sister. That's why he had also kept Reza in the business. 'Let me introduce you to my friend, Fibi, she is from Dherapur.'

'Good evening', Fibi said it in polished English shaking hands with Firoza and Shan Reza.

'You are really beautiful, did you meet my brother Pearce, he was also in Dherapur?'

Fibi's face changed; suddenly she remembered the long night she has had spent with Pearce. 'Yes I did, I was working in the hotel, very nice man, your brother.'

'Yes, he praised you as well…you used to work there, no?' Firoza's expressions and tone were difficult to read.

Fibi did not like the way she referred to her work in India. 'Yes, I was a waitress there.' Fibi said it smilingly as though she was the owner of the hotel. Her smile was very strange, it showed the confidence and it was intimidating to the other person.

Firoza admired her frankness and confidence. She realised that Fibi was quite a match and it would be foolish to provoke her any further. This was not the time or the place. 'My mother is from India, in fact, in her young photos, she looks a bit more like you.' She immediately changed the subject.

'I am from a respectable family from Kashmir.' Fibi also decided to let it go and changed her expressions and tone.

'You must come to our place sometime. I am sure she would love to meet you.'

'I would love to.' Fibi smiled again.

Vincent was pleased that the conversation had cooled down. He had noticed that the two lionesses were ready to pounce at each other. In a few minutes, Vincent excused himself and took Fibi from there to meet other guests.

The party continued. In a short while, there was an orchestra and the guests started dancing.

Your beautiful lips on mine, your warm hands on my shoulder,
Your breast touching my chest, your thighs getting closer and closer,
Your eyes looking deep inside me; your perfume all around me,
I can't hold myself, I shake, I slip; my heart beating faster and faster,
I am falling darling, please hold me tight.

The Keyman

Jimmy Noble and Pearce Noble, brothers run a family business called Chezan Investments Ltd, based in Mayfair of London. The company is under huge debts to its bankers. In fact, they had been skimming the profits into Swiss bank account quietly. When the bank presses for the repayment of loan, instead of bringing the money from Switzerland, they think of a new idea of hiring a key executive and take out a substantial Keyman insurance policy. The insurance broker, Marc Kohnvich is their accomplice.

Vincent Muller is a chartered accountant who gets hired as the key executive being the CFO and the director of the company. The brothers try to kill him to cash in the policy. The bank, the company and their associates all treat the female staff as benefit in kinds. But the sister, Firoza Noble, is a very willing party to bribe the bankers. When Vincent visits Caribbean island to do due diligence on a business opportunity he gets very friendly with Talisha but her ex-husband tries to kill him when he sees them making love; did someone ask him to do it?

The second project takes Vincent with Pearce to Dherapur, a beautiful hilly small town in India. Where a refugee Fibi, working as a waitress falls for Pearce. She has been trying to make both ends meet even if it meant 'selling' her body occasionally, but is in tears when she finds her younger brother doing the same. The elder brother, without the knowledge of his younger brother Pearce Noble arranges his hatchet man to get Vincent killed in Dherapur. But Fibi saves him.

In the end, Jimmy Noble gets killed but by whom? Vincent Muller takes over the business from the receiver with the help of his uncle. The corporate world, the bribes, champagne, expensive parties, the lust of the bosses and revenge are the key ingredients. It shows human nature at its best or at its worst, or perhaps both!

Other work by Kamal M Malak:

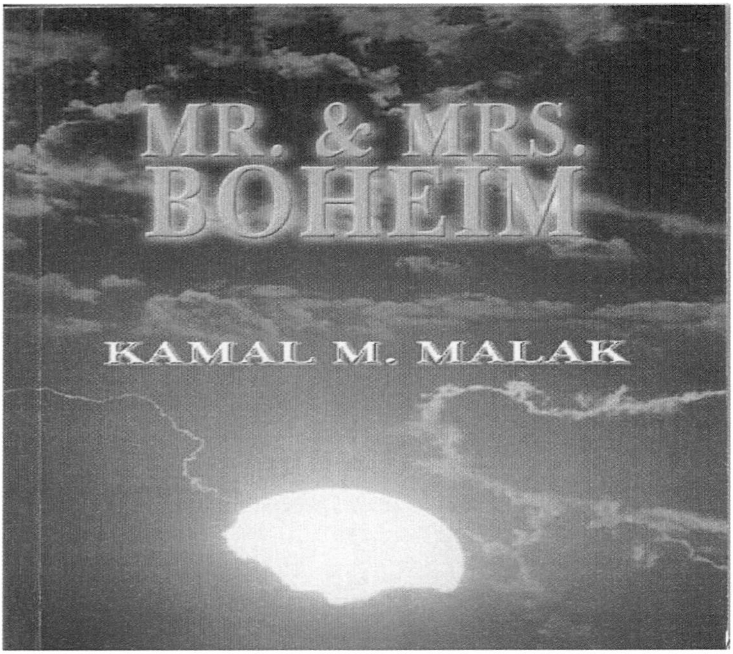

Steve, a chartered accountants, in the City of London is married to Kate, a software engineer. One day, they quarrel after Kate having been very depressed and suffering from Claustrophobia, and Steve very frustrated having been passed over for the promotion to become a partner in his firm… and they divorce. After a few years, they meet again tell their stories since their split.

Kate's first boyfriend was a very handsome model and she falls in love with him straight away but he turns out to be gay. Her second boyfriend was a slave driver who takes her on a trip to Middle East and 'sells' her to his boss, a rich Shaikh. And finally, she meets a scrounger who lives off on many women like her. Steve turns to a gay clergy for spiritual help. Then he meets a smart, sexy young woman connected with some con men. She tries to swindle him out of a small fortune. Finally, he finds a divorced girlfriend who is, slightly older than him, her young teenage daughter gets infatuated with him and the relationship ends in a disaster.

ISBN 978-0-9954528-1-7 Available at Gardner's Books, Amazon and Kindle.

Other work by Kamal M Malak contd.

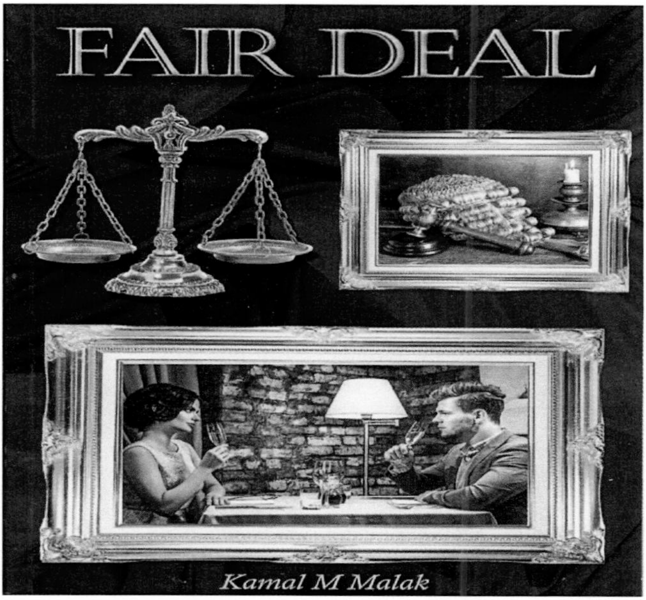

The story is about a group of lawyers working in the City of London. Terry is a department manager, number two to Sir Henry Sheldon. His wife, Sharon, a beauty who is never satisfied with one man. During a Christmas party in the office, she gets carried away in a secluded filing room with her husband's colleague, Lenny. Another colleague, Chris sees them in their intimate activity by accident.

Lenny gets fired, loses his girlfriend Joan, and leaves the country. Sharon is very hurt, physically beaten by her husband and missing her dashing young lover. She blames Chris for it and befriends his neglected wife, Meina. She takes the revenge on Chris by getting him also fired. She uses Meina and an Ex-Agency divorced lawyer from New York. The way Sharon takes revenge and uses Meina is very interesting and thought provoking.

ISBN: 978-0-9954528-0-0 Available at Gardner's Books, Amazon and Kindle.

Other work by Kamal M Malak contd.

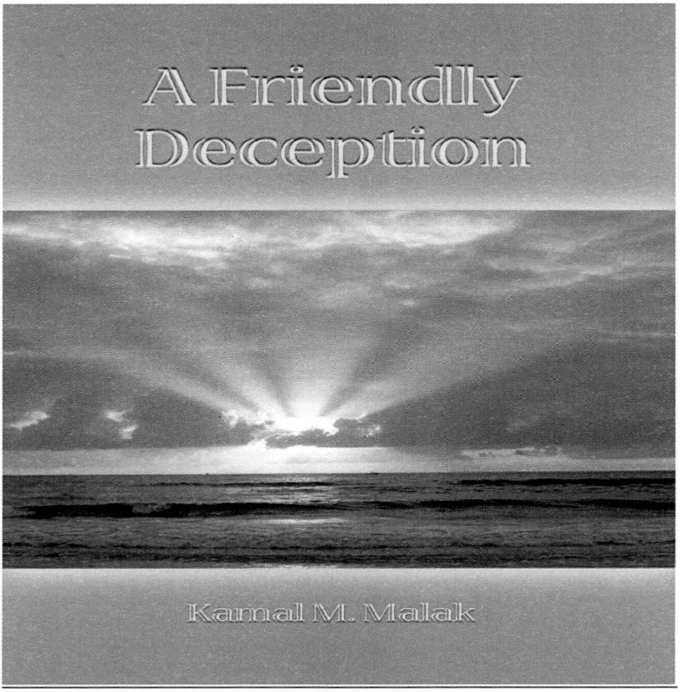

The story is about Sean, a banker in the City of London, and his desire to have a daughter who would call him "mon papa cheri". When all the natural efforts fail, he and his wife Gina, take their close friend Rohit's advice and visit India, where in a renowned temple, Pundit runs a business behind a façade of devtas, dasees and bhagats. God rewards them with a beautiful daughter, Sophie; but who fathered her? Is it Pundit, Harry the driver, or one of the many devtas in the temple? Other characters include Sherou, an Anglo-Indian who makes his living by whatever it takes; sharp, razor- brain secretary Judy who believes that bankers can afford two women, and an extremely ambitious Mariena, who has her eyes set on 10 Downing Street...

ISBN: 978-1-4349-6329-1 Available at Amazon and Kindle.